"I HAVE SOME BAD NEWS LARISSA," the alien, Oshrii, said. "You won't be fighting Karen again."

My stomach lurched. Was I on the second string just because of one loss?

"Karen was killed in a bar fight last night," he continued. "Apparently she was doing some bragging to the wrong people and Makrit decided to make her prove her claims."

"I see."

"I know you wanted to revenge yourself on her," he said. "If you want to call blood feud on Makrit, I will arrange it for you."

"Oh no, I'm pleased he did it."

"Very well," said Oshrii. "Oh, I almost forgot. I have your ear in stasis."

"You do?" I said, trying desperately not to sound hopeful.

"Yes. You can have it back when you've earned it. You're dismissed now."

ROC (0451)

FANTASY AND SCIENCE FICTION FROM SIGNET AND ROC

LARISSA

Emily Devenport

A ROC BOOK

ROC
Published by the Penguin Group
Penguin Books USA Inc., 375 Hudson Street,
New York, New York 10014, U.S.A.
Penguin Books Ltd, 27 Wrights Lane,
London W8 5TZ, England
Penguin Books Australia Ltd, Ringwood,
Victoria, Australia
Penguin Books Canada Ltd, 10 Alcorn Avenue,
Toronto, Ontario, Canada M4V 3B2
Penguin Books (N.Z.) Ltd, 182-190 Wairau Road,
Auckland 10, New Zealand

Penguin Books Ltd, Registered Offices:
Harmondsworth, Middlesex, England

First published by Roc,
an imprint of New American Library,
a division of Penguin Books USA Inc.

First Printing, October, 1993
10 9 8 7 6 5 4 3 2 1

Printed in the United States of America

for Ernie

Chapter 1

This may sound deranged, but I think I owe my interest in knives to the serial killer who murdered my mother when I was nine. The newspeople called him The Butcher; and when the vid about him came out recently, the posters said: "THE BUTCHER . . . HE DELIVERS . . ." I believe that last part referred to The Butcher's habit of killing his victims in their own homes, with their own cutlery.

The artist who designed the poster must have visited Hook at least once, because in the background, behind the shadowy figure of The Butcher, was the harsh, cloudless skyline I grew up seeing. To the left were the Q'rin fortresses, and to the right, the ugly prefab buildings of the Human side of the city. An eloquent depiction of my childhood.

I watched the vid last night, to see if I was in it. I was the only one who had ever survived one of his attacks. In the vid, the little girl was rescued by the tough actor-hero. But I remember what really happened.

I was playing in my room when I heard Mother screaming at someone. I had thought she and I were alone in the house, so at first I thought she was yelling at me. Then I heard her say, "Try it you son of a bitch! I can cut, too!" This didn't makes sense to me, and she sounded so angry. I hated it when she was angry, so I didn't respond when I heard her call my name.

"Larissa, don't—"

There wasn't a sound after that, and my heart turned to ice, even though I still had no idea what was going on. I tiptoed out of my room and across the hall carpet. I can remember every hole and frayed spot in that rug. When I got to the top of the stairs, I looked down. He was already on the way up. He had been moving as quietly as I had.

He was naked, and he had my mother's butcher knife in his hand. Her blood was on it. I knew she was dead, then. My eyes went from the knife to his face, and I backed away from him. I ran into my room and closed the door behind me, but my door didn't have a lock on it; so I climbed onto the ledge outside my window. We were six stories up.

Funny, they stopped constructing buildings with ledges after they built ours, and if we had lived in one of the more modern ones—something Mother wanted very badly—I would be dead now.

I crawled as far away from the window as I could get. It was 110° F. outside, and the heated concrete burned my hands and legs, but I didn't care. I hoped feverishly that he wouldn't look out the window and see me.

But he did. He looked at me, then looked at the street far below. There were people down there, kicking sand up from the hot streets as they plodded along about their business, oblivious to what was going on above their heads.

"If you come out here, I'll scream!" I said. "Those people will look up and see you!"

I wished I hadn't spoken, because he looked at me again. "Come inside, sweetheart," he said. "Your mommy wants you."

I started to cry at that point, because I knew she was dead. "You killed her!" I said.

"Shit," he said under his breath. "Look, honey—you're gonna be in trouble if you don't come inside. Your mommy will spank you. She might even slap you."

"You're full of shit," I said.

I cringed when he smiled.

"I'm gonna fuck you," he said. "Then I'm gonna kill you. Just like I did your mommy."

"If you come out here, I'll scream!"

"Come in here right now you little cunt."

So I screamed, and he started to laugh. Then he mocked my screams. But when people on the street noticed what was going on up there, he ducked back inside.

"Call the police!" I heard someone say from below.

Eventually, the police broke into our apartment and found Mother. They tried to coax me back in through the window, but I was sure *he* was hiding in there somewhere, waiting for me. They had to use a fire ladder to get me down, and it was another hour before they could persuade me back into the apartment. Mother's body had been photographed and removed by then.

They asked me to describe him.

"A white guy," I told them.

"What did he look like?"

That really hung me up. To me he had just been a white guy who looked like a million other white guys. He had a crew cut, like most of the other Humans on that military planet. I could have described his penis, which had been rock hard as he climbed the stairs after me. For years afterward, I thought men's penises were always hard like that, and I couldn't figure out how they hid them under their clothes.

I could have described the look on his face, too. I think it was because of that look that I learned to think I could control people by using knives. I wonder if I wear that look myself, when I'm fighting. Not the part of it that told me, at the age of nine, of his total and all-consuming hatred for women. I mean the part that said, *I've got you right where I want you.*

I heard two of the detectives talking during one of the lulls between their many attempts to get some useful information out of me.

"You know what really burns me up?" one guy said. "I don't even think these murders would be happening on Hook if we weren't so backward in every area but the military—"

"Sshh," his partner said. "They'll hear you." He was referring to the military police who were milling around the apartment, not really doing anything useful, but occasionally coming over to smile at me and pat me on the head.

"I don't care. If this woman had had a food synthesizer, she wouldn't have even owned a butcher knife. Shit, we can't even dust for fingerprints, because we don't have the equipment!"

"They sign the checks, man."

"But fucking fingerprint equipment, man! The most primitive police equipment in existence, and we don't even have *that*!"

The military guys were starting to look at them. "I just wish she had a decent cooler, man," the second guy said nervously. "It must be ninety-five degrees in here."

"So, little girl," the first guy asked me, "do you remember what color his eyes were now?"

None of this was in the vid. In the vid, the police and the military cooperated perfectly. But the truth is, on Hook, if you're not Q'rin or military Human, you're a second-class citizen. And if you're a miner, you're third-class.

Anyway, they never caught The Butcher. One day he just stopped killing—at least on Hook—and blended back into society. I think it was just about the time the new detection equipment arrived. Maybe it was Mother's murder that finally convinced the accountants back on Earth to send the modern stuff.

The Q'rin might have been able to help them find the killer, if they'd been interested in doing so and if they'd been asked, which I don't think they were. They had the resources, and they own the planet. But I guess the Ragnir war was still too recent for that kind of cooperation. The losers never feel comfortable asking favors from the winners.

So I went to live with my dad, who was a major in

the marines, and who had a better cooler. Mother and Dad were divorced right after I was born, so it was like meeting a stranger. I still don't know him. He wasn't cruel or negligent; he was just never there, even when he was sitting across the breakfast table from me. I understand what must have driven Mother to leave him, even though her secretarial job paid almost nothing.

I don't think Dad understood it though, because he looked so surprised and hurt the time he had to bail me out of jail when I was arrested for assault at the age of fifteen. Where had he been for the past six years?

"Larissa," he said, "you know right from wrong. Why did you do it? Why?"

"They tried to rape me, Dad! They jumped us! We were just defending ourselves!"

"You nearly killed them! You cut them to ribbons! How could you, after what happened to your mother? How could you even touch a knife?"

"But Dad, those miner brats—"

"Did you call them slaves?" he demanded. "Is that why they attacked you?"

"No!"

He was almost crying. His face was purple, and so twisted with pain—it really shocked me. Dad is the original poker face. Nothing ever wrinkled that smooth, chocolate brown surface; nothing ever seemed to faze him. I never saw him cry when Mother was murdered. I didn't know what to say to him when he was like this, so I just stopped trying.

"Promise me you'll stay away from those kids you've been hanging around. Friends don't get friends in trouble like that!"

I promised. And he got me off through some good connections he had with his military comrades, plus eyewitness accounts that those three miner brats really had jumped us—they did! But they picked on the wrong girl—and I went home with Dad, who went back to being Mr. Poker Face. Only occasionally did I see him with that look behind his eyes that seemed to say, *What has this planet done to my little girl?*

Yes, that vid poster for The Butcher summed it up pretty well, only he should have been in the background and Hook should have been up front. Hook was stronger than him, maybe stronger than all of us. I've been to a dozen planets since, and I'll probably never go home; but I measure everything by what Hook taught me with its hot, dry summers and cold, dry winters, its no-nonsense collection of flora and fauna. When I see the flowers of other, lusher planets, I always feel a twinge of disapproval. They seem self-indulgent.

"Hook makes you hard," the Q'rin always said. "It teaches you to endure." They love it. It seemed to me, when I was little, that the Q'rin had always been a part of that world; but always separate from us, just as we were separate from the miners. I thought the Q'rin had been on Hook first. But they weren't. It was Dad who told me that.

I was ten years old, and we had gone to a Double-G game in the Q'rin sector. Sometimes they invited military Humans and their families into their fortresses to view sports and do business, sometimes even to dine, if they thought a lot of you. I had seen their fortresses looming over the horizon for years, and seen the warriors in Hook Central conducting whatever business brought them there; but I had never been *Inside* before. I held tight to Dad's hand as we got off the tran with the others who had been invited, including Captain Rogers, who was Dad's best friend and the ranking officer of our group.

Q'rin warriors guarded the east gate, and other Q'rin marched inside, finishing the end of their day. We walked right up to the gate, where our escort was waiting for us.

"Rogers," their captain greeted ours. "You're five minutes late. Follow me." And they promptly turned their backs on us and marched off.

This may sound rude, but it was actually their standard form of courtesy. It was gruff, and very off-putting to most Humans, but we were used to it.

Captain Rogers signaled us to follow the escort, and we all marched to the arena, with the sound of Q'rin boots ringing off the massive walls and in our ears. Our escort didn't look at us while we were with them; but everyone else did, every moment we were there.

The complex seemed fantastical to me, unused as my young eyes were to the architectural aesthetics of a race whose existence is centered around conflict. It was huge, and Spartan; but I still think it was beautiful. I guess I'm warped.

I thought nothing of it at the time, but they sat us in fairly good seats. This was a sign of respect not to be taken for granted. I had to sit in Dad's lap so I could see, because of all the seven-foot people around us. Good thing Dad was six-foot-six and the seats were graduated. There was a lot of noise before the game started, Q'rin arguing with each other in their gravelly voices; but I wanted to be quiet. I was feeling delightfully solemn. I did ask Dad one question, though, because I had never seen a Double-G game played before.

"How come I don't feel heavy, Dad?"

"Because this isn't a real Double-G game. They play the real thing in space, with the rotation of the sports station creating an artificial gravity. The farther out you are from the center of the station, the heavier you feel. I've been to a few of those games, but most Humans like to watch a real Double-G game remotely, so they won't feel the discomfort."

"Uh-huh," I said, wondering if I should tell him I didn't understand. That might tip him off that I wasn't paying as much attention in school as I should.

"On Hook, they simulate Double-G and Half-G games by using light- or heavy-suits that interact with electromagnetic fields. Remember how they told you in school about Hook's electromagnetic field, how quirky they are?"

"Uh-huh—"

"I'm no expert, so you should ask your teachers.

But I think they have something to do with the way this planet is shaped. It's irregular."

"Yeah!" That I did remember.

When the game started, he got real quiet. I was so caught up in the thrill of watching Double-G played by the people who had invented it, I hardly even noticed. In person, the Q'rin players seemed like giants, and the heavy ball looked like a boulder.

But I picked up the bad feeling again as we were walking back out the east gate, something about the way Dad interacted with the Q'rin escort. He was so polite to them, it made me nervous.

I watched him from the corner of my eye as we said good-bye to the escort and trooped back across the sand to the nearest public transport. Only Q'rin noblemen and the very top Human military brass own private transports on Hook, so we all had good legs. Dad's heavy silence continued when we got on the tran—and through most of the ride—but finally he said, "They act like they invented this planet."

"Huh?" I said.

"The Q'rin. They weren't here first, you know. We were."

A couple of older military men who were close enough to hear him nodded as if he were speaking to them.

"They came to this planet because we were mining metals out of its moon to supply our efforts in the Ragnir war. They took the planet from us, and we lost the war."

My half-learned history lessons suddenly trickled into my memory. "But the Aesopians kept on fighting, right? They were our allies, but we couldn't fight anymore so we went home, and they fought the Q'rin for another year. Do the Aesopians really look like lions and bears and stuff, Dad?"

He was frowning at me, and the other military men looked mad. "I'm telling this story," he said. "Just listen. *We* fought the Q'rin on this planet, and we lost—"

"But they still let us live here," I offered. He gritted his teeth at that. But to me, the Ragnir war was just another thing I hadn't paid enough attention to in school; and the Q'rin were those people who didn't quite look like us, but who were interesting and lived a comfortable distance from my part of town. If they were our enemies, how come we had just visited them at their house?

"You're only ten, so I'm not surprised you don't know any better," he said quietly. "But the Q'rin executed the military Humans who were caught planetside, and then they enslaved the miners. That's why I never want to hear you calling the miners *slaves*. It just stirs up bad blood. The miners were still slaves when we came back, and I don't think they'll ever forgive us for that. And in a strange way, we never forgave them, either."

"For what?"

"For living as slaves."

It made sense to me then, as we rode on that segregated transport. But a year after that conversation, our public schools and transports were opened to miners; and I began to learn that they hated us more for standing by and saying nothing than we hated them for submitting instead of dying. If I had studied my own family history, I would have known that my own great-great-grandparents would have understood how the miners felt. But it was something I had to relearn.

I wonder if Dad has been promoted from major by now. That's about all I wonder, because I don't know anything else that mattered to him. Maybe I mattered, but I was out of his house by the time I was sixteen. After my arrest for assault, I stuck to the letter of my promise to him that I would quit hanging around with that particular gang of kids. I replaced them with new, worse ones. Same thing with my knives. By the time I was sixteen, I was already six feet tall, and well versed in the art of cutting anyone who looked cross-eyed at me.

But back when I was eleven, before I had my growth spurt, things were different. My breasts began to develop then, and when I looked in the mirror, I could see my mother coming out, which pleased me. Mother was so beautiful, with her night black skin and her round, firm breasts. That's why the butcher killed her. When Mother was still alive, I watched every move she made and copied it. Boys and men began to watch me when I was eleven, and I wondered if they wanted to kill me.

I saw the blood on the knife as The Butcher came up the stairs toward me, naked, with *I've got you* on his face, and I thought the blood *was* Mother. Mother was the blood. I suppose some people would see Freudian overtones in that image, but I think it stands on its own.

So I believed I was helpless, that I could be overpowered at any time because I was a girl. I knew I was beautiful, like Mother, so for the next two years I took every precaution to avoid conflict.

This was hard work. I had to walk to the public tran every day, which let me off in the Central District, the run-down part of town where the miners landed after the Q'rin let them out of the bowels of their fortresses. When I passed miner brats on the street, I crossed to the other side. When groups of Q'rin men looked at me in that way that made me understand why they never let their women come into town, I learned not to make eye contact with them. When military brats asked me out on dates, I told them my father wouldn't let me go.

It was exhausting. The only peace I had was during lunch hour, when I would hide out in the school library. That was when I developed an eclectic taste for books that I still enjoy today.

I also developed a reputation for being a prude and a chicken, which on Hook is pretty bad. But I managed to keep it up for those two years, and finally my growth spurt began. At thirteen, I was the tallest kid in my class. Just in time.

One day a bully walked up to me and poked one of my breasts. "Hey big tits!" he said, so everyone would hear. "You'd love it if I sucked on one of those titties, wouldn't you?"

My face got very hot. Up until that moment I had thought my breasts were beautiful, and this creep made me wish they would just deflate and never come back. I slapped him. We were both surprised when the blow knocked him on his ass.

When he came for me again, I held him at arm's length. I didn't know what else to do. Finally a teacher came and broke us up, and I wasn't even scratched.

That night I crept into the kitchen and opened the knife drawer. I had been afraid to touch a knife before then. As I looked at the shiny, sharp things in the drawer, I realized that I wasn't afraid of what they might do to me; I was afraid of what I might do with them. It seemed like a betrayal of Mother to feel that way, but I couldn't help it. And now I had a good reason to carry a knife, because I knew that bully with his injured pride would be back at me again.

I picked up one of the smaller meat cutters and sneaked it back to my room. Once there I began the modifications I had observed so many times in the past without being aware I had observed them.

Chapter 2

My decision to get myself a knife at the age of thirteen was the beginning of a new self-image for me; a strong one—and the start of my career as a bully. A thug, in fact. And I remember every minute of it, though I wish I could forget how easily I was manipulated by both friends and enemies. You want to see a spectacular fight? Want someone beaten up, but don't have the stuff to do it yourself? Just arrange for Larissa to hear them talking about her tits. This shouldn't be hard, since she goes out of her way to display them.

I stayed in Central High School the whole time I lived on Hook. Why shouldn't I? I got regular meals there. In fact, I bet the schools on Hook had about a ninety-five percent attendance rate for that very reason. Also it didn't hurt that the schools had heaters and coolers that worked. At noon the miner brats would come in, fresh from their 5:00 to 11:30 A.M. compulsory shifts in the mines, and head straight for the showers. For most of them, it was the only way they had of getting clean.

The people I wanted to be with were at school, both friends and enemies. I enjoyed the reading, and the math was easy. I never made any effort to do anything that didn't please me, and I know I didn't complete more than half the assignments that came my way, yet I still made average grades. This is how I qualified for the Double-G and Half-G teams.

I was a freshman when Coach Thiele approached me after my regular gym class. I knew he was the Half-G coach, so my heart started to pound when he took me aside.

"You're a killer, you know that?" he asked me. "You didn't have to push that kid right through the net."

"Hey," I said, "my side was losing. What else was I supposed to do?"

"Exactly. I want you to try out for Half-G. Your grades are good enough, and you have the moves. What do you say?"

I said yes.

I thought I was pretty special as I turned out for my first practice, all rigged up in my cute little harness and my light-suit. I was smiling and everything. I noticed there was only one other girl on the team, and she was almost as big as me. At least half the players were miner brats looking for the sports ticket off Hook. They didn't look happy to see me. In fact, none of the guys did. They had this O-shit-not-*another*-girl look on their arrogant faces. I put my smile away.

The interference grid under the floor opened up, and we got to feel the electromagnetic fingers of Hook grabbing our light-suits. It really is almost like Half-G. You can jump higher, move faster, perform acrobatics you could never do under normal conditions. I loved the sensation—though I wished I hadn't had such a big lunch—and I almost got lost in it. But then the first whistle sounded, and it was Let's-show-the-girl-why-she-shouldn't-try-to-play-with-the-guys time.

The ball was injected into the game from low on the A wall, and someone on my team got it, so he was center. He instantly headed for the goal area, the two guys on either side of him acting as guards. I started moving as soon as I saw my team had the offensive for this play, and headed for some player scoring areas. I knew that much. I had watched my very favorite game in the whole galaxy played many times, and I wanted to hit my targets on the far walls and the ceiling as many times as I could before the play ended. The other team got into their roles as interceptors with enthusiasm, and it looked like our roles could reverse sooner than usual, the way they were going after that ball.

But this was the Surahi Variation—which is outlawed on the Human side of the Sector—so both teams could score certain physical points against each other. The other team went straight for my tits and my crotch. The crotch is always a penalty area, and the chest is if you touch it with your hands or elbows. These penalties count against your team's score, and they also enable the fouled person to hit you back *anywhere,* legally. But if you are hit hard enough, you may not get the chance, and that's what they were trying to do to me. I got hit so many times in that first minute, I didn't know which way was up. And my own team didn't do a thing to help me.

But I kept moving. I think they believed I would curl up and float away, but instead I took as many of my legal hit backs as I could reach, and even scored on some of the bonus areas. After a while, my team started to help me out. By the second half, I was officially accepted.

And black-and-blue all over. Fortunately, my dark skin concealed a lot of that. For the first day, anyway.

After that game, the other girl came up to talk to me. She had been on the other team, but she had played fair. Her name was Mary.

"Sorry you had to go through that," she said. "They always do that to the girls. They're not half as hard on the guys who try out."

"How many girls have tried out?" I asked as she and I walked into the girls' locker room. I was almost limping by then as the adrenaline leaked out of my system.

"Besides you and me?" she said. "Eight. And they all tried hard. Shit, one girl got kicked in the head so many times, she was in the hospital for weeks. At the end of that game, the score was negative twenty-seven to negative three. What's the point? It makes me sick."

"But you still play." I looked at her as she was

stripping down for the showers, and her pale skin showed every bruise she had.

"I didn't want to give them the satisfaction, you know?"

I did. It was a lesson in fairness and sportsmanship I never forgot.

After a semester of Half-G, my standing in the school was pretty high. The miner brats on the team made it known that they wouldn't go against me in any gang fights, and I had a bunch of instant friends among the other kids. I still got into plenty of fights, but I tried to keep them off campus.

Eventually, the Double-G coach, Coach Wilson, approached me. "Playing Half-G is good, kid," he said. "But there are a lot of kids out there who play Half-G. If you can play Double-G, too, you can write your own ticket."

"Isn't it a bitch to adjust from one season to the other, though?" I asked.

He slapped me on the back. "You can take it. You keep playing like you've been playing, and you'll make the pros. You'll have more options after you graduate high school."

So I agreed, and started working out with the Double-G team during their pre-tryout session, right after Half-G practice. It was hard, but Coach Wilson made it plain to me that I already had a place on his team. I wondered why he had approached me in the first place, because the two games really are so different. During the last week of the Half-G season, I got my answer. Coach Thiele made an announcement just before practice.

"We've made it into the Q'rin circuit," he said, looking straight at me.

The guys started cheering, while Mary and I exchanged looks. She gave me the high sign. "Friday we're not gonna play Central South," Coach continued, still looking at me. "We're gonna play the Scorpion Sector. I want double practice this week."

So I went to Coach Wilson and told him I couldn't make his practice that week.

"Yes you will," he said.

"No I won't. If you still want me after a week, I'll be there. But I'm not gonna blow off this Q'rin game."

He was mad, but he let me go. I had known he would; I was just being polite. He and I both knew I was going to get the Double-G team into the Q'rin circuit, too. We were making history, because no Human team had ever been good enough to qualify for the Q'rin circuit before. The Q'rin don't believe in exposing their students to *inferiors* at a tender age, because they think it weakens them. So we had a lot to prove.

We had a whole week to be nervous about the game, and we were scared to death as we walked into the Scorpion Arena that fateful afternoon. The bleachers were crowded with Q'rin who had come to see what was so special about this Human team. Coach Thiele had been breathing fire and shitting bricks all morning, and we all knew he would murder us with his bare hands if we didn't play twice as good as usual.

Then the Q'rin team came out.

"Shit," Tommy Higgins whispered to me. "And they're not even full grown yet."

These guys were all six-and-a-half to seven feet tall. They were big, ugly, bony young men with cheekbones like boulders and ridges over their eyes that made them look like eagles. Their gazes were just as unblinking. But to me, those fierce faces were oddly tempered with naïveté, and they were Human enough for me to read something else in them.

"They're afraid we're going to embarrass them," I said.

"I could have told you that," said Jim Hughes. He was a miner brat, and hadn't been the least bit surprised by any of it. "They think they're being punished. Playing against us is a step down for them."

This made the military brats on our team mad, but it kind of tickled me. I could see a hint of nervousness in the way those Q'rin boys were checking us out, especially when they looked at Mary and me in our tight little light-suits. I relaxed when I noticed that, because it showed me they did have a weakness. On Hook, the Q'rin don't allow women to play sports.

We got into our pregame positions and waited for the grid to open up. Right across from me was this Q'rin who had shaved his head except for one long braid. I would never want to give an enemy something like that to grab onto, but the Q'rin don't care if you pull their hair. Their heads are so tough, they don't give a shit.

When we were all at Half-G, the arena tilted. The Q'rin like to play Half-G on about a forty-degree tilt. The walls, ceiling, and floor were transparent, which showed how much fancier their arena was than ours. We only had transparent walls.

So there we were, crouched down with one leg bent, trying to keep our bodies balanced while we glared into the faces of huge, crouching Q'rin warriors-to-be. The whistle sounded, and *kaboom*! We all flew into action.

Jim Hughes got the ball first, so I hurtled toward the player targets, which were marked with holographic lights (another fancy difference). The first thing Mister Long Braid did was foul me in the chest area with his hands. He did that all through the game—poor guy didn't seem to be able to help himself. I took my legal hit-backs; but I went for points instead of trying to hurt him. Punching that rock-hard body would have done more harm to me than him—we all figured that out fast. Unfortunately, so did *they*, and before long Tommy Higgins was out of the game with an injury. Oscar Jones flew in to replace him, grinning like mad.

But he was out by the end of the first quarter, and so was Tony Fiore. We realized then that we would have to play a more defensive game, and that we probably weren't going to win. We did have two advantages: Mary and me. Those Q'rin boys were disgruntled at the sensation of colliding with soft female bodies, and Mary and I scored about twice as many points as the guys on our teams, from penalty hit-backs and from scores on the walls and the goal. Plus we were faster than the guys, Human and Q'rin both. I got to be center six times, and I scored ten points alone in the second quarter by kissing Mister Long Braid on his big nose when he tried to block me from the goal. He grabbed me, a double foul, dropped me like a hot potato, then grabbed me again, too late.

But just before the end of that quarter, he grabbed me and kissed me on the mouth. They had to make up a penalty for that one, because it never happened before. "I don't care," he whispered to me when we heard it was a double foul. "You're going to lose anyway."

And we did. But we got a higher score than any Human team has ever achieved against a Q'rin team, and *I* scored the most points of any player in the game. Even if you didn't count the points they lost by fouling me. After it was over, Coach told us we were going to start out against Scorpion Sector again next season, and we were scheduled to play four other Q'rin teams.

He took me aside and said, "You've got a good shot at the pros, kid. There aren't many women in the pro circuit, but I think that's to your advantage right now. I sure hope you're going to go for it."

"I am," I told him. And I certainly meant to.

We got into the Q'rin Double-G circuit too. We had a great team, with a lot of the same guys who played on the Half-G team also playing Double-G, despite the adjustment difficulties between seasons.

Double-G is a Q'rin game, hardly ever seen outside their territory. It's a lot slower and more cerebral than Half-G, so maybe Human spectators just don't have the patience for it. It's like a combination of chess and basketball, played in lead suits with a medicine ball. (That's what it's like on Hook, anyway. In space, it's a lot worse.) You don't bounce the ball, but you do pass it, and you can score if you're on a scoring square.

Each team has a commander and a sub-commander, but the rest of the players' designations depend upon which square they land on. That first game, I wasn't one of the commanders, so I didn't get to plot the game. I was squared off against Mr. Long Braid again. I wondered if that was deliberate. I was sure they had spent at least as long plotting pregame strategy as we had.

"What's your name?" I asked him as we all stood waiting for the filter grid under the floor to open all the way.

"Abriin," he said.

"I'm Larissa."

He eyed my heavy-suit and grinned. "You've lost your advantage in this game, Larissa."

"Huh?"

"I can't see your body very well in that suit, and bouncing against you will only cause me to hurt us both. No fun at all. I think we will kill you this time."

There are a few independent moves a non-commander can and sometimes must make in a Double-G game. Threats and intimidation are two of them. I made a few of my own.

"No way," I said.

"You think not?"

"You boneheads are in trouble. It takes brains to win this game."

"You forget," he said, "we invented it. It trains us to command and to be commanded. Perhaps one day you and I will face each other gun-to-gun or ship-to-ship, and we'll test what we've learned today."

"Could be," I said, but before I could think of something clever to add to that, I felt the pull of my heavy-suit and almost grimaced. I had been practicing so long in the heavy-suit, I was supposed to be used to it. We had even trained the way the Q'rin teams do, taking long hikes out into the Rust Mountains to build up our endurance.

Abriin was still grinning at me. "Females should not play sports with men," he said. "Before long, we'll get used to you, and we'll end up treating you just like males. You'll get hurt."

I had already heard that argument from my own team, so I ignored it.

The goal of Double-G is not only to score with the ball, but also to have your team in the position that best suits the players' individual talents. I wasn't the best shooter that first game—I was only second or third best. But I got my chance to score almost immediately. I was advanced into a ten-point square, and no one was there to intercept me. I threw the ball and hit the goal on the far wall dead on; so ten points for us. But when Jim Hughes advanced to a twenty-point square, an interceptor moved into position to stop him. The interceptor jabbed him in the gut with a pain rod. Jim still tried to make the shot, but he missed it by a foot.

I got a chance to be interceptor with Abriin two moves after that. He was on a fifty-point square. I studied him for the ten seconds I was allowed, then stuck my rod against his right elbow. It hurt bad enough to make him want to kill me—I could see that—but he still managed to score the shot. Two moves later, a dozer pushed me off my square, and Abriin made another fifty-point shot.

Jim Hughes scored off a hundred-point square after that, and Lali Eo scored off a ten-point square. I was the next to move, and I had to make an individual choice. I could move to a capture square and steal twenty points from the other team, or I could move to a hundred-point square and take my chances with the interceptor who waited for me there. I decided to go for the hundred-point square.

I didn't know the interceptor. He regarded me for about five seconds, then thrust his pain rod against my right breast.

The pain was agonizing, and I had to wait the full ten-second-recovery period before I could make the shot; but my anger loaned me a little extra strength, and I scored.

Two moves after that, an executioner got me, and I was out of the game. Abriin got it two moves after that, and the two of us watched the rest of the game together from the sidelines.

"How is your breast?" he asked me. "Shall I rub it for you?"

"No thanks," I said. "How's your elbow?"

"I'll live. You Humans can't do any lasting damage. We'll capture your commander in another five moves."

Actually, it took ten. Our sub-commander was out in another five, but not before he managed to capture their commander.

We lost that game, but we lost it well. We scored high and made a name for ourselves. Coach Wilson wanted me to consider a Double-G career, too, but even Q'rin Double-G players develop internal troubles after ten years of pro-playing. I shudder to think what it would do to me. I heard Abriin made it into the pros, and I wish him well.

But none of that sports-career stuff went anywhere for me in the long run—not in the normal sort of way—because I got in big trouble. I killed Korry Vather and had to run away from Hook forever.

Korry Vather was a tall white boy with a lot of zits that were always either bleeding or getting ready to pop. But the zits didn't bother me. It was his mouth. It was soft and pink. And while most guys reveal with their eyes the fact that they want to rape you, Korry always did it with his mouth. The way he held it, the way it moved—I don't know. It really bothered me.

Now I can admit I was perversely attracted to it, too. I sometimes wondered what it would be like to be devoured by that nasty little mouth.

Korry wasn't a big man with his gang—a bunch of miner brats who thought he was a pussy for being the son of an army clerk. He dressed just like them, in work overalls that they wore because it was all they had, and he let his hair grow long just like theirs. It was kind of pathetic. But he knew how to use them to get what he wanted, and he wanted me. I think he must have planned for a whole year before he made his move. That's the kind of guy he was.

But I knew it was coming, because stupid Artie Smith made an obscene call to me the night before and told me what he was going to do to me. Must have thought I wouldn't recognize his voice, but who could miss a speech impediment like his?

"I'm gonna lather you up wis my own thpecial thoap, baby," he said, "then thcrub you clean."

Could he be stupid enough, I wondered, to tell me that they were planning to attack me in the showers? I decided he was. So the next day my buddies and I were waiting for them, soaking wet but fully clothed, in the girls' shower room, the water running just hot enough to be steamy. They crept in and tiptoed to the stalls, thinking I was in there. When they were all in, we turned off the main valve for the cold water and waited for them to come screaming out of there.

It was murder, literally, because the moment I saw Korry's pink mouth, I knew it had been the mastermind behind the attack. I'd like to be able to say that I didn't mean to cut the throat beneath that mouth, that I had just been defending myself against his vicious attack; but I don't remember if he had a weapon or not.

I don't ever remember how long we slashed and cut at each other; just that abruptly I was alone with a bunch of wounded wet people and at least one dead one. I was just sixteen. I think I may have peed my pants at that moment, but it was hard to tell, since they were already wet.

Chapter 3

I have been more scared in my life only two other times. The first I've already told you about. The other was yet to come.

That day in the shower room I reverted to the coward who was really living inside me. I ran out of there without even looking to see if anyone had seen me, and went straight home. Dad was still at his office. I dressed in my warmest clothes, packed some food, and packed my best knives. Then I went to Dad's secret stash, in the strongbox at the bottom of his closet.

He had five thousand credits in there. It was his life savings. It's too bad he didn't trust the banks, because I took all of it. I didn't feel good about it, and I probably wouldn't have the guts to face him again even if I had the opportunity. But I thought I was looking at execution or a life at hard labor in the mines if I didn't get off Hook fast.

I left Dad's apartment without a glance back.

The streets outside seemed like the same old streets. It was winter, so there was no heat distortion to make people look wobbly as they approached you. I hopped the crosstown tran, expecting the police to come running after me at any moment. All I could think of was to get out of town—even though that meant leaving civilization. There's nothing outside Hook Central except abandoned mines, mountains, sand, and thorny plants.

That was just what I wanted, a place out past the Q'rin fortresses, out past the mines. I was bundled up thick and had my hood up, hoping it would disguise the fact that I was a woman. Some of the remote Q'rin sentries might have seen me as I skirted the hills north of the fortresses, but no one bothered me.

I got to the mines just as the sun was going down. The night shift was changing places with the day shift. I watched men, women, and children trudging back and forth; the adults so covered in grime, their eyes shone forth like ghost lights. *Take a good look,* I told myself. *That's where you're headed if they don't execute you.*

I turned away and walked into the desert. The temperature was dropping rapidly, so I hurried. I headed for the abandoned mines about ten miles north of the new ones. I started to run when the light disappeared completely, and the temperature dropped below freezing. The stars came out and blazed down on me, making the bear-claw cacti and the scrubby rustwood trees stand out with spooky clarity. I half expected them to reach out and grab me. I wasn't in a cheerful mood.

I ran for a long time, mentally thanking my coaches for all those early morning runs they had put me through. But that brought hard thoughts. I was never going to be the Half-G star I wanted to be. Maybe I was never going to be anything.

The old mines finally came into sight. They had been destroyed during the Ragnir war. How long ago had that been? Fifteen years? More like twenty, I thought. My dad had been young when he fought in them, probably not much older than me. Coach Wilson had brought us here numerous times on hikes, so the sight of that ruined place wasn't new to me. But I had never really felt it personally before, never had a reason to connect it with my own life.

We always left materials for building fires there. I built one, trying not to think about the cold as my numb hands fumbled with the lighter.

As cold as I was, Korry Vather was colder.

I sat in front of my little fire, utterly miserable, and wondered what to do next.

* * *

Morning in the desert was spectacular. The light shining through all that dust in the air is what does the trick. The Rust Mountains turned bloodred, then mellowed as the sun climbed higher. I sat on my frozen butt and tried to enjoy it, because I thought it could be my last.

I had thought up a plan by then, but I was scared to actually get started. It was too uncertain. I had Dad's money tucked under my clothes, enough to buy an ID. Jim Hughes had talked to me about that once, when he had been a little drunk and feeling friendly.

"If I don't make it to the pros, I'm gonna find a coyote and get off this rock," he had said.

"A coyote?"

"Yeah. They hang around the spaceport looking for desperate runaways. I guess that describes me pretty well."

"I guess it does. What do they get for getting you off planet?"

"Money. A whole lot of it."

"How are you gonna get money?"

He had taken out his knife and fingered the point. "How do you think? I know miner brats who have gotten out that way. I'm saving it for last choice."

"Yeah, but, if you get caught—"

"I get hard labor in the mines! Right?"

Right.

The ground warmed up a little bit as I sat there agonizing about it, and I watched a rootfox dig under a bear-claw cactus to get at the moisture stored there. It looked at me calmly as it chewed, and I almost hated it for being so innocent while I sat there a murderer. But life goes on, and I still wanted to be part of it.

So I got up and moved my feet back toward town.

I had actually only been to the spaceport once, to meet a friend of my father's who had been assigned to Hook. Once you get assigned there, you tend to be stuck for a long, *long* time. Most people don't make enough to take vacations; so in a way, the spaceport is almost a separate town, with hotels, casinos, restaurants, and shops for people just passing through or for the local big brass who can afford it.

Once I got there, I had no idea what to do next. I stood around and looked unhappy, hoping that would attract the coyotes. I didn't have to fake the look. The port was new and shiny, and made me feel like I had spent my whole life being scruffy without knowing it.

Of course, I was completely lost. The port was much bigger than I remembered it being. I had to ride a tran to get to the off-planet passenger lounges, and once there I jumped at the sight of anything remotely resembling a police uniform. I used a little of Dad's money to buy myself brunch in one of the overpriced snack bars and bought a pair of dark glasses in a gift shop in a futile attempt to disguise my features.

I was sitting in an overstuffed leather chair, watching rich people go by and feeling deprived, when the coyote finally approached me.

"You look lost," he said as he sat in the chair next to mine. He didn't look at me as he spoke, and for a moment I thought he might be talking to someone else. But no one else answered, so I said, "I'm looking for someone."

"Really?" he said to the ferns hanging overhead. "Anyone in particular?"

"No. Just someone who can help me."

"Hmmn." He steepled his fingers and studied the carpet. "That's nice."

I waited another fifteen minutes for him to speak again. I sneaked looks at his bald spot and the gray chest hairs peeking out of his low-cut muscle shirt—he wasn't the kind of guy most people like to see dressed that way—and I wondered if I hadn't stumbled onto a pimp by accident. He increased my doubts when he asked, "Are you a working girl?"

"No," I said emphatically.

"I was just wondering. No insult intended. It's just

that you have the most spectacular body I ever laid eyes on. Beautiful face, too.''

He said all this as casually as you would talk about the weather, which made me nervous. Then he shut up again, until I couldn't stand it anymore.

''Look,'' I said. ''I've got to get somewhere. I need someone to help me get somewhere.''

''Somewhere as in anywhere?''

''Yeah.''

''Follow me.''

He got up and walked casually toward the nearest bathrooms. I was hoping he wouldn't take me into the men's room—I was beginning to develop a horror of plumbing. The lounge was crowded anyway; people were certain to see me going in there with him. But no, he walked right past it and down a narrow service hall. He stopped in front of a closet, opened the door, and motioned for me to go in. I glanced behind me—people were walking past the entrance to the hall, but no one was looking our way.

''The trick is to look like you have every right to be doing whatever you're doing,'' he said, and pushed me into the closet. ''Free advice, kid.''

He got in there with me and shut the door, leaving us in pitch darkness. I tensed, waiting for him to grope me; but instead, he switched on a pocket flashlight.

''Let's see,'' he said as he fished in his pants pocket. ''You're about seventeen, right?''

''Close enough.''

''Okay. I think I've got something here.'' He pulled out three IDs. Two were for white people, one man and one woman. But the third was for a black girl who even looked a bit like me. He shone the light in my face and said, ''That will be two thousand credits.''

I froze. This was too easy. What if this guy was an undercover agent? I just stood there and sweated and shook, while he took it all in calmly and waited. Finally, I pulled the money out and handed it to him. I had had enough. If this was it, this was it. I couldn't take it anymore.

"Thanks." He wadded up the money and stuffed it into his other pocket. "Here's your ID. Good luck, kid."

He walked out of that closet and didn't even bother to close the door behind him. I followed a few seconds later, on shaky legs. He was already gone.

I took my ID and the rest of my money up to the Surahi Lines desk and bought a ticket to Moasaii. That cost me another thousand for coach, but I considered myself lucky to get that price. When you're going from nowhere to nowhere, you have to be prepared to pay everything you've got.

I must have looked like a zombie when the ticket agent examined my new ID. But she barely glanced at me as she handed it back. "Gate six," she said. "The *Obsidian Butterfly* is leaving in half an hour. You should have plenty of time."

I walked with stiff legs to the tran and rode to gate six, my face as blank as the mind that rested behind it. I must have looked like the "Saint of Last Resorts." I went through the security checkpoint, where they checked my ID again and x-rayed my meager belongings. Once again, I was sure they had found me out. But they all looked bored, and seemed only too happy to get rid of me.

"Down this corridor another five hundred feet," said the guard as she handed me my things.

I opened my mouth to say thank you, but nothing came out. So I just went.

The *Obsidian Butterfly* was a middle-aged ship, and it was twice as luxurious as anything I had ever seen. It didn't have what I would call fighting lines, but it wasn't bad. Didn't look much like a butterfly, though. It was more like a bird. A really *big* bird. A big black bird. Took me half an hour to walk out to where it was sitting on the field. I was still expecting the police to grab me, so I tried to calm the beating of my heart. I didn't want to get my hopes up only to have them destroyed at the last moment.

I walked up the long ramp and smiled back at the

stewards and stewardesses in the main lock. "Welcome to the *Butterfly,*" said a blond lady. "May I see your ticket?"

I held it out, smiling numbly.

"That's deck four," she said. "Take the main elevator down at the end of this corridor, ride up to level four, then go right."

"Thanks!" I said nervously, but she had already forgotten me.

So I went up to my room. It was actually a lot bigger than I had thought it would be. It had a nice-sized bathroom, too. The bed had safety webbing over it for takeoff, and on the bedside table were a variety of sedatives to make takeoff easier. I didn't take them for that reason, though. I thought I could handle the takeoff forces. I took the sedatives because I was just plain scared.

I lay there for forty-five minutes. I didn't think the police were coming anymore. That would have been too easy. No, I was going away forever, away from my career as a sports star, away from the only friends and family I had known. And I had done it to myself; that was what hurt the most. I had fucked my own life. I barely felt it when the ship moved out to the launch area. I fell asleep before we took off, wondering what I was going to find on Moasaii. I had picked it because it was the cheapest fare.

I still don't know what Moasaii is like, because I never got there. But that was John Lovelock's fault.

Why do we always do the things we swear we never would? I was a virgin when I left Hook. Maybe that explains my rotten disposition. I was very scared and confused as I walked into the Butterfly Bar and Grill, and with my background you would think I would have avoided strangers at all costs.

But instead, I talked a mile a minute to the man who sat down next to me at the counter. John never stood a chance. I don't think he would have come onto me if I hadn't attached myself to him.

"Where you headed?" he asked me.

"Moasaii."

"You going to work in one of the topless bars there?"

"Ah—maybe."

"You'll make more money on Z'taruh. A lot more money. Moasaii isn't any richer than Hook. In fact, it might be poorer."

"You headed to Z'taruh?"

"Yes," he said, guardedly.

John wasn't what you would call a handsome man. He was forty, about twenty pounds overweight, and wore conservative suits. He had a bad back. His blond hair was thinning in front, and his breath always smelled like tobacco. Probably his most attractive features were his eyes. They were steel blue, and very commanding.

He never came out and admitted it, but John was a drug dealer.

"I'm in politics," he told me. "I'm working for Bernard Goldbar."

Yes, John, who used and sold drugs liberally, had a sixteen-year-old girlfriend (me), knew the inside of every topless bar between Earth and the Q'rin Empire, and had a passion for illegal hand weapons, was working for the most conservative, right wing, religious fundamentalist you could imagine: Bernard Goldbar.

For a couple of years after we broke up, I was ashamed of the submissive, deferential way I had behaved toward John. But when I really examine what happened the first evening we spent together, I realize *he* was the one who had no choice. His male ego would not permit him to let me pay for that first brunch—or any of the meals we had together afterward—and this may have been what made me decide to stick with him. I had two thousand left in my stash, and I had absolutely no idea what I was going to do to earn more.

"You really do have a great body for exotic dancing," John told me, as brunch spilled out into late afternoon and we were working on our sixth cup of coffee.

"Thanks."

"You don't seem surprised to hear that." He seemed a little angry at my lack of modesty, but I'm afraid that was a characteristic I never learned to fake.

"I know I'm beautiful," I said. "In fact, I'd like to show you just how beautiful I am."

"Really?" He blew smoke in my face. I loved it. "I'll let you know how you rate."

So we made a date to meet for dinner. I went back to my cabin and tidied up as well as I could. My clothes were terribly drab compared to what the other women were wearing on the *Butterfly,* and I wished I had some extra money to spend on pretty things. I was looking in the mirror at myself when it suddenly struck me that I was planning to sleep with John.

My mouth went dry at the prospect. I also suddenly felt as horny as four years of teenage frustration could possibly make me. It never occurred to me that he might say no, though I'm sure it occurred to him, despite his fascination with breasts. Anyway, the whole idea made me feel very shy, and I went to dinner with my knees trembling.

I scored points by ordering a medium-priced entrée. He actually took my hand for that. But he frowned when he felt the calluses in my palms.

"What's this?" He turned them over to examine them.

"I played ball in school."

"I'd better not get into any fights with you, then."

This was true, but I knew enough not to say so. I smiled and arched my back subtly, catching his attention with my best features.

"I bet the boys loved bouncing off of those on the court," he said huskily.

This was actually a pretty tacky comment, but I didn't care. For once I could listen to a come-on without feeling like I had to save face by fighting. Hot waves began to pass through my body.

"Of course they did," I said, then gulped my water.

I was hungry, but I couldn't eat much. John ate with a good appetite, though I think he might have been holding back a little out of embarrassment. I couldn't have known at the time, but I think he must have had some doubts about whether or not he could perform to my satisfaction. This was probably why he made me sit through three after-dinner cups of coffee.

"I sure would like to see your cabin," I said finally, with all the subtlety of a Q'rin shock tank.

"Don't worry, kitten." He winked at me over his last cup of coffee. "You will."

I got the message and stopped pushing him. After a face-saving amount of time, we got up and left the restaurant.

As soon as we got to John's cabin, he turned me on to his supply of first-class loki.

"You ever smoked that before?" he asked as I coughed like an old woman.

"No. Had to stay clean for sports."

"Oh, yeah," he said as he sucked in half a stick's worth of smoke. "I played ball once. Football."

"Huh?"

"You wouldn't know it, kid. It doesn't involve artificial gravity. You have to have *real* mass to play football."

Sounded pretty lame to me, but I didn't say so. I just held in as much of the smoke as I could, hoping it would counter the overdose of caffeine I had consumed during the day.

But I don't know if it helped me relax or not. I thought I wanted to make love, but it turned out to be much more of an inner struggle than I had thought it would be. John acted like Mr. Cool once he had the loki in his system. He kissed me and stroked my breasts right through my clothing, which felt great, but also tensed me up.

I doubt he ever had any notion of how close he came to getting killed that first night. I should have had the foresight to leave all of my knives in my cabin before going to supper, but foresight was not my great talent back then.

"Relax," he kept saying. "Have some more loki."

So I had some more loki, and I kept still as he pulled off my shirt and then my bra. His eyes glazed over when he saw my naked breasts.

"Look at this," he said. "I can't believe it."

He had completely missed the two knives that were concealed in my sleeves. I threw the shirt across the room to resist the temptation, the knee-jerk reaction of cutting him. This was hard, because loki can cause some very realistic inner visions. I didn't think about my mother at all, but I did think of Korry Vather and his pink mouth; which only led me back to knives again.

But as my clothing came off piece by piece, along with my knives in their secret pockets, I let them go. This was my release. Soon we were squirming around in his bed, naked black and lily white, licking and kissing and fondling each other like a couple of sex maniacs. I quickly became attached to John's other best feature.

So much for my sexual fears of being either frigid or a sadomasochist. John showed me I was normal. For that, I will always be grateful.

"You're going to have to go back to your cabin," he said when we were done. "I can't sleep when other people are in the room. Makes me nervous."

At the time I thought he was afraid I might rob him while he was asleep, but now I think he was trying to dismiss me as a one-night stand. I went, because I've always needed my own space. Besides, I was belatedly worried about something I hadn't discussed with John.

Birth control. I didn't have any.

I went the very next morning to the ship clinic and bought a three-year supply of the once-a-week pill. I almost got the once-a-month pill, but I was afraid I would forget to take it. If the gynecologist found left-over sperm in my vagina, she didn't say so. But she did give me some pamphlets on abortion, adoption, and womb transfer. I read them all, carefully.

I called John. "Want to have breakfast with me?" I asked.

"I'm not sure I'm up to company this morning," he said.

"Well, I can understand that. After all, you did get your brains fucked out last night." What can I say? I was sixteen.

There was a long pause. "Well, I always give as good as I get."

"You sure do, daddy."

It was a pattern that was to last our entire relationship. John never wanted a girlfriend. His ego would have preferred a different woman every night, like his friend Dominik had. But Dominik was twenty-five and looked like Michelangelo's *David.*

"I'm starving!" I said finally. "You coming or not?"

He insisted on bringing Dominik and Dominik's latest lady friend along. When he introduced them, both of them stared at my breasts; but Dominik wasn't a bad guy. He actually paid attention to my conversation.

"Where you headed?" the lady friend asked me.

"Z'taruh," I said, before John could say anything.

John gave me a hard stare.

"I'm going to check out the topless bars there, get a job," I quickly added.

But instead, I stayed with John for another two years.

Chapter 4

So it was John who introduced me to Z'taruh, the planet of my destiny. But I didn't actually live there until after we broke up. In between that time, I traveled with John on his drug–pseudo-political circuit, and Z'taruh was an important stopover. For one thing, it was where he bought his own private supplies of numbrain and loki, wholesale, from Cliff Goldbar, who just happened to be Bernard Goldbar's grandson.

My first sight of Z'taruh impressed me very much. As a military brat from a backwater planet, I was ignorant of many modern conveniences. I didn't even mind how damp Z'taruh was. The Spacer Sector in Capital looked like Shangri-la as John and Dominik led me from one expensive bar to another. Towering above us was the glittering Hill, where the Human power brokers live.

"I've got a friend up there," John told me. He kept trying to call this friend as the night wore on, and was very upset when he couldn't get an answer. It didn't help that his back was hurting from the planet gravity. The starliners are really John's favorite habitat, because they have about three-quarters of the average Earth-type gravity. He hated having to come down.

Anyway, I was so dazzled, I hardly noticed how frustrated John was becoming; just as I hardly noticed that the bars we went to were mostly of the topless or nude variety, and John kept trying to introduce me to the owners. I had already forgotten my lie to him about my job goals, so I didn't take the hint.

"This is nice," I kept saying. "I could get used to

this." I hadn't seen Deadtown or even Midtown yet, so I was unaware of the poverty that was the reverse side of this splendor. There were Deadtowners and Skids on the streets, but they were just part of the exotic background as far as I was concerned.

One thing I did notice was how much John disliked Q'rins. He wouldn't go into bars that had too many Q'rin customers. I asked him why not.

"They stink and their women are ugly," he said, then excused himself to go make another call to his *friend.* Dominik and I sat back to watch some lady strip multicolored latex-like stuff off her otherwise naked skin. It was kind of disturbing.

"So," Dominik said, "you gonna try to get a job in one of these bars?"

"Shit," I said. "I forgot about that."

"Meaning you never intended to in the first place."

"Well—" I couldn't make up an excuse to put him off, so I shrugged.

"I knew you were lying when you said you wanted to work in a titty bar," he said. "And you knew it, and John knew it. But you know what? I think you could be useful to us in another way."

"How's that?"

"As a bodyguard."

That surprised me. In the six months since I had left Hook, I had crawled into the role of soft passive female for John, because hard women turned him off. I had put in some time in the Half-G ball rooms on the *Butterfly,* and even a little in the Double-G rooms, but they were different from the simulations I had played on Hook, and no one on the ship was worth playing; so I wasn't anywhere close to my old form.

Still, his suggestion sent a thrill up my spine.

"You carry a knife or two, don't you, Larissa." It wasn't a question.

"I like to feel safe."

"You know John has a bad back. He was a tough man in the old days, but now it's mostly just talk."

I certainly knew that. He had disappointed me the

night before by insisting that his back hurt too much to make love. But he had gotten me all worked up first, and I was still a little resentful.

"That's why he does so much numbrain," Dominik was saying. "Because it kills the pain. And he doesn't like what the doctors tell him."

"That he might end up paralyzed someday?"

"Yeah. He almost got into that new nerve-replacement program, but he withdrew at the last minute. I'm gonna tell you why, because I think you're gonna stick around for a while, and the more you know, the better you'll do your job." He sipped the red liquid in his glass, which was turning his tongue pink.

"He was afraid they would tell him he wasn't a good candidate for the operation," he said. "He would rather sedate himself than find out he's incurable."

"Then he should have the good sense to stay out of fights," I said. Actually, John did. But I had seen him stare people down often enough, and I believed it was only a matter of time before his blue eyes lost their steel.

"Why don't you act as his bodyguard?" I asked, though I knew damn well, and he knew I knew. He had enough pride to give me a hard look before he answered. It didn't scare me a bit, but I kept a neutral look on my face.

"I'm a lover, not a fighter. Besides—*honey*—you outclass me. I've seen you in the Double-G room. John has seen you, too."

"You think he wants to offer me the job?"

"No. You'll have to ask him. And he'll probably say no the first time."

I nodded.

John was on the way back to the table, and the stripper was down to a pink layer.

"We're going up the Hill," he said, not sounding exactly happy about it.

"Good news," said Dominik, who was now refusing to look me in the eye.

I wasn't sure that Cliff Goldbar was such a good friend. For one thing, we had to walk from the end of the public transport line all the way to his house. It took almost two hours. Didn't bother me, but I could tell John was hurting.

Cliff answered the door himself. Later John told me Cliff lived there alone. He had a maid who came in once a week, and he did all his own cooking. He looked up at me from his five-foot-four vantage point and asked John, "Who's this, your bodyguard?"

I seized his hand and shook it before John could answer. "That's right," I said. "Call me Larissa."

He was respectful to me from then on, but he played weird games with John. He was in the interesting position of being rich without ever having earned a penny on his own. The only thing he was good at was small-time drug deals. If he had tried the big stuff, the real bosses would have chewed him up.

John respected Cliff's money, but he didn't respect Cliff. And they were friends. It was very strange.

After all that time John had spent trying to get in touch with Cliff, and all the pain of dragging his bad back up the Hill, I expected him to get right down to business. And maybe he tried to do that, in an indirect sort of way; but Cliff wasn't having any of it. After two hours of watching the three of them consume imported beer and listening to them talk about swamp rats and old girlfriends, I doubted that Cliff Goldbar had a serious thought in his head.

"Got me a fat one last week," he said, along about two in the morning. I had been dozing, and I wasn't sure if he meant a girl or a rat.

"So what are you gonna do with it?" asked Dominik.

"Play it. Maybe breed it. It's the biggest goddamn fucker you ever saw. This one is a winner."

"Man, you always say that about your fucking rats," said Dominik, "and I ain't never seen one."

"Come to Medusa's tomorrow. Rodney's in the amateur round."

"Rodney?" I said. It was the first time I'd spoken since I'd introduced myself, and it made them jump. "Rodney the rat? I gotta see this. You fight rats? I mean, whataya do, hit them with a stick?"

John threw me a disgusted look. He rarely paid much attention to me when we were with his friends, but he liked to think I listened closely to everything that was said. "No," he said, "we throw them in a pit with teenaged nymphomaniacs and watch them fuck each other to death."

I was beginning to wish he'd take some numbrain instead of the stims the three of them were eating along with their beer. I knew he wanted it. The stims could only have made his back pain worse. I could see the strain around his eyes and mouth. Cliff should have been able to see it, too, unless he was completely insensitive, which he might have been. They bullshitted and drank and stimmed themselves until dawn while I dozed and stifled impatient questions that I knew I wouldn't get answers for anyway.

Sometime around 7:00 A.M., Cliff prepared a lavish breakfast. I consumed most of it myself, because they were too stimmed to have appetites.

"You're a great cook," I told Cliff.

"Thank you," he said, and seemed genuinely pleased.

"Don't know if you're gonna want all that food in your stomach when we watch the rat fights at Medusa's," Dominik said around a cigarette.

"Huh? When was all this arranged?" I asked John. I was angry that he seemed not to care that this neurotic rich fool was putting us through one unpleasant experience after another, just so John could get his fix. But John simply stared into space and guzzled black coffee.

"Do I even get to take a shower first?" I demanded.

"No," John said. "First show's at eight."

"Who the fuck wants to see a rat fight at eight

o'clock in the fucking morning? In fact, who wants to see a rat do anything?"

"Shut up," said John. "We're going."

Everyone was quiet for several minutes. I was trying to decide if I was mad for being told to shut up. John was still staring straight ahead, looking like a bad imitation of the strong silent type. Dominik was staring at the bright yellow kitchen table, and Cliff was shoving dishes into the recycler, his back stiff. I wondered if his feelings were hurt.

At about 7:45, we roared out of Cliff's garage in one of his private trans and down the Hill to the Spacer Sector. The morning was warm and humid, just like the night had been, and the humidity made me wish again for a cool shower. But I kept my mouth shut.

Medusa's was a little disappointing from the outside, kind of run-down. There were a lot of Skids and Deadtowners outside. The former were digging through the trash, and the latter were eyeing us the same way I used to eye people on Hook. It made my spine tingle.

Inside, the place was fancier and a lot more interesting. It was inhabited by an odd assortment of aliens and humans from just about every social class. There were lots of Q'rin there. A lot of Lyrri, too; and I stared my fill at these people I had only seen in vids before. They were even whiter than I had thought, and they looked kind of like dolls—you know, too hard and too perfect. They gave me the shivers.

I saw an Aesopian elephant man sitting in the corner, near the back. He was gigantic, and he was dressed in a short kilt, just like the ones the Egyptians wear in those ancient bas-reliefs. I would liked to have stayed and looked at him some more, but the guys kept moving through the room toward the back door.

The rat pits were out there.

It smelled awful around those pits. Fancy cologne and old sweat clashed as their owners rubbed elbows. It didn't matter how rich or poor they were; their eyes all glazed over as they stared into pits from which came an ominous hissing and snarling. I had to get a look at what was in there. I shouldered my way to one of the rims and looked over.

Z'taruhn rats are about the size of a small dog, maybe twenty to thirty pounds. They have sharp teeth and very smart eyes. They use their hands. I think they're probably about as smart as orangutans, maybe a little smarter. A pack of them can bring down an armed man, easily. Z'taruhn entrepreneurs hunt them down and train them to tear each other apart in pits while people bet on them.

Me, I felt sorry for them.

"Which one is yours?" I asked Cliff.

"Huh?"

"Which one is Rodney?"

"Oh. That one." He pointed to an overweight fellow who was crouched near the wall. Rodney lashed his tail and hissed at any rat who came near him, but he didn't attack. The others left him alone, probably because he was no threat.

Two others were going at it with teeth and claws, moving almost too fast to follow, pausing occasionally to pant and look disoriented.

"Are they drugged?" I asked.

"Don't have to drug them. They're always like that."

Before too long I was bored—and disgusted with people who could get so excited over watching animals hurt each other. I stared at the crowd when I wasn't watching John, and wondered how much longer he was going to put up with this nonsense. He looked horrible. He had developed a tic under one eye, and he looked about sixty. The picture of a numbrain addict in pain. I was beginning to despise Cliff Goldbar.

"Hey," Cliff said after two hours of this torture, "want to go on a rat hunt?"

"No!" I said before the others could get a word in. "You and John have some business to attend to, and then we need some more food and a lot of sleep."

I was giving him my no-argument-don't-cross-me tone, and he was giving me back a blank look.

John was furious with me for a moment, but then sort of sagged. "Yeah," he said. "It's time, man."

I think Cliff was mad that we made him leave before his precious Rodney was done "fighting," but he took us back anyway. Dominik gave me a wink when the others weren't looking, and John squeezed my hand as we sat in the tran together.

John bought his numbrain and dosed himself. He was out in seconds. Dominik had disappeared into the depths of Cliff's place just as soon as we got back, and I realized that we were to be guests in this big house that was as empty as its owner's personality. It gave me the creeps, but I was relieved to step into a good shower and then slip into a clean bed next to John. The two of us slept until noon the next day.

And then we went on that stupid rat hunt.

The tone for the day was set when John and I attempted to make love that morning. He was too stiff in every place but the one that counted. The failure made him angry—if at me, I wasn't sure—but I thought that at least this meant we wouldn't be running around after any rats.

But John was even more excited about the hunt than Cliff. In fact, Cliff had almost changed his mind about going by the time we were up and around. Dominik and I would have been thrilled to do just about anything else, but John was not to be denied one of his very favorite vices: illegal weapons. He had one of his force rifles unpacked in the middle of the living room floor, and he and the other two fussed over it for a solid hour while I sat with my chin in my hands and tried not to think uncharitable thoughts.

"Wake up, Larissa!" John said.

Grow up, John, was what I thought, but I said nothing. Having been raised on a military planet, I knew something about weapons. John's experience was mostly theoretical. He read about guns, collected them, but hardly ever used them. That explained why he wanted to go hunting with a force rifle, which is anything but a hunting rifle. I expect a rat hit with a force bolt would explode. No trophy. John was probably just interested in shooting and killing something for the hell of it. Not my idea of good sporting fun.

But I went along with it anyway, and within another hour we were packed up and on our way to the swamp in Cliff's ridiculously luxurious Land Rover. With the top rolled down.

I got my first look at what lies outside the Spacer Sector.

At first glance, Capital isn't that different from Hook Central, especially in the way the Human and Q'rin sectors are divided. As I looked at the massive fortress walls that designated the Q'rin-only areas, I felt a pang of—not homesickness, exactly. Of *I know that.*

Midtown and Deadtown were quite a letdown from the Spacer Sector. Midtown, cleaned up and slightly more modern, could have passed for Hook Central. But Deadtown—yes, that's what makes Z'taruh a planet of extremes. The rich are ridiculously rich, and the poor are astonishingly poor.

There were other differences, too.

On the Hill, I saw only rich Humans. In the Spacer Sector were Humans, Lyrri, and Q'rin, plus a variety of people just in from the nearby landing fields. Midtown is where you'll find the most diversity, with Aesopians thrown in to flavor the mix, along with a smattering of other races that were not as familiar to me. I saw a lot of Aesopians walking around in kilts like the one the elephant man had worn in Medusa's; but most of them were wearing ragged versions of what my military background told me must have once been uniforms or fatigues. I wondered if they'd had them from the Ragnir war. They don't make uniforms that last that long anymore.

Only children live in Deadtown. They eyed Cliff's Rover as if they wanted to strip it, and us, to the bone. We were attacked three times, but only in a half-hearted manner, as if they were testing us. Fortunately, the Rover proved that it had more going for it than just good looks.

Several times John took aim at rag-wrapped urchins who looked like incomplete mummies. They laughed at John, knowing somehow that he wouldn't fire (which was more than I knew). They also wore ragged vests and belts torn from the plasti-fix that was supposed to be covering holes in the decaying buildings. Those of them that had shoes didn't have a matching pair. But they had dignity, I had to give them that. They reminded me of the miners, back home. They met John's threats with open contempt, and after a while he stopped aiming that damned rifle. His mood had fallen appreciably since we got started.

We left Deadtown and entered Outskirts, the ring of warehouses that completely surrounds Capital. On this side, most of the structures were abandoned or wrecked, but some of them were heavily guarded. We hurried through this section a lot faster than we had through Deadtown, and splashed on into the marshes.

The mist wrapped itself around us until we could barely see ten feet in front of us. It smelled ripe and moldy, and made me long again for the dry climate of Hook.

"What else is out here but rats?" I asked.

"Loki farms," said Cliff. "A few redweed farms, too. They make numbrain out of that and ship it off planet. Sometimes the Skids come out here and gather redweed wild, make meltdown out of it. Sometimes the rats get them."

"Skids?"

"Old people. You saw them in Midtown."

"Where are the loki farms?"

"Mostly on the other side of the planet. We wouldn't want to get close to them anyway. They shoot first and don't ask any questions at all."

John elbowed me in the ribs, though Cliff was the one doing most of the talking.

I shut up and let boredom descend on me like a wet

blanket. I felt inclined to do this because I mistakenly believed that at least one of these men had been on a hunt before and knew what he was doing. What I didn't know was that when Cliff had bragged that he had "caught him a fat one," what he had really meant was that when he hired some professional hunters to take him out on a rat catch, they had allowed him to push a few buttons. He then paid them a substantial fee, and took the rat home.

I'm just guessing about most of this, since I had to piece it together much later, but this is what I think happened:

Rich fools like Cliff want to engage in some sport (but not *too* much danger) so they hire professional catchers. Any catcher who spends five minutes with Cliff knows he doesn't know a fat, lazy rat from a sharp, fighting rat; so they go after the easiest rat they can find. They try to make it look exciting and difficult; but Cliff, who is only selectively stupid, sees through this deception. He buys himself a Land Rover just in time for us to visit and go with him on a rat hunt.

So there we were, four people who knew nothing about swamps, rats, and Rover repair, making our steady way toward some tall vegetation. With the top down.

"Let's see what kind of path this thing can cut!" Cliff was saying. At the back of my mind, a little voice was asking, *Don't you already know*? But I was too busy brooding about the possibility of exploding rats to pay it proper attention.

We plowed into the vegetation, and ground to a halt.

"Does that answer your question?" I snarled, as debris rained down on our heads.

Cliff just laughed and fiddled with his controls. I began to suspect all was not well.

The three of them argued and pushed buttons for about fifteen minutes, but all they found out was how to work the windshield wipers.

"Why don't we just back up?" I asked.

"Because the rats are in here," said Cliff.

"What, in the trees?" I looked up, and sure enough, not six inches from my nose, suspended from a broken branch and looking every bit as surprised as me, was a big, fat rat. "Oh," I said. "Here's one now."

Chaos in the cockpit. John swung his rifle up and smacked me right in the jaw. He tried to aim it at the rat, fired, and hit Dominik in the face with the rifle butt. At almost the same moment, Cliff threw the Rover into reverse, and we all went crashing to the floor.

Then the engine died.

Outside the Rover we heard *ka-sploot, ka-sploot, ka-sploot* as the rat ran away across the swamp.

John kicked open the door and went after the rat. He made a large *splat* as he landed in the muck.

"Hey!" I said. "Is it safe to go out there?"

"I don't think so," said Dominik. Cliff just messed with the controls.

"Well, tell him to come back here!" I said to Dominik.

"Hey John!" Dominik yelled. "Come on back! We'll chase it in the Rover!"

"No way!" John panted. "That thing makes too much noise!" This as he went *shmuk, shmuk, shmuk,* across the swamp.

"We have to go after him," I said.

"You're his bodyguard," said Cliff.

"Yeah," said Dominik, refusing to look me in the eye.

So I went after John. My feet sank in the muck up to about mid-calf. It was an utterly disgusting sensation, but my panic was beginning to rise in proportion to the distance John was putting between himself and the Rover. I slogged off in the direction of the *shmuk shmuk* noises as fast as I could.

"John!" I shouted. "Get the hell back here! You're crazy!"

"Shut up, bitch!" he called back. "You'll scare them away—*aaarrgh*!!!"

He stopped making noise. I froze and listened hard. I could hear a faint *ka-sploot, ka-sploot,* but it was going farther away.

"John? You okay?"

"—my back."

I started to move forward again. "Keep talking," I called.

No answer.

"I said keep talking!"

"What the fuck do you want me to say!?"

"How about 'I'm over here'? Say whatever the hell you want, but say something!"

"Something," he said. "Something. Something, something, something. Something? Something!" And he kept doing that until I caught up with him. I was ready to smack him.

"You can stop now," I said.

He did. He was looking over his shoulder, toward the open swamp. "Do you hear that?" he said.

I did. Coming toward us from several directions: *ka-sploot, ka-sploot, splash*!

"Shit." I hauled John's arm over my shoulder. We began to "run" with me half dragging John along.

"Dominik!" I screamed. "Where the hell are you!?"

"Over here" came the answer. It didn't sound as far as I thought it would, but with the rats getting closer all the time, it might as well have been a million miles away.

"Come on," I kept panting to John. He did his best to comply. Dominik kept yelling, "Over here!" And the rats got close enough for us to hear their hissing.

As it turned out, we were only about fifty feet from the Rover. I don't know how far away the rats had started out; but we all got back to the Rover at almost the same moment.

Dominik and Cliff hauled us through the door and slammed it shut. Half a second later, a hundred rat feet pelted the outside of the Rover. I looked up and saw several pairs of eyes glaring down at us.

"I see you figured out how to get the top up," I said.

"Yep," said Cliff.

Somewhere along the line, John had lost his precious gun. By the time Cliff got the engine started and headed us back to town again, John had lost most of his spirit, too. He stayed on the floor and stared into space.

The rats jumped off the Rover as soon as Outskirts was in sight, and ran back into the swamp.

Cliff, Dominik, and I were careful not to speak to John, or even very much to each other. I stared out the windows at the spectacle of Deadtown at dusk, privately relieved that we were done with the nonsense. I figured that once John got some food, numbrain, and sleep, everything would be all right again.

But it wasn't. John never forgave me for saving his butt when he couldn't save it himself. We were never quite friends again.

Ultimately, we were enemies.

Chapter 5

It took another year and a half for my precarious relationship with John to come undone, and those months were an object lesson in why so many mismatched people stick together long after they know better. Funny what Human beings will do just to keep having sex three times a week.

John barely spoke to me when we got back to the *Butterfly*. He did name me as a member of his party to the ship's clerk, which meant my fare was paid for by the Bernard Goldbar Campaign Fund.

"So I'm a member of the team now?" I asked him.

He gave me a down-the-nose, don't-get-uppity look and rubbed his lower back. "God, this ship gravity feels good," he said, and staggered to his cabin. I knew without asking that I shouldn't follow. He probably just wanted to numb himself and go to bed.

"What a complicated guy," I said to Dominik.

"Sure you still want the job?" he said.

"Better than stripping latex off my body six nights a week. By the way, when's payday?"

He took out his wallet and slipped me a hundred credit note. "Here. Don't ever ask John for it, or he'll act like he don't know what you're talking about."

I put the money away, privately relieved that this wasn't something I'd have to argue with John about.

Dominik winked at me and strolled on down the corridor, giving all the women plenty of time to check him out. He smiled at one lady who must have been fifty, and I wondered if he might not have alternate sources of income.

That night we all met in the Butterfly Bar and Grill, as usual. John seemed to be feeling better, and was actually cheerful. I thought he was just enjoying the lighter gravity. I didn't figure out until much later that it was because of the girl Dominik had brought along.

Her name was Solange. She had light olive skin and dark brunet hair, brown eyes, and a trim figure. But I dismissed her immediately, because she was one of Dominik's girls; and because, quite frankly, I've never seen anyone nearly as beautiful as I am. Not that I've been looking.

I hardly remember anything about that evening, except that John was cheerful and that's the first time Solange came into the picture. I think I had steak.

The next thing I remember was several months later, when we got to Odin.

Everybody knows Odin is a prison planet. I knew it, too, but the reality just didn't sink in until we were almost there. I had some panicky feelings about it, and I even went so far as to tell John I couldn't accompany him down there.

"I think I'm coming down with the flu," I told him, and my gray complexion and shaky hands helped with the illusion.

"All right," he said. "Stay in bed and take care."

He made much less of a fuss than I had expected. In fact, he was downright distracted. If I hadn't been so wrapped up in my fear, I would have wondered why.

The next day I didn't meet them for breakfast. John had said that they were going to head down to the planet surface afterward, and I was afraid they might ask me to come along. When I heard the knock on my door, I thought maybe John had come to say goodbye. I put on my best sick face and answered it.

The steward was standing there.

"Sorry to bother you, miss. I just wanted to warn you that the agents will be here soon for your security check."

"The agents?" I choked. "For *my* security check?"

"Yes, ma'am. It's standard procedure when we go into orbit around prison planets. They want to make sure no one is smuggling anything on or off the planet, so they search the entire ship before and after—"

"Looking for drugs and stuff?" I interrupted.

"Right. And fugitives who might—"

"When will they get here?"

"About half an hour."

"Thanks."

I practically slammed the door in his face. I was dressed and out of my room within ten minutes. I ran to the shuttle deck, praying they hadn't left without me. I made it by five minutes.

"I thought you were sick," John said as I shoved in beside him.

"I just couldn't stand the thought of being alone all day," I told him. "Besides, I'm starting to feel better. Maybe it was one of those twenty-four-hour things."

I was careful not to look at him, so I don't know if he believed that or not. Solange and Dominik seemed not to even be hearing what we were saying, though I'm sure Dominik heard every word. I gazed out the window at the ice planet below, wishing I was somewhere else.

Odin is beautiful, though; maybe the most beautiful planet in the whole System. It's so cold, the oxygen is frozen. The center of the planet is warmer, and it has ice volcanoes that erupt regularly. The prison complex has huge super-tough windows to let all the glorious view in, but the atmosphere inside is even drier than on Hook. Made my nose itch.

When we stepped off the shuttle and into the Visitors' Center, I was congratulating myself for having outsmarted the authorities. I suppose I just assumed that we would find our hotel and no one would ask us anything about where we had come from. The Visitors' Center looked so friendly and sparkly, I could hardly believe there was a prison attached to it, except that I had seen it on approach. We got into a long line. I was so relieved to have escaped the agents on the

Butterfly, I didn't even wonder what it was for until I was boxed in on all sides. Then it was too late to go back.

"What are we waiting for?" I asked John.

"Security checkpoint."

It took several moments for that to sink in, as my eyes darted back and forth from the two walls that now closed us into a corridor so narrow, I couldn't possibly have forced my way past the people who were behind me. I kept moving my feet forward with everyone else, hoping that this checkpoint consisted of a couple of bored security guards who would just look at my ID and pass me through.

No such luck. They had a retinal scanner. I had a retinal file, just like every military brat. They were going to get me. They were going to slap the cuffs on me and say, "So you're the bitch that murdered that boy back on Hook! We've been looking for you!"

I moved my feet. The others went through the scanner, one by one: first Dominik, then Solange (who had already lasted months longer than any of Dominik's other girlfriends), then John. And then it was my turn.

I stepped onto the square with my head held high, feeling utterly numb as the scanner zapped me right in the eyeball and read my pattern, assessing the damning information I knew had to be there. I gazed out the big windows as I waited, unwilling for the others to see my guilty expression, and I saw an Odinian ice cat not ten feet away from the complex. It was chewing ice in its powerful jaws, eating its daily requirement of oxygen, and watching me with its huge, onyx eyes. It was as big as a horse, and it had six legs, but those eyes said *cat, cat, cat* to me. *I'm a cat! What are you?*

"Clear," announced the security man. "Step on through."

I couldn't believe my ears. I could have sworn that the search had taken twice as long for me as it had for the others, and I had been sure that they had come up with the goods. I stumbled as I got off the platform, and the technician gave me a penetrating look; I could feel the mask of boredom that had slipped down over my face, and he glanced away, sure of my stupidity.

The mask stayed in place as I joined the others, and I had no power to exchange it for something else, so I left it there. It must have irritated John, because he said, "This is the most maximum security complex in the system, you know. Show a little respect."

I had respect all right. I was so relieved I could hardly walk. But he gave me the jolt I needed to straighten my face up a bit; when I couldn't keep it straight, I just turned my mug toward the spectacular scenery outside. The entire complex seemed one giant picture window, but I wondered if the prisoners were permitted such a view. What would be more punishment: to look out at all that glory from your cell and envy the ice cats, who were free there; or to have only blank walls to look at? It still makes me sad to think about it.

So we hustled ourselves to our adjoining rooms in the hotel in the Visitors' Center, and the first thing John did was call the guy who presumably set up the rally John was supposed to speak at that night; because, believe it or not, John was still going through the motions of being Mr. Campaign Worker. He got off the phone, mad as a hornet.

"We're canceled," he said.

I was still looking out the window, but this time it was because I didn't want him to see that I wasn't surprised. For the whole two years I knew John, I never once saw him give a speech he was scheduled to give. In fact, I never saw him do anything at all that could be remotely connected with campaign work.

"Maybe you ought to hop in the shower, big guy," Dominik said.

John was shooting looks at the door between our rooms, acute embarrassment creasing on his face. Solange was in the other bathroom, taking a shower herself, and he almost seemed worried that she might have heard what he said about the cancellation.

"Yeah," John said. "I think I will."

Once we were alone, I asked the question. "Look. Why the hell would John be giving a campaign speech on a prison planet? These guys aren't even allowed to vote!"

"Whatever you do," Dominik said, "don't ask *him* that."

"I'm asking you."

"I don't know what's going on. I didn't make the arrangements."

"Well, then why is he so upset? His arrangements always get canceled."

"He's got a bad case of I'm-being-watched-itis."

"Huh?"

"Never mind. Just follow my cues, okay?"

Yeah, right. Cues. Dominik was the worst cue giver ever born. He always just did what he wanted, then asked why I hadn't picked up on his damn *cues*. My brat upbringing was no help with the more subtle of Human relations. Now I'm grateful for those two years with John, otherwise known as Mr. Oblique.

"Okay," I said, my face still frozen in the *bored* mode.

"And wipe that look off your face!" he laughed.

I tried. I really did.

It wasn't more than two hours after we had checked into that hotel in the Visitors' Center before John was having a tête-à-tête with some prison guards in another room, selling them drugs. Snoot and loki, I think, and maybe a little numbrain—though he was always careful not to deplete his personal supplies of that stuff. We had met them in the hotel coffee shop, and I'm still not sure whether the meeting was accidental or not.

"I'm Ben Jones," their unofficial spokesman had said. "This is Oscar Teal, and this is Mattie M'Benga." Mattie smiled at us, and in fact, always seemed to be smiling at some private joy. Oscar had the look of an ex-miner. He and I disliked each other instantly. Ben was a handsome man, with skin the color of caramel. He made a point of looking at my face more than he looked at my chest, which I appreciated, because I liked him. Later I found out I had good reason to.

I don't know whose room we ended up in—I doubt it was rented for more than a couple of hours. There were no clothes or personal effects. Ben made free use of the hospitality cabinet, especially the scotch, and Mattie spent most of the time with her hand up against a picture window, pretending to touch the paw of an ice cat that had come up to the other side as soon as it saw her through the transparency. She and the cat gazed into each other's eyes, giving me the uncomfortable suspicion that one or both of them might be telepaths. I was tempted to watch them closely, but Oscar was too much of a distraction. He was looking at me out of the corner of his eyes, like a dog that's getting ready to bite.

"Did anyone ever tell you that you have Nefertiti features?" Ben asked me after I declined a glass of scotch.

"No," I said. "But it's true, isn't it."

John frowned, the way he always did when he felt I was being immodest, but Ben smiled. He sampled a small amount of loki and then a small amount of snoot.

"Very nice," he said. "From Z'taruh?"

"Yes," John said.

"I hate that Z'taruhn shit," Oscar said, his eyes showing their whites.

"Peace, Oscar," Mattie said, without turning her gaze from the cat's.

Oscar's face twisted, as if he were trying to take her advice; but then it fell right back into its old lines.

Ben was snorting more snoot, and, of course, John and Dominik and Solange had to have some, too. John and Dominik were drinking steadily, more heavily than Ben, but not as much as Oscar. Mattie and I stayed sober. Ben was saying "Very nice. Quite decent. Very good." John was making small talk, telling little anecdotes about this guy or that fellow who "put him in touch with'' this variety of snoot or that variety of loki, and everything was going quite smoothly; until Oscar, on one of his many trips back from the whiskey bottle, sat down next to Solange and slid his hand down her thigh. Solange's usually placid face dissolved into abject horror.

''What's your name again?'' he said. ''So-long?''

If I had been her—seeing as how I was a bit more mature by then—I would have simply gotten up and walked to the other side of the room; especially if I were as small as Solange was. But she just sat there, throwing her stricken look not to Dominik, but to John.

I glanced at John, too. His face was dead white, his jaw set like a bulldog's. His eyes were radiating blue steel. *What the hell's going on here?* I wondered.

Oscar shook Solange's knee. ''I asked you a question!'' he insisted.

''Don't be like that, Oscar,'' warned Ben, who was busy rolling another stick of loki. John continued to glare at Oscar, but blue steel is no match for rabies.

Oscar dug his fingers into Solange's kneecap and said, ''I bet you have one hot little cunt, don't you honey?''

John jumped up, but Ben and I were there quicker. I had my fist in Oscar's soft stomach before he was more than halfway to his feet. Ben clamped his hand down on what was undoubtedly a nerve cluster on Oscar's neck, and Oscar sank down on the couch, his eyes bulging.

Mattie *tsk-tsked* from her place at the window. ''Oscar. Oscar.''

Oscar's eyes glazed over, and he slumped. He didn't wake up for the rest of the meeting.

''Sorry about that,'' Ben said to me as we sat down again. ''He's a little messed up. Had some hard times in the mines.''

I smiled and shrugged.

Would you believe Solange still didn't get up from the couch? She just sat there with her lips pressed together, her body turned slightly away from the now snoring Oscar. *I'm-being-watched-itis.* Solange was watching John, making him feel like he had to pass her tests, prove his manhood. And who's standing in his way, beating up the bad guys, making him flunk the test?

Me, that's who.

John wouldn't look at me or Ben directly after that. He wouldn't look at Dominik or Solange at all. But he did stare at Oscar, his face frozen in its bulldog expression, as if to say, *What wouldn't I have done to you if they hadn't gotten to you first!* It was silly, and it was embarrassing to watch. So I ignored John and talked to Ben for the rest of the time we were there.

"You've got to teach me how to do that neck pinch thing," I said.

Ben gave me his beautiful smile and said, "Want to learn to be a prison guard? We could use you."

I told him I would think about it, but I knew I didn't ever want live on that beautiful, sad planet. Not even to find out if Mattie M'Benga really could talk to ice cats.

"You sure seem preoccupied lately," Dominik said to me not long after Odin.

John hadn't noticed. He was too busy looking at himself through Solange's eyes.

It wasn't that I was thinking of going home to Hook to see if I was really clear, if I could pick up the pieces and salvage my sports or anything. I liked being out on my own, acting like an adult, going places. I didn't even miss playing ball, if you can believe that. It had been over a year since I had left Hook, and most of the old interests were fading. I only worked out in Half-G or Double-G to stay in shape.

"John, are you sleeping with someone else?" I asked him one night when he had, once again, failed to make love to me because his back hurt him too much.

"Is that any of your business?" he asked me stiffly, but I could tell the question pleased him.

"It's just that if you are, I'd like to know."

"Look, kitten," he said, stroking my breast. "I've never been physically faithful to anyone."

"So, are you sleeping with someone else or aren't you?"

He sighed. "No. I'm not. But—do you want me to be perfectly honest?"

"Okay," I said, already tired of the conversation.

"There is someone else I've been wanting."

He waited for me to ask who, but I didn't feel like being his confessor.

"She belongs to someone else," he continued, "and I think too much of our friendship to do anything about it."

Our friendship meant his and Dominik's, not his and mine.

"Oh," I said. "Does that mean you still want to sleep with me?"

He took a long look at my body. "I'd be a fool not to want it."

"Well," I said, "okay." And I got up to get dressed. I still didn't actually *sleep* with John in his quarters. I had my own, and I liked that situation as much as he did; especially now that all the affection had leaked from our relationship.

"See you at breakfast," I said.

"Uh-huh," he agreed.

I left him sprawled on his bed, still feeling pleased with himself. But he was being stupid. Dominik wouldn't have given a damn if Solange slept with John. I could see now why he was keeping her around past his usual girlfriend expulsion time. He knew his boss wanted her. It almost gave me satisfaction to think of the way Solange had looked that evening at dinner, staring at John but secretly watching Dominik through her peripheral vision.

When John and Dominik had gotten up to get drinks

from the bar, I had winked at her and said, "Hey, want to play a fun trick on them tonight?"

"What do you mean?" she asked cautiously.

"You go to John's room tonight, and I'll go to Dominik's," I said.

"I don't think so," she said, pressing her lips together. If John could have seen that exchange, he would have been crushed. She wasn't about to let him touch her.

That's why I thought John might be sleeping with yet another woman, to boost his ego. But it wasn't jealousy that made me want to know about his affairs. I just didn't want to be fucking him if he was fucking someone else. I wasn't about to be the fool in the little play he was writing for Solange and himself.

To me, John was just Mr. Big Dick. I mean that in the complimentary sense of the term.

I took my time getting back to my room, just strolling and enjoying the old-fashioned grandeur of the *Butterfly*. Once she had been the grande dame of luxury liners; now she was old and somewhat frazzled, and I liked her that way. I wouldn't have traded her for a ride on one of the new liners, even if I had had the money.

Korry Vather was dead, and I really didn't like John very much anymore. I wondered half seriously if I wouldn't be happier in another job, one where I could get more respect. But I let go of the notion by the time I got to my room. I was seventeen then. Another year would do just as well.

For the next six months or so, things continued on as they had been, except that John and I went down to making love two times a week instead of three. We went back and forth between Z'taruh, Ragnir, El Dorado, Thor, Kali, Odin, and half a dozen others—once, even Hook. I hid in my cabin during that stopover, pleading another bout of the flu. I don't think anyone bought it, but no one asked me about it.

Along about the seventh month, Abdul came into

the picture. Never could remember his last name—Aziz? Azuz? Anyway, he was a rich guy, had about the same amount of money as Cliff Goldbar, but a lot more smarts. He fell in lust with Solange. Actually, he tried for me first, but I couldn't stand him.

"I can throw away a thousand dollars a day if I want to," he told me. "Come to my cabin?"

Plus Z'taruh was his favorite place to go whoring, but he didn't frequent any of the Spacer Sector houses, which left only one thing. The baby houses: the places where you could find child prostitutes. This did not make me a big fan of Abdul's.

But Solange was tempted, I could tell. She kept lowering her eyes demurely when he spoke to her, and he only had to ask twice to get her to go out with him.

"Don't you know about his *hobbies*?" I asked her.

"What hobbies?" she said, with a look that told me she didn't intend to know anything she didn't want to know.

Abdul had a big deal he was working with John, a numbrain haul to Ragnir, one of the places numbrain is illegal. Apparently the Ragnarians think numbrain is poison. Not that the job was a dangerous one, or even that we might get arrested. It's just that Ragnir is under Q'rin rule, and they charge heavy taxes for the illegal stuff. You get charged double if they catch you trying to sneak it in, and that's just if they're being nice.

I don't know what made John more furious, the strain of negotiating with Q'rins or the sight of Abdul playing rich Arab with Solange. I mean, the guy didn't even look like he was from one of the Arab worlds, what with his blond hair and Arian features. He spoke with an accent right out of an old vid, but Arab-worlders speak impeccable Standard. So I don't know what he thought he was.

Of course, Solange insisted on having him meet her in the Butterfly Bar and Grill, where she knew we would be eating our regular supper. He whisked her off to the fancy restaurant on the Grand Deck, the one with the star panoramas all around you as you eat your overpriced food. John had steam coming out of his ears after they flounced off, and even Dominik was miffed. He was used to being the one who did the dumping.

"Shit," John finally said. "If I had known it took money to get her to sleep with me, I would have offered it long ago."

"If she wanted money from you, you would have known by now," I said. I was the only one enjoying my meal. "You want the rest of your onion rings?"

He was still trying to decide whether or not I had insulted him. "Hands off," he said.

Later I almost felt sorry for him as he made love to me. He really felt he had to prove something. "Look," I said as he smoked his cigarette, "so she fell off her pedestal. Are you surprised? Don't you know what she's been doing all this time?"

"No. What has she been doing," he said coldly.

"Come on. How long do Dominik's girlfriends usually last? And don't they always think they're going to end up as his one and only?"

"Solange is different," he said.

"Yeah. Because she's the one *you* wanted."

Silence. I was just stating the obvious, or he wouldn't have made his comment about buying Solange in front of Dominik, at dinner.

"Okay," he said. "So why won't she take my money?"

Because she doesn't want you or your money, I thought to myself as quietly as I could, but he picked up on it. It just hung there between us like a big fart.

"You think I'm too old for her?" he said, looking down at his naked body, which was actually as pink and smooth-skinned as a child's.

"No—look. Think of it this way. Now you don't have to act like Mr. White Knight anymore. You can just be yourself. Won't that be a relief?"

"Yeah," he agreed. "It will."

Then he kicked me out of his room.

After that John was like his old self for a couple of weeks. Just in time, because Solange had dropped her game with him as soon as Abdul came along, and her new game was working better than the old one. Dominik was—well, not exactly jealous, but he did seem to be caught up in a battle of wills with her. And the funniest thing was that Solange's will appeared to be the stronger. Dominik didn't date another girl until close to the time I left.

But I'm getting ahead of myself. First we met Abdul on Z'taruh, at Cliff's house. That was another funny thing about this run to Ragnir: Cliff insisted on it. John felt weird about trusting Abdul (and not just because he was jealous of him). Cliff had just met the guy himself.

"Can you believe it?" he said while Abdul was out on the terrace showing Solange the garden. "A blond Arab!"

"Well, he says he's an Arab," I demured.

"He's got enough drugs to be an Arab." Cliff stimmed himself, as if to punctuate his point.

"Actually," I said, "Islam forbids the use of drugs or alcohol—"

But he wasn't listening to me, or to John's objections. "Shouldn't we get to know this guy better before we make such an important run with him?" John had asked. "If we get caught smuggling this stuff in by the bloody Q'rin, we're going to lose our profit."

"Well, if you want to get to know him, go talk to him," Cliff said. "Besides, my grandfather's good for it." He gave John a hard look when he said that last part, and the threat was obvious. Granddad was paying for the whole trip, but John's free ride could end anytime. He might actually have to go to *work*.

"Hey, I'll bet he even has a harem," Cliff continued enthusiastically. "Hey Abdul! When do I get to visit your harem?" He went out on the porch to ask this. I didn't hear Abdul's reply.

So we were stuck with this guy for at least six

months. Solange started playing Dominik and Abdul off each other, and John appeared to be out of her picture completely; until one night about two months from Ragnir, when we heard a knock on the door. We had just made love, and John already had his pants back on. I was still naked, but the son of a bitch went to open the door anyway.

Solange was standing there. "Are you busy?" she asked.

He looked like he'd been hit in the face with a brick, but he recovered quickly and threw me a disdainful look. "No," he said.

I got up slowly while the two of them stared at me. Solange turned white when she saw my body, which gave me some satisfaction. I got dressed while they talked.

"I have a special date with Dominik," she said shyly, "and I really want to impress him. I want to be elegant, you know?"

"Oh," he said knowingly, "so you've made up your mind." He implied that she had decided to stay with Dominik. He also implied that he was happy about it.

She pretended she didn't know what he was talking about. "I want to wear black—maybe a gown with those, you know, spaghetti straps? And my hair in a French horn? But I've never done a French horn. I thought maybe you or Larissa could help me."

I was bending over, putting on my pants, but I still hadn't put my bra or blouse on. I let them take a good long look at my breasts, how firm and shapely they were even when I was bent over in that position. "Why the hell would I know anything about a French horn?" I said. "We don't wear those in my family."

"Well," she said, "I just always heard that black girls were real good at hair."

I let that pass. She realized too late that she had been rude. "I mean at doing fancy hairstyles. You know, because your hair is so—I mean the texture is different, so you had to learn—" She floundered to a halt.

I started to put on my bra, looking at her, saying nothing. Her eyes flew to my military haircut, which was so short you could see my scalp through it. I liked it that way. It showed off the beautiful shape of my head. She turned red.

"Hey." John frowned at me. "Can't you take a compliment?"

"Of course I can," I said as I slipped on my blouse.

"Then what do you say?" he demanded.

I couldn't believe it. *What do you say?* "I say fuck you," I told him.

"Only if you're lucky," he snapped back.

I put on my shoes and walked from the room.

Later I saw John and Solange outside the Butterfly Bar and Grill. Abdul was standing a short distance away, a cynical smile on his face. John was taking pictures of Solange in her fancy dress and French horn, a goofy proud-father expression on his face. I went to stand next to Abdul.

"Such a father should not be trusted alone with his daughter," Abdul whispered to me. So I wasn't the only one who was thinking it.

Solange and John turned and saw us. Abdul put his arm around my shoulders. "I wish I had such a beautiful bodyguard," he called to John.

John's jaw got very tight.

Yes, I could have played that game with him, but I didn't. I didn't sleep with Abdul; and for that matter, I didn't sleep with John anymore either. Not after what he had said to me.

It's over, I said to myself then. But I was wrong. We still had the Ragnir fiasco to get through.

Chapter 6

I almost died when I found out how John was planning to smuggle the numbrain into Ragnir. I was summoned to Abdul's room (somewhat peremptorily, for my tastes), and when I entered, I found them all sitting around a table. The table was loaded down with little plastic baggies of numbrain.

John, Dominik, and Abdul were swallowing them.

"God Lord" was all I could think of to say.

John pointed to a pile set aside from the others. "There's yours," he said.

"No." I backed away.

"Yes."

"I said no!" I shrieked. They all stopped and looked at me; including Solange, who I had noticed didn't have a little pile of crap *she* was supposed to swallow (unless she had swallowed it already, which I very much doubted).

"I am not going to swallow that shit!" I said, feeling madder than I had in years. "Do you understand me? I'll be your bodyguard, keep the bullies and the geeks off you; but I won't be a repository for you. I'm not going to eat that and then—God!—shit it out later on demand! What a *rape*!"

Abdul began to swallow baggies again, as if to say that he *liked* being raped. The others glared at me.

"It has to be done this way," John said. "There's no other way to smuggle it in."

"Then you eat it," I said. "You think it's worth it, okay. That's your business. I won't do it."

"Do I understand you to say you're quitting?" said John.

"If that's how you want to interpret it."

"So you want your walking papers now?"

"I'm not going to swallow that crap." I turned and made to walk out the door.

"Wait a minute," Dominik said. "Larissa, just hold on, will you? Please? You don't have to swallow the stuff."

I stopped and turned to look at him. John was looking at him, too, furious at being contradicted.

"Can I talk to you alone for a minute, buddy?" Dominik said. He and John exchanged silent information with their eyes, until John finally grimaced and said, "Fine." They got up and left the room.

I sat down across from Abdul and Solange, my back stiff. Abdul was still swallowing the baggies, practically gorging himself on them. When he was done with his pile, he consumed a third of mine.

"Do you know why I did that?" he asked me.

"No."

"Because our friends in the other room have just realized that they need you to be on their side. Understand? Against me. Me and Solange."

He put his hand on her upper thigh, and she didn't move away. I shrugged. I knew she had decided to pick him. She decided that night when she got all fancied up for Dominik, and he still wouldn't ask her to marry him.

"Three against two," he said.

"Doesn't that bother you?" I said, not really caring if it did or not.

"No. Not if it makes them feel better. They're amateurs. I don't want them to be nervous."

"So you're a pro?"

He smiled, but didn't answer. After a while, John and Dominik came back into the room. John didn't speak to me, but Dominik winked. They started swallowing the baggies again, but John was having problems. Dominik finished his pile, while John still had half to go.

"I have to go to the bathroom," I said. I stayed away for half an hour. When I got back, John's pile was gone. I didn't say anything about it, but as we got up to leave, Abdul whispered in my ear, "Did he always have performance anxiety?"

I pretended I hadn't heard him.

Ragnir security was even stiffer than Odin's. They wouldn't let *Butterfly* land either. We took the regular shuttle down, into the hot, wet atmosphere; and their tractors guided us to a landing in cleared swampland.

A cloud of insects flew in the lock as soon as it opened. They were closely followed by a squad of Q'rin warriors. Their leader regarded us with a stony face for a moment.

"Follow me," he ordered.

I obeyed without looking at the others. I could feel John bristling, and it gave me an inordinate amount of pleasure. He didn't know when he was being insulted by a Q-rin or when they were just treating him like regular folks, which is what they were doing now. I glanced back at him and felt a stab of pity. He looked shrimpy next to the Q'rin escort. I'd never seen him that way before.

We emerged from the landing area and were marched into the processing center. It was huge, a city unto itself. It was elevated above the swamp waters, the traditional, flat-topped pyramid design of the colonial Q'rin somehow looking just as right there as it had on Hook. It made me feel nostalgic, and something else, too. Something that originated from between my legs. Inexplicably, I thought of Abriin, my old Double-G nemesis.

Inside, we joined a throng of Human and other offworlders. There were Ragnarian officials standing around too, looking like a cross between tall, skinny frogs and alligators. They wore loincloths and thin sashes. I envied them their wardrobe. My own clothes were already soaked through.

They herded us through the standard metal detectors. When we got to the luggage area, the Ragnarian clerks were already going through our luggage.

"You have anything to declare?" hissed one as he held up a bag of loki.

"It's all written on the forms," John said, handing the clerk his folder. We stood there for fifteen minutes while he went over everything, then stood in the "FINES AND FEES" line for another twenty. Finally, we were directed toward what we thought was the exit. But when we went through the door, we found a huge waiting room full of weary, overheated offworlders.

"Oh, my God," said John. He and the other two "carriers" were beginning to look hideously constipated.

"This is a new regulation?" Abdul asked him with a painful smile.

"It is," said someone behind us. We turned and found the captain of our escort. He seemed more relaxed. "You could be here up to six hours. Quarantine."

God only knows how the guys kept their faces straight. But he wasn't looking at them anyway.

"There are ways to speed up the process, though," he told me. "I can brief you while we have a drink."

For a moment I just blinked at him. It had been so long since John had paid me any attention, I had almost forgotten what a lovely package I was walking around in. The captain was tall, lean, and bony, a splendid example of his race. He wore his hair long, with rings of precious metal braided into it.

"What a lovely idea," I said, and smiled at him.

"The rest of you can wait here," he said. "You'll be taken care of." Whatever that meant.

I waved at them as I walked off on his arm. John's face had a cold dead look that I had never seen before. I told myself he was just in pain from the numbrain baggies. I also told myself that I was only going off with this soldier because I was trying to speed them through quarantine. But as I gazed up into that rocky face, I felt that feeling between my legs again—that wonderful, marvelous feeling.

All kinds of people snapped to attention as my captain and I walked by, some because of him and some because of me; and I must say, in spite of everything that happened later, I was enjoying myself more than I had in almost two years. We went up several stories, to a much more elegant and less crowded floor. We went into a bar with a mixed clientele, a place where people of influence went to get a taste of the exotic. I ordered a rum and Coke, because I like the way that drink makes my mouth taste. He ordered a whiskey.

He sat close enough to touch me, but far enough away to look me in the eye when he was talking to me.

"Your friends seemed very nervous," he said.

"They're not used to doing business on Q'rin-dominated planets."

"And you are?"

"I came from—from one." I took a big swallow of my drink, realizing what a goof I'd made.

"Really?" he said. "Which one."

My mind went blank. I couldn't even think up a lie, so I stuck to the truth. "Hook."

"Oh yes," he grinned. "Yes. Now I remember. I believe I may have seen you before. You played Half-G, didn't you?"

My spine turned to ice.

"Yes," he continued. "You were quite good, for a human. I was pleasantly surprised." He smiled wider, apparently enjoying my discomfort.

After a moment of very acute fear, I started to think clearly again. This man wouldn't give a damn about who I may or may not have killed. The Q'rin never did. In fact, he might have even admired what I had done.

"Which game did you see?" I asked.

"I don't remember, exactly. I only remember you.

Would you like another one of those?" he indicated my drink, which was only half-gone. I said I would.

We chatted about how different the weather on Ragnir was from Hook's dry climate, while we sipped our drinks and stared at each other's bodies. This man was scaring and impressing me more every minute. He seemed to know a great deal about Humans.

"I must say, you are the most beautiful woman I've ever seen, even though you belong to a different race. I'm a bit surprised with myself. I normally don't go for the exotic. But you're not surprised, are you Larissa."

"No, I'm not."

"Good." He touched my face with his big hand. I felt like a fancy vase, being examined by an art lover. I found myself leaning into the touch.

"Now," he said, "about your friends."

"Yes."

"The big, middle-aged man. The bigot. The one whose relationship with you has apparently gone sour. He's hiding something. He should cancel his plans and go back where he came from."

"I don't know if he would accept that advice from me," I said.

"He'd better. We aren't as gentle with smugglers as you people are. We have ways of—extracting—information that you wouldn't want to know about."

I was very glad I was not the sort of person who liked carrying drugs around inside my intestines.

"My goodness," I said.

He just sipped his whiskey.

"How much longer will they have to stay in quarantine?" I asked.

"If they want to go back to their ship, they can go right this minute," he said.

"Well, maybe they'll want to do that. I mean, seeing how uncomfortable the weather is here."

"Yes," he agreed. "But they can wait a little longer, don't you think? While we chat and finish our drinks."

"As far as I'm concerned, they can."

"And then later, I'd like to see you again. When I'm off duty." His eyes glittered to show me just how much of a concession he was making for me. Just because he was an art lover.

"Are you going to feed me?" I asked.

"Yes, Larissa."

We finished our drinks casually, then strolled back to the quarantine area.

"I'll leave you here. Meet me at the same bar at seven o'clock? Tell them Vahsra gives you clearance."

"See you then," I agreed. I admired the way he had turned a Q'rin order into a courteous question with just a slight modulation of tone. I wanted this man, and the look he threw me just before he walked away told me the feeling was mutual.

I went back to where John and the others should have been waiting. I found Solange, all by herself.

"They left me here to wait for you," she said, neutrally. "Abdul has a buddy who got us through quarantine. They went to find the doctor, to—you know."

"Jesus," I said, a premonition of bad things to come lifting the hairs on the back of my neck. "Solange, do you know where they are?"

"They left directions—" she pulled out a tattered piece of paper.

"Solange, the Q'rin are on to them. They know they smuggled something in, and I think they even know how."

"Oh no!" she said.

I thought that summed things up pretty well.

I didn't have a lot of choice about what to do next. I couldn't risk calling them on a public line, and I couldn't just leave them to their fate, mad as I was at them. So Solange and I hired a private transport and went to find them.

The Ragnarian driver wanted fifty credits when we finally found the address.

"Thirty," I said.

He blinked at me with his sad, froggy-gator eyes. "Okay."

He left us there, and I took a good look around, reminding myself that this was the planet over which the Ragnir war had been fought; and I couldn't even remember why. Maybe all those swamp plants contained valuable medicines, or maybe the planet was strategically located. You couldn't even tell there'd been a war where we were standing. Maybe the swamp had swallowed up the scars. We trudged through the muck, trying to avoid inhaling insects, and searched for the private address we were seeking. We could sort of tell we were on a street, because there were a few signs here and there with Q'rin writing on them.

When we finally found the house, I decided it probably predated the Q'rin occupation. It looked like the vids I had seen of mansions from the American South. It was overgrown with vines and weeds, and when we fought our way to the front door, moisture dripped on us from the warped wood. The porch was dark, and so were the windows. We couldn't see another house from where we were standing, so I was worried when no one answered my first two rings.

But Abdul answered the third one, grinning when he saw who it was.

"You shit it out already?" I asked him with some astonishment.

He shrugged. "My byways are well oiled." His eyes spoke of jaded histories. My stomach tensed at the notion.

"How about the others?" I asked.

"Dominik is almost done. Poor John, as usual—"

"Oh great," I said. "You guys couldn't wait for me, could you. That Q'rin as much as told me that he knows you smuggled drugs inside your guts. He made some very suggestive, if not overt, threats—"

"And you came here? You stupid cow!"

"Look, mister." I loomed over him, and he backed up a step. "I bought you idiots some time, and you turned around and fucked up. Didn't you hear me? I said *he knew you had illegal drugs in your intestines.* He knew while you were standing there in *quarantine*. Understand?"

He blinked. "Go on."

"He told me to collect you and immediately leave. If I had gone back to the ship, I would have been safe, but you guys would still be here, and guess what he would do?"

"You should have gone somewhere else, led him astray."

"Abdul, *he knew*. We have to pass back through Q'rin security before we leave again. You know what will happen when you come back *without* the drugs you smuggled in?"

"Hmmn," he said. "You have a point. What do you suggest we do, then? Swallow them again?"

"Well," I said, feeling a little queasy. "Maybe it would be—oh hell, I suppose you have to."

"John won't like this."

"Tell me about it."

"I'd better go break it to him before he passes any more of them."

Solange and I sat down. She had a crease between her brows, and I realized she was worried. I'd never seen her worried before.

"No!" John's voice boomed from the other room. "Where is she? Get her in here!"

Abdul came out with as much dignity as he could muster, but he looked shaken. "He wants—" he said.

There was a knock on the door.

None of us moved.

The knock came again, and a Q'rin voice boomed, "Open the door!"

Abdul's shoulders slumped, and he obeyed.

John was lucky he had already passed the last of the baggies when Vahsra and his men came marching in. I mean that he was lucky in terms of his dignity. Once they got done fining him, his dignity was all he had left. On top of that, they confiscated all the numbrain.

"The next time you bribe someone in quarantine," Vahsra told him, "be sure he earns more than five thousand credits a year. The temptation to collect twice for the same deal is a strong one."

"Quarantine, huh?" John said, glaring at me and not believing it.

The three of us were alone in Vahsra's office. "You think your bodyguard betrayed you?" Vahsra said. "You should have waited for her instead of trusting some slimy little traitor in quarantine."

"Slimy traitor is a good description," John said, still glaring at me.

Vahsra laughed, shortly. "You are a fool, Human."

John didn't hear him. He left without saying another word.

"Well," I said, "another chapter comes to an end."

"As all chapters should." Vahsra got up and took my hand, kissing my palm. "Now I believe you and I have a dinner date, Larissa."

Solange stuck up for me. I never expected that.

"I knew there was something wrong with that guy in quarantine!" she said. "He acted like he was some important hotshot, but he had a *hole* in his pants!"

"So," Abdul sneered, "other than the fact that you disapproved of his wardrobe, what didn't you like about him?" Unlike John, he didn't worship Solange. He just slept with her.

"He was a creep," said Solange.

She and I were seated on the couch in Abdul's suite, and had been for two hours since I got back from my date with Vahsra. John, Abdul, and Dominik sat in chairs, facing us. The third degree. But, despite appearances, Solange was not on trial. She may have even known that; but I almost liked her at that moment, anyway.

"I've already told you what happened," I said. "I told you thirty times. I'm not going to tell you again."

Abdul looked away, bored. He had already cut his losses. He wanted to go on to the next thing.

Dominik knew I was telling the truth, but he said nothing in my defense.

John was another matter.

"I just want to know one thing," he said.

"You've been saying that all night, and it's always something different."

"No it isn't," he snapped. "Just one thing. Did you fuck him?"

"None of your business."

That answer almost seemed to please him. In fact, I think it must have, because it gave him a cue for the next line he must have just been aching to say:

"So. Did you fuck that Q'rin-nigger before or after he paid you?"

I felt the others tense, but all I could see was the satisfied glitter in John's eyes as he saw his poison had hit its target. I almost called him names back, but I held myself a moment and thought up something better.

"*Pay* me," I laughed. "Are you kidding? He didn't have to pay me. That big strong man? Do you have any idea how pathetic you looked next to him, with your balding head and your broken back? You fat old creep."

Abdul was grinning now. John's eyes had turned almost black. I couldn't help myself; I laughed again, even though I knew what that would provoke him into doing.

John got slowly to his feet, then suddenly threw the chair across the room. I assumed that was supposed to intimidate me, but all I could think of was how much it must have hurt his back.

"You're fired," he said.

"No shit?"

"Wipe that look off your face."

That was just the end. Even Solange laughed at that one, letting her control slip a little. For John, that must have been the last insult. He came at me with his fists balled, and I had to sock him in the throat. He didn't fall down; he just sort of froze, his face turning purple.

Just imagine. He had so much pride, he wouldn't even fall down.

"You'll be all right," I promised him. "In fifteen minutes or so."

I walked out of Abdul's suite, not exactly feeling proud of myself, but relieved to have been pushed in some direction, at last. I didn't wonder if John knew what the word *nigger* had once meant to people of my color. I was sure he had chosen his words carefully. It was weird to hear it stuck on the end of *Q'rin,* though. What did it mean? Q'rins have sort of dusky copper skin, not black. And the word *nigger* has no power over them. I was to hear it again, on Z'taruh, but it took me a long time to figure out why.

It was an insult Human Ragnir vets used, even the black ones. Losing the war made them feel helpless, and calling the people who beat them Q'rin-niggers lets them pretend they're powerful. You almost have to feel sorry for them.

I still had some money left, enough to pay my meals back to Z'taruh. I had a feeling something was waiting for me there, though I had no idea what. I wasn't even worried.

I saw John one more time after that, leaving the Butterfly Bar and Grill with Dominik. He didn't see me.

Later, Cliff told me his grandfather had decided to fire John from his campaign staff.

"Why did he hire him in the first place?" I asked.

"Well—actually, I snuck him on the payroll. I was hoping Grandfather wouldn't notice."

Ah.

CHAPTER 7

When I stepped off the shuttle and into Z'taruh's warm damp climate that last time, I had a different attitude. After the hot wet hell of Ragnir, this didn't seem so bad. (I had some other hot wet memories of Ragnir, but those were pleasant.)

By now I had a plan. I had become accustomed to being a bodyguard, so I would try that. In fact, Cliff was my first choice. After all, he knew me, and he was just weird enough to hire me, despite his relationship with John. Possibly even because of it.

Yes, this trip to Z'taruh was different. I felt alive as I made my way to the public transport, through crowds of people of every imaginable shape and color. I held my head up when the men checked me out. I felt proud and strong. No more dogging John's shadow or worrying whether I was being too aggressive to please him. I was just myself, and I felt even more at home than I ever had on Hook.

Deadtowners rode on the transport, going nowhere. They were trying to pick up spare change, intimidating people, or picking their pockets. They didn't approach me, but they watched and watched—smiling as if we were sharing a joke. Made my spine tingle.

They were gone by the time we reached the Hill. Armed men had gotten onto the bus and chased them off when we were well into the Spacer Sector. The Deadtowners barked at them halfheartedly on their way off.

"The doggies must like you," one guy said to me. He meant the "police."

I figured I would run into John at Cliff's house, but

I didn't. Cliff let me in the front door, actually looking happy to see me.

"What's going on?" he said.

I said something noncommittal. "How's Rodney?" I asked him.

Rodney the rat wiggled his tail at me from his place on the chair in front of the fireplace. He was fat and sleek, and had a diamond collar around his throat. After that first bout in the ratpit, Cliff had decided Rodney made a better house pet than a fighter. Oddly enough, he was right.

I patted Rodney on the head, and he squeaked with pleasure.

After I had drunk a couple of his imported beers, I asked him for a job.

"I thought you worked for John," he said.

"He fired me."

"Oh, yeah. Now I remember. He told me what happened."

"Yeah," I scratched Rodney's chin. He was now sitting on my lap. "We didn't exactly part on friendly terms."

"Yeah, me, too." He sighed.

"What?"

He told me John had been fired and the rest of it. "He really got mad. He kind of went for my throat, you know? I mean verbally. I guess you really find out who your friends are when the chips are down."

"You sure do. So, do you need a bodyguard?'

He brightened. "Yeah, as a matter of fact, I do! I bought some farmland on the other side of the planet. You know, the Big Boys."

"You going over there to manage it?"

"No, I've got someone else to do that. I'm just gonna collect the income."

I had already known Cliff long enough not to comment about any of his plans, so I just nodded. We sat there in front of the fireplace he never had any reason to use in that climate, and sipped our beers until Rodney started to snore.

* * *

I slept in my usual room, the one John and I used to share when we visited. I would get up early in the morning, shower, and go downstairs for Cliff's usual proudly prepared breakfast. That man really could cook. It's too bad he was born rich, because I really believe he could have found happiness behind a grill.

On the days when Cliff was just puttering around the house, I would spend a few hours in the gymnasium he never used. I was six-foot-three by then, and weighed in at just under one hundred seventy. Skinny, but nicely stacked. Rodney always watched me from his perch on top of the monkey bars. The rat and I were becoming close.

I liked it best when Cliff had business in town, when we could get out and around Capital. He had his bank business, his lawyers and investment brokers, his shops and bars and restaurants.

But his favorite place to eat was the fast-food stalls, probably because they prepared the same kind of food he liked to make at home. The fast-food stalls deserve their own chapter in the *Z'taruhn Restaurant Guide,* not only because you can find the best hamburgers, hot dogs, and submarine sandwiches in the entire System there, but also because you can have the very best food in the entire System torn right out of your hands by hungry Deadtowners. They hunt the stalls like hawks (or sharks, even), and attack at the slightest sign of weakness.

Despite this, the place is always crowded with customers of every known race and origin. (I'll never understand why hamburgers and hot dogs are so damned popular. I'm a crab and veal girl myself.) Cliff liked to go there at least two or three times a week.

"Now that I have you, I can relax more," he told me. That was basically true. Deadtowners never bothered me. They just gave me that secret smile, sometimes even winking or waving at me. There was one girl who especially gave me the willies. She was small and pale, no figure to speak of, with the most abominable haircut I've ever seen, even on a Deadtowner.

But she had a weird sort of class, and I could always feel her eyes right through her dark glasses. Sometimes I heard other people call out to her, "Hey, Shade, what's going on?" or "Hey, Shade, been betting at the pits again?"

One day while Cliff was glomming his way through a meatball sub and I was trying to do the same, I felt those eyes on me again. Before I knew it, that weird little mummy-wrapped girl was sitting next to me.

"Greetings, fellow Deadtowner," she said.

I gave her a narrow look. Poor Cliff had almost choked on his meatball. I patted his knee to reassure him.

"I'm not a Deadtowner," I said. "What makes you think I am?"

"Oh, beg *pár*don," she said with an exaggerated accent. "It's not that you don't dress nice or anything like that. It's just that you look like a knife fighter. Nice haircut, too."

It was uncanny. She was making the hairs stand up all over my body, including the back of my neck.

"So," she said. "You want the rest of that sub?"

I had been thinking of leaving it anyway. I gave it to her.

"You ever fight at the pits?" she asked me.

"The rat pits?"

"Hell, no! The people pits. The Q'rin pits. Bet you would make a good knife fighter."

"I've never even heard of it," I said, feeling slightly queasy at the way she was stuffing that sandwich into her face. And she was such a skinny thing.

"You should go," she said, and having delivered her prophecy, she got up and walked away. I saw her swoop down on another sub three tables away.

"Hey," Cliff said, a weird light burning in his eyes, "can you knife fight?"

"Knife fighting is something you do to protect yourself, not something you do to have fun or make money," I said. But I felt a weird excitement burning in my gut.

He was a little subdued after that, and I remembered that he used to bet at the rat pits. I think he was feeling guilty about putting poor Rodney in the pit with those other mean rats. He had really gotten attached to Rodney since then. I wondered if he had the same kind of attachment for me.

"I've got to talk to my partner today," he said with a mouth full of meatball. "You know, my farming partner."

"I thought he was your employee."

"Well, yeah, but he's so knowledgeable about the business, I upgraded his status."

"You mean he invested in the business?"

"Well, no—"

"Then technically, he's not your partner."

He waved that away. "I couldn't run the business without him. So I made him a partner."

I was so used to Cliff getting in over his head, I didn't even think anything about it. It seemed like there was always money to bail him out, always some excuse for just dropping all his plans and leaving them where they lay. I didn't think this case would be any different.

But it was.

We found Cliff's "partner," Vlad Florescu, in Jugs, one of the cheesier topless bars. He watched the floor show the whole time Cliff was trying to talk to him, then stared at my breasts for the rest of the time. I swear, I felt like I had a vid set strapped there.

"Don't got the figures with me today," he said when Cliff wanted to know how business was going on his farm. His bloodshot eyes squinted at my chest, and for a moment I was afraid he might try to adjust the dials.

"Well I don't need the exact figures, man," Cliff said cheerfully. "You know, just a general idea."

"Business fine," said Vlad.

"Well, like what kind of money are we talking about?"

"Didn't bring the figures."

I couldn't believe this. Vlad looked like a broken-down old walrus, with the whiskers and bloated nose of a bull who's been in too many territorial fights. Thinking back, that was probably his exact history.

"How's the loki coming along? I heard there was a hurricane last week—"

"Not growing loki. We're doing numbrain."

"Man, I thought I bought a loki farm."

"Never grew loki out there. Redweed plants. Could make meltdown out of it instead. If you want."

"Okay," Cliff said.

"Meltdown is cheap shit, man," Vlad sneered. "Skids drink that shit. What do you want to mess with cheap shit for?"

"But you just said—"

"Numbrain makes a lot more money. A *lot* more. Refinement process is expensive. Gotta cover that, but, you know, once you got that covered, you make money hand over fist. I mean, an *obscene* amount of money. Gotta cover that refinement process, though. You bring your checkbook with you?"

Cliff had. He actually started to write this guy a check for five thousand credits.

"Oh wait," said Vlad. "I forgot. I need ten thousand."

I couldn't resist. "You *forgot*?" I said. "How did you forget ten thousand credits?"

"Girl," Vlad addressed my breasts, "once you get through the refinement process, you make *money*."

"Now you know why I'm rich," Cliff told me, handing the walrus his ten-thousand credit check.

No, but I knew how Alice had felt at the mad tea party.

I suppose I'm at least partly to blame for what happened later, because as soon as we got outside again, I said, "Cliff, I don't believe you! You just handed that man a check from your personal account for ten thousand credits, and you don't even know what he's growing on your farm!"

"Well, he said numbrain—"

"Have you even been out there?"

"No. I saw pictures. I knew what I wanted, so I went to my real estate agent and set up the deal."

"And what did your agent say they were growing out there?"

"Loki." Cliff unlocked the doors to his Land Rover, and we climbed in. I waited until I had my safety belt on before I made my next point.

"Loki," I said. "But Vlad says numbrain. He says loki was never grown there. So who's right?"

"Vlad runs the farm. He would know."

"What did you see in the pictures your agent showed you?"

He didn't answer that. His brow was all creased up. He sighed in an irritated fashion and pressed his lips together.

I should have let it go then, but I said, "Cliff, even if he's growing numbrain like he says he is, why didn't you write him a check from your business account? Or why didn't you write it to your company, instead of to him personally?"

That's when I realized I had pushed too hard. His face got bright red, and his hands started to tremble. I had been an insensitive clod, because it wasn't until that moment that I realized why Cliff had given Vlad the money.

He was terrified of Vlad. Even with me sitting right there with him. The walrus man, without even lifting a finger, had poor Cliff mentally and emotionally outclassed, and Cliff was helpless in his hands.

"Look," I said. "I have a feeling I've let you down. I don't think I did my job back there."

He was quiet for a time, but his hands stopped shaking. "Don't be so hard on yourself," he said.

"The first thing I want to know is can we get payment stopped on that check? Right now? Then, if you still want to, you can write him a check from your business account. What do you think?"

He didn't answer, but he turned the Rover around and headed back to banker's row, right in the heart of the Spacer Sector. Driving through those sparkling streets lifted both our spirits considerably. Cliff was whistling by the time we got to his bank.

I guess Vlad was still busy inside Jugs, because he hadn't tried to deposit the check yet. Cliff stopped payment. "I was drunk when I wrote it," he told the girl at the window. She smiled at him and patted his hand.

We both felt better by supper time, and I believed I had done the right thing by interfering: until later, after my evening exercise session, when Rodney and I came into the kitchen for a snack. I heard noises in the garage, and went in to investigate.

The garage was actually more like a warehouse, big enough for Cliff's vehicles and a couple of light planes. But he had something else in there, too, something that had been added since the last time I looked. It was a helicraft equipped with a couple of force cannons. He was climbing all over it and talking to himself.

"What are you doing?" I asked, startling him.

"Oh! I was just checking out my surveillance craft." He had a manual in his hands, and was pushing various buttons.

"Surveillance craft?" I asked uneasily. "What is it supposed to surveil?"

"I thought we could fly down to my farm and take a look at it from the air."

"You know how to fly that thing?"

"I think so," he said. One of the cannons swiveled over to point at me and Rodney, and Rodney squeaked from his place on my shoulder. He was probably remembering his own capture. Poor thing.

"Sorry about that," Cliff said. He pushed another button, and the cannon moved back to its forward position. "It's not warmed up. It wouldn't fire. Sorry Rodney! Pookapookapook!"

Rodney chirped unhappily, but his claws retracted from my flesh.

"So," I said, "you want to take a look at what Vlad is doing."

"Yeah!"

"Are you going to tell him you're coming?"

"I doubt it. He might get mad."

"But Cliff, won't they have ground defenses? Weren't you the one who told me that the drug farmers shoot first and ask questions later?"

"Hey, we'll be broadcasting my ID code. I'm a fellow farmer now. They don't shoot at each other."

"Um—"

"Besides," he said, "this thing is fast, and we've got the cannons."

"Oh shit," I said. The other cannon swiveled back and forth.

"We're just going to look, okay?" he said. "We'll be broadcasting peace messages. We'll go straight to the farm, take some pictures, then fly straight back. Then, when we talk to Vlad again, we'll know what's going on."

He looked at me with his earnest, goofy face, and I wondered why I shouldn't just go along with his plan. It seemed reasonable to want to find out what was going on out there. I didn't realize how sophisticated the drug farmers' setup was. I also didn't realize that they were constantly at war with each other, and that Cliff didn't know the protocol.

"Okay," I said. "Let's do it."

That night I dreamed I was riding behind Cliff on an inflatable aircycle. It kept deflating before we could get off the ground. "Don't worry," Cliff would say. "I've done this plenty of times."

We never did get off the ground.

If I had spared Cliff's plan even one moment of critical thought, I would have realized that his house doesn't have a clear space for landing and taking off, even for a helicraft. So the process of getting the damned thing to an appropriate area was an adventure in itself. Cliff had to *drive* it, and it wasn't made for driving—at least, not much driving.

So we shimmied back and forth along the road, inviting more than a little criticism along the way (especially from the lady whose rosebushes got slashed to pieces by the rear rotor), and occasionally I even had to get out and push.

"Make sure that damned rotor is off!" I told Cliff, not wanting to end up like that lady's rosebushes.

We only had a few blocks to go, just to the parking lot outside of an unrented mansion; but it took us two hours to get there. And once there, Cliff insisted on looking at the grounds.

"Maybe I'll move into this place," he said. "I could probably even land my light planes here."

"That's some pretty strange criteria for picking out a place to live," I panted. "Shouldn't you look at the inside? It looks like a whole town could get comfortable in there."

He looked at the place for another hour, then seemed to forget about the whole notion.

"Let's not waste any more time," he said, as if it were my fault. "We've got work to do."

I kept silent as I strapped myself in, nursing more than a little hope that perhaps he wouldn't be able to get the craft far enough into the air to get us killed. But he got the thing up without a hitch, and by the time we were breezing over the Spacer Sector, I was almost having fun. The view was gorgeous, all those glittering lights and those ultraclean streets.

Once we got over Midtown, it wasn't so pretty anymore, and, of course, Deadtown was like flying over a graveyard for dreams. We left it behind and headed out over the marsh, which gradually changed to swamp. Things got very boring at that point.

"When do we get there?" I asked Cliff.

"I don't know. A few hours?"

"You don't know?"

"Well, we're going a couple hundred miles an hour—"

"Did you check a map before we left?"

"I've got it programmed into the navigation computer," he said, sounding a little hurt.

"Oh. Sorry. I'm a little nervous in the air."

"Are you kidding?" he said, waving to the greenery that was blurring as it flew past us. "This is *great*! We could go even faster if you want!"

"That doesn't sound like a bad idea," I said. And he increased our speed to about three hundred miles per hour.

So, unknown to either of us, we were heading straight into private airspace at top speed. You see, over the drug farms, you apparently have to fly a convoluted course, skirting your neighbors' farms. Seems like common sense to know that, right?

About three hours into our trip, we received the first warning. It came in the form of a force bolt, fired directly in our path.

"What was that?" Cliff asked me breathlessly.

"Get on the radio!" I screeched. "Tell them we're not hostile!"

"Oh, yeah," he said. "I forgot." He put on the com set and tried to give me a reassuring smile. "Don't worry!" he squeaked.

"This is Cliff Goldbar, vehicle number CG 4773—ah, 4773 something or other—ah, sorry, I just got this thing, and—"

Another shot went past us, this one closer.

"Ah, yeah! Anyway, we're peaceful! I'm your new neighbor! Howdy neighbor—!"

"Get out of this airspace immediately!" The voice boomed from the speaker; and, unfortunately, Cliff's headphones. He fumbled with it before he spoke again.

"But I'm just going to my place! I'm not—"

"This is not an acceptable travel route!! Leave this space immediately or you'll be destroyed!!"

"Cliff," I said. "Let's turn around and get out of here."

"Okay," he said, fumbling some more. "Let me just figure out how to interrupt the navigational programming."

"What!?"

"Don't yell at me!"

"Cliff, you're going to have to put it on manual—"

Another shot came, and this one burned our left

side. Cliff screamed, and his fist came down on the controls. Our force cannons began to swivel and fire at random. The green world around us erupted into a red nightmare.

"Cliff, for God's sake!!"

"*Aaaaaaaggghhhh!*"

"Turn off the cannons!"

"I can't! I can't!"

"That button! Is it that button?"

"I don't know!"

"Turn us around!"

We were still going about three hundred miles per hour, and the cannons were still firing. Some more bolts flew past us, but maybe we were going too fast for them. Cliff's hands flew all over the controls, and we were suddenly swerving at a terrifying angle.

"Straighten out! Cut the speed!" I screamed, not having any idea what I was talking about. An alarm started honking, and a calm recorded woman's voice said, "You are now off automatic pilot. You must pilot the craft yourself now. Repeat, you are now off automatic pilot."

The cannons fired, and we swerved back and forth, while the lady's voice repeated over and over again that we were off automatic pilot. I'm sure our erratic behavior is the only reason we survived that day. That and dumb luck.

Abruptly, we straightened out, and Cliff managed to turn us back in the direction we had come—right back through enemy airspace. The cannons were still firing.

"Cliff, you've got to take us in another direction!"

"I can't!"

"Why not?"

"*Warning!*" the recorded lady's voice interrupted, much louder this time. "*Fuel supply is dangerously low. You have three hours of flight time left.* Repeat—" and she did, for another five minutes, while Cliff and I gritted our teeth and sweated. I could have asked him how he had expected to get back from his farm without refueling in the first place, but I didn't.

Our cannons suddenly stopped—or at least I thought they had until I looked out the window. They were still swiveling and aiming, but they were out of juice. "Uh-oh," I said, just as another bolt from the ground flew past us. "Can you speed this thing up?"

"We won't have enough fuel to get home," he panted.

"So, we'll walk part way!"

Another bolt singed us, and he complied, getting another fifty mph or so, as we blurred past their guns.

Just as we were about to leave their space, the speaker crackled. "Hey!" a man's voice said, conversationally. "Hey, Cliff Goldbar? You there, man?"

Before I could react, Cliff had flipped on the com. "Yeah, man!" he said. "Hey, look, I'm real sorry about the misunderstanding back there."

"Oh, hey," the friendly voice said, "no problem. Accidents happen."

"Yeah, well, I hope I didn't do too much damage—"

"Oh, no." The voice hardened. "You just destroyed the main house and several acres of prime loki, man."

Cliff didn't answer that, but his face went dead white.

"Cliff?" snapped the voice. "You still there?"

"Yeah," Cliff whispered.

"You're dead, man." And the radio went silent.

Cliff and I had a long talk on our way back to the house, after we abandoned his million-credit toy where it had run out of fuel, in the marshes. He was asking me if I thought I could handle this kind of heavy-duty threat from an unknown enemy, and I answered him honestly.

"No, Cliff. This is the big time, way out of my league."

"Can you at least protect me long enough to get Rodney and some important discs out of my house?" he asked, his tone uncharacteristically calm and rational.

"I will," I promised.

So we went back and got Rodney and the discs. No one bothered us. We went straight to the spaceport. Cliff made a few short calls from there, unloading everything he owned at an astonishing rate and transferring all his assets to his off-world bank accounts. "I've left you five thousand in your own personal account," he told me. "Is that okay?"

"Fine," I said. We had agreed that I would stay on Z'taruh. I wanted to, and he seemed to have given up on the bodyguard idea. I hadn't been able to protect him from his own schemes.

He sat there in the waiting lounge, with Rodney on his lap, looking like a ruined little boy. I patted them both, and tried to say comforting things. When it was time for them to board, I walked Cliff to his cabin and helped him get settled there.

The steward poked his head in for a moment and glared at Rodney. "Hey," he said, "what kind of animal is that?"

"He's a dog," I said, slipping him twenty credits.

"Oh, yeah," the steward brightened. "A Chihuahua, right?"

"He's had all his shots!" Cliff said, hugging Rodney, as if he were his last buddy in the whole universe.

The steward left, and I gave them both one final pat. "Take care," I ordered. "And—stay out of trouble, okay?"

I smiled at them, and Cliff gave me a weak smile back.

"Okay," he said.

And that was the last I saw of them.

Chapter 8

Five thousand credits sounded like a lot of money to me then, but I quickly found out it wasn't going to last me long. The cheapest apartment I looked at was one thousand credits a month. Utilities were even higher. I figured out that if I really cut corners and scrimped, the money would last about two-and-a-half months.

I could get another bodyguard job, of course, but I couldn't seem to rouse myself to do that.

So I checked myself out of my cheap hotel in Midtown by the third day (after Cliff's flight) and walked myself over to the fast-food stalls to munch and watch and think. Like I said before, I'm a crab and veal fan; but with my money running low, the stalls were the cheapest and best place in town.

I was putting away a turkey-and-avocado special when that weird girl came to sit next to me again. Shade. She still had on those dark glasses. I wondered if anyone had ever seen her eyes.

"I'm going to eat all of this sandwich," I told her warningly.

"I know." She shrugged. "Just wanted to say hi. Besides, I've had two subs already. Won't be hungry again for another hour."

"Uh-huh," I said, keeping a tight hold of my sandwich.

"What happened to the rich guy?" she indicated the empty space to my left, where Cliff had habitually sat.

"He's gone. Got into trouble with the Big Boys." I mentally cursed myself for blurting out that last part.

She was making the inside of my skull itch. I couldn't help but tense my fighting muscles with her around.

But she seemed perfectly relaxed. "Deadtowners don't spread stories about other Deadtowners," she said, making me twitch again.

"I'm not a Deadtowner," I said.

"You are now. Been looking for apartments? Amazing, isn't it? Of course"—and she lowered her voice here—"you could probably get a job as a dog. You know, one of those armed mercenaries. I shouldn't be telling you that. I hate those bastards."

I blinked at that. This girl was crazy.

"But I was just thinking," she said in a normal tone, "about your talent for knife fighting. Been to the pits, yet?"

"No."

"Well, some day. Me and Knossos will bet on you for sure."

"Knossos?"

"The elephant man. He's my betting partner."

"An Aesopian?" That sounded unlikely. This strange, skinny little mummy-wrapped urchin didn't seem the type to hang out with Aesopian nobility. Even *fallen* Aesopian nobility.

"Yeah," she was saying. "I can't go there by myself. The Q'rin don't like Humans. And besides, I wouldn't want to get mugged for my earnings, afterward. He keeps 'em off me."

"Oh."

"But listen, about apartments. Believe it or not, you can find some livable places in Deadtown. Stick to the edges, near Midtown. Lots of Deadtowners even tap into city power and water—not me, I don't have any talent for tinkering—so it can even be comfortable. You have your knives where you can get to 'em easy, right? So, you're set."

I didn't feel set. But she had tickled my curiosity. "Maybe I'll check it out," I said. "But why are you telling me all this? You thinking of setting me up and robbing me? If you try, I'll kill you."

Her little mask-like face didn't even quiver. "I'm telling you," she said, "because you seem like a nice girl."

She got up from the table, already turning her sharp eye toward other things. "One more thing," she said. "Rag-wraps are real comfortable in this weather."

And off she went.

I finished my sandwich and then took my time sipping my coffee. I was trying to imagine myself cruising the tables for scraps like these kids were doing, and it wasn't appealing to me. But I did have a notion. I thought I might check out those Deadtown buildings, after all. If I could live rent free and utility free, my money would last a lot longer, maybe even a year. Then I would have time to decide whatever it was that I was trying to decide about my life.

As for the rag-wraps—I wouldn't wear them until I knew I could earn them. And coming as I did from Hook, I had a pretty good idea how I would be expected to do that.

So here are the rules: If you're going to go into Deadtown, do it while most of the inhabitants are off doing something else, like cruising the fast-food stalls. That's what I did the next morning, after my conversation with Shade. I put on neutral clothes, strapped my favorite knives in, and set off to do some apartment hunting. I obeyed another rule, too. I didn't take any money. Just in case.

I looked around for a couple of hours, and I actually saw some pretty decent prospects. I'm not talking luxury; I just mean that there were some buildings with roofs and windows still intact. Several of these had "guards" outside, urchins in rag-wraps who all gave me warning looks whenever I got too close. I ignored them. When I found the building I liked, I simply walked past the guard and in through the front door.

"Tell your boss I want to talk to him," I said.

The kid didn't answer.

This building was very much like the one I had

grown up in—not with Mom, but later, with Dad. I guess the same company must have put it together. It had eighteen floors, ten of which were quite habitable. I began to wonder if I hadn't miscalculated. A place this nice must have some pretty fierce protectors.

But I let myself inspect the place for a bit longer. I tried the faucets and the toilets, which worked in seven of the apartments, and tried the lights, too. Same story. Obviously someone here was good with gadgets. That was a plus.

I was considering leaving and checking out the inhabitants from afar, at a later date, when I heard the sound of feet on the stairs. Too late. So I peeked over the landing and saw two guys coming up the stairs. They were both mummy-wrapped. One guy had the typical Deadtowner haircut. He was about my height with about forty extra pounds on him. The other one was a delicate-looking guy with no hair. I mean literally, this guy's scalp was a mass of scars. Probably was an interesting story there.

The big guy was climbing to my left, near the wall, so I waited until I knew they would be climbing right below me, and then I pulled a lovely backward flip, grabbing the bottom of the landing and bringing my legs up right into the big guy's face. I got him with both feet right under his chin, and he tumbled all the way down the stairs, ending up at the bottom, with his head against the wall; alive but out of the picture.

The smaller guy had his knives out half a second after this. He must have been surprised, and I was lucky he was, because he didn't hesitate to come at me with both blades. I kicked him in the chest with one of my long legs, shoving him back several paces, and attacked him in return. I was wearing a good jacket, and he had his rag-wraps, so the wounds we were giving each other on the arms weren't too deep. We cut and circled a couple more times, checking each other out, and then he hesitated.

"You the one who came about the apartment?" he said.

"Yeah."

He came at me again, and I managed to get in a good, solid kick to his groin. He wilted, his legs curling under him, then fell on his back with his knives pointing straight up.

"I want the one on the sixth floor," I told him. "I can tell no one is living in there right now. And I intend to be left alone. Anyone who comes up there to see me without my permission is dead."

He breathed heavily, and turned his head to look at me. Finally he said, "Are you a Deadtowner?"

"Yes," I said, without hesitation.

I heard the big guy coming hesitantly up the stairs. His face appeared over the landing, looking confused and light green. "Buster?" he said, then took in the scene. "Oh, man. I'm sorry."

"Don't be ridiculous," said Buster. His face was completely blank, which worried me a little. Had I picked a maniac to abuse?

"Don't worry," Buster said. "It's just my training. I always react this way to pain." He sat up, and his face twitched into an expression that wasn't much more readable. I knew how I would have felt in the same situation, so I just assumed he hated my guts.

"Nice equipment," he said looking at my breasts.

"I know. Remember what I said about invitations."

"Alfred," Buster said. "Meet our new neighbor."

"Howdy," said Alfred. "Didn't catch your name."

"Larissa."

"Larissa. You an acrobat or something?"

"Yeah."

"Oh. Cool." He walked past me, and I tensed until he had walked down the hall and out of sight. I heard a door opening and shutting.

Buster got to his feet. He limped past me, then threw me a strange look over his shoulder. His expression was so inappropriate, I couldn't interpret it.

"See you later," he said.

* * *

I moved my few belongings into the building that very day. The kid out front had been joined by six more, ranging from very young to about my age. But they didn't trouble me. I had already convinced the most formidable guys in the club.

I passed Alfred on my way up. "Give you a hand with that?" he asked me.

"No thanks. I've got it covered."

He nodded and went down the stairs.

I had some good locks on my door—which is why I wanted that apartment. I had a working shower, too, for those days I needed to go into the Spacer Sector to visit my bank. I had lots of space for my clothes, and a few books and trinkets I had grown fond of. I had at least three exits from the apartment: the front door, a side door, and the fire escape. I bought screens for my windows, which kept most of the bugs out.

On my way out the front door to get lunch at the fast-food stalls, one of the little ones ran up to me and said "Hey! Hey! Hey! Heyheyheyheyheyhey," about seventeen more times, until I picked him up by the loose ends of his rag-wraps and gave him a little shake. "Hey!" He said in a different tone, an outraged one.

"I don't like being nagged," I said, "and I don't like being harassed. If you want to ask me something or tell me something, start out with, 'Hey Larissa.' "

"Hey, Larissa!"

"Then try something like, 'Do you know,' or 'Have you seen,' or 'Will you tell me—' "

"Do you know, have you seen, will you tell me what Buster the buster did before he was a Deadtowner?" he chanted.

"No, I don't know. I assume he was a knife fighter."

"Nope!"

"Well, then what was he?"

He pressed his lips together and skipped backward. He put his fingers against his closed lips as an extra measure, and kept skipping. Finally he turned his back on me and ran back to the stoop, where he joined the other kids. They all stared at me, to see what I would do next.

I just walked away. I would find out what "Buster the buster" used to do sooner or later, I was sure of it. Whether I wanted to or not.

Your dreams tell you what you already know. Well, mine do, anyway. They speak to me in very plain emotional language that I can easily understand if I really want to. Trouble is, I usually *don't* want to. That first night in my new apartment was no exception, as I lay dreaming about Buster and what he had been.

But at first I didn't know it was about him. At first, I was just aware of sleeping on my stomach—even though I was really on my back. I tried to open my eyes several times, or thought I did; but I couldn't keep them open for more than a few seconds, and I couldn't make sense of the images I saw, as if they were upside down or scrambled. I thought I was facing a different direction in the room, too, and sometimes thought I was in a different room. None of this was very restful.

I felt the pillow under my cheek. Then I felt someone under me. I opened my eyes—I think—and saw Buster's scarred face. He was lying in exactly the same position I was—on his stomach with his head turned to the left—and I was lying right on top of him, making love to him. How I was doing this, I'm not certain, but it all made me feel vaguely guilty. His eyes were open, and he might as well have been dead for all the expression in them.

Suddenly the eye nearest me looked directly into mine, and he said, "Don't worry. It's just my training. I always react this way to pain."

Again, that guilt feeling. Like I was doing something wrong but couldn't help myself.

Then I was lying on the mattress, alone again, still on my stomach, still with my head turned to the left. He was sitting against the wall, in my line of sight, rag-wrapped only to his waist. I remember thinking how graceful his torso was, like a dancer's. He was cutting himself on the face and arms, then licking the blood off the knife and smiling radiantly.

"They love to drink your blood," he confided.

His expression aroused me, until I got so excited I woke up.

I was really lying on my back, with my head turned toward the wall. *Maybe he's on the other side of that wall,* I told myself, and almost got up to look. But I waited and thought about it for a while, and the more I thought about my feelings, the more uncomfortable I got. How come the dream had made me feel so horny and yet so guilty? I don't usually sit around dreaming up ways to sexually dominate people, and the thought of doing what I had done (seen?) in the dream cooled me off.

Finally, confused and frustrated, I decided it would be best to avoid Buster and just get on with my own plans. I had suddenly realized what they were.

I had decided to try my hand as a knife fighter, at the pits.

But first I wanted to watch a few games. I would try to get Alfred to go with me soon. Those were my plans, and they made me feel better.

So I went back to sleep and dreamed about nothing at all. Nothing I can remember, anyway.

In the morning I found Alfred easily enough, but he was less easily persuaded than I had thought he would be. "I'm busy," he said.

"Doing what?"

"Cruising for breakfast."

"I'll buy you breakfast. In fact, I'll buy you lunch, too."

"I don't know," he rubbed his chin and looked at the closed door of the apartment he shared with Buster. "I don't know how that would look."

I understood what he meant. On Hook, how things looked were just as important. Deadtowners weren't that different from military or miner brats. In fact, many Deadtowners *are* military or miner brats.

"I think it'll be all right," I told him. "I'm gonna wear these neutral clothes, so no one will think you're eating with a dog or a government clerk. In fact, Ninjas wear this kind of outfit, did you know that?"

"No kidding?"

"It's true."

"What's a Ninja?"

"An assassin. Kind of like a Deadtowner, only meaner and quieter."

"Oh. Cool. You gonna ask Buster to come along?" He made to knock on the door.

"No. I don't want this to get too complicated. Not to mention expensive."

"Oh." He seemed disappointed, and something else, too. I could hardly believe it when I realized it, but Alfred was very shy. I was later to see him in brutal fights, mugging people, and hunting the fast-food stalls like a killer shark; but Alfred could also be bossed around, if you were patient enough with him.

"We've got to get going if we're going to miss the rush at the stalls," I said. "You hungry?"

"Yeah," he said, and followed me out of there.

We didn't have any trouble at the stalls, from anyone. Two big customers like Alfred and me don't invite a lot of harassment. He ate like a horse, but would hardly speak to me. His eyes kept looking around, as if he were a child looking for a lost parent. Suddenly his face brightened, and he waved at someone.

Buster came over to the table, and the hair on the back of my neck stood up. "Hey!" He made a half-hearted swipe at my turkey and avocado, then slapped Alfred on the back. "What are you up to?"

It was me he asked, not Alfred. "Just having breakfast," I said.

"She wants me to take her to the pits, Buster," said Alfred. I felt like kicking him.

"Really?" Buster said. "I'd like to come along, if you don't mind."

"Sure," I said. What else could I do? If I had said no, Alfred would have refused to go, too. I tried to relax, because I knew it wouldn't do any good to sit there all tensed up, waiting for him to strike.

I half expected Alfred to share his food with Buster, but he didn't. He gobbled it up without even offering, and Buster didn't look in his direction. This was Deadtowner protocol. Never share, never stare at another Deadtowner's food. Nothing personal, just business.

"You ever been to the pits before?" Buster asked me.

"No."

"You'll like it. It's exciting. You sure won't see anything like it anywhere else."

That was the truth.

Riding the transport to the Q'rin side of town was an unexpectedly nostalgic experience. It was the same kind of transport I rode on Hook; and the Q'rin architecture was identical—as it is on every planet they colonize—as if to say, *Adapt to us, we won't adapt to you.* It's not just that, though. Their cities are designed to protect them from enemies on the outside and the inside. Creativity isn't a priority. Fully half the Q'rin city lies outside the fortress walls, but each shop, each home, each office is built to withstand attack—and possibly even to initiate it.

"Hey!" Buster said right next to my ear, making me jump. "They look sort of like sawed-off pyramids, don't they."

I twitched, but then realized I had been staring at the buildings, so of course he knew I was thinking about them. No mind reading going on there.

"They do," I agreed. "Or almost like Mayan ruins, only built out of steel instead of stone. Well, I don't mean *ruins*—"

"I know what you mean."

His cool attitude was beginning to get me mad, but I was relieved that at least he and Alfred had finished picking pockets and were now seated peaçefully like normal passengers. The rest of the people on the transport were a mixed crowd of Deadtowners, Skids, and a few Aesopians. The latter hadn't gotten on until my two companions were seated peacefully, thank goodness; because they were lion men, and I had already seen a fight between a lion man and six Deadtowners who hadn't paid him proper respect. The lion man won.

I couldn't help peeking at them from the corner of my eyes. I swear, their heads were just like the heads of lions I had seen in books and vids. The mouths were maybe a bit more mobile. Their manes were so long they fell down their backs, those giant, manlike backs that sat atop manlike butts and legs. They wore kilts; and their furry, clawed hands with three fingers and one thumb rested on their powerful thighs as they sat staring at other passengers who always looked away uncomfortably. Except for me. When they turned their deceptively calm eyes to me, I couldn't look away. All I could do was sit and wonder where the lion women were.

They nodded to me, and I nodded back. Then they went back to staring down other passengers, until we finally reached our destination. They were the first to stand and leave the transport, everyone waiting respectfully as the bus shook with their heavy steps, down the aisle and out the door. Buster, Alfred, and I were next in the pecking order.

"Well," I said as I surveyed the field surrounding the pits, "this really *is* the pits."

"It looks better on the inside," said Buster.

It would have to. I had never seen anything so sleazy. Well, that's not true. It's just that I was so used to order and clean lines when it came to—*Q'rin* things. This was mud and chaos, crummy shacks set up as cheap bars, and bums hanging out everywhere. Even the Q'rin warriors—Q'rin-dogs they call them on Z'taruh—seemed touched by the disorder. They swaggered, laughed and joked just like the Human-dogs.

The Q'rin back home would have been so shocked! That's what I thought then.

The three of us joined the throng headed toward the entrance. Once we were closer I got a glimpse of the building itself, and it was much more like what I had expected. It was rather like the Roman colosseum, but with trapezoids instead of arches. It was a beautiful sight, and made up for all the squalor.

Pretty soon we were all squished together, and I guessed Buster and Alfred's hands were pretty busy again, because when we got up to the ticket office, they had enough money to get in and then some.

"You gonna bet?" Buster asked me.

"I don't know. I really just wanted to see what it's like."

"I wonder if Shade is here," Alfred said, which made me twitch, because I had been wondering the same thing. I could picture her sitting in the crowd, watching everyone from behind those dark glasses. Watching me.

I followed their lead in the choice of seats. There was a mostly Q'rin section, a mostly Lyrri section, and a general section. The Aesopians sat with the Q'rin, and I rather wished I could sit with that group. But we chose general seating, and I toughed it out.

That first time was very exciting. I smelled the smells and saw the sights, feeling happy and dazzled and alive, and for some reason I kept thinking of John Lovelock. *Just look at this,* I wanted to tell him. *You aren't half as alive as even the dirtiest, poorest man in this crowd!* And *you aren't half as manly as—* I let my eyes drift over to the Q'rin section. Maybe I was a traitor to my race to feel the way I did—and still do—but I am what Hook made me.

After a long time, the crowd quieted down and the gates were closed. We were all locked in with each other. I looked down into the pit, wondering what the rods were that lined the inclined edge, when suddenly energy flowed into them. They hummed—and sparked occasionally—answering my question. It wasn't until that moment that I really understood I might see people die in the pit. That explained the feeling of vitality flowing through the people there. This was the *real thing,* not a game. I was at the crossroads. I could practically see the line I was to step over. Before I knew it, they were announcing the first game.

"First game of the day!" the announcer cried in Earth, Q'rin, and Lyrri Standard. "Timmy and Sasha, lectrowhip! Fifteen units to place your bets!"

Timmy and Sasha came out of the fighter's door and walked out onto the sand. They were dressed in lectrowhipper outfits; short, black tunics that left their arms, legs, and neck exposed. There was a lot of excited talking and calling as the bet takers stalked back and forth through the stands. I was glad I had decided not to complicate that first trip with wagers. Not that I was a gambling woman to begin with. To me, betting money is like putting your coin in a gum-ball machine and then not getting a gum ball. What fun.

All I cared about was the two fighters. Actually, I was fascinated by their weapons. I had never heard of a lectrowhip before. They looked just like big whips, except they were a bluish metallic color. There was something very ominous about them, even when they were switched off with their tails trailing in the sand. It wasn't until betting time was almost up that I noticed Timmy was a Lyrri—though whether Timmy was male or female, I wasn't sure at that point. I would have noticed sooner, but she had her hair shaved on the sides, pit-fighter style, and cropped on top. Lyrri usually wear their black hair long.

I noticed right off the bat that Sasha was a wolf man. It would have been hard to miss that.

"Hey," I nudged Buster in his remarkably unyielding side. "That's an Aesopian, right?"

"Yeah. Don't see many of them on Z'taruh. Wolf men, I mean."

"How come?"

"I'm not sure, but I've heard wolf men don't like to take orders from anyone but other wolf men, so they don't make good soldiers. If that's true, you wouldn't see many wolf man vets, right?"

"Oh." I wondered if he was implying that I was stupid. For all I knew, he was making all that stuff up, anyway. Much later I heard some more about why wolf men are scarce, from the horse's mouth, so to speak. And it was quite a different story.

I had been about to ask Buster a question and had my hand on his wrist to get his attention. But dead silence fell as Timmy and Sasha's whips snapped up over their heads with a hum that easily drowned out the hum of the rods lining the pit sides. The whips danced about like live things, making me forget my original question and making me wonder if the fighters were moving them or if the whips just moved that way on their own. I kept meaning to ask and meaning to ask, until Buster had to pry his wrist out of my grasp as I accidentally bruised him.

Timmy and Sasha circled. They hated each other, that much was plain. Timmy wasn't smiling the way I had seen other Lyrri smile—almost constantly, like crazy people—and anyone could have interpreted the snarl on Sasha's face. I thought, with so much hate, they would cut each other to pieces. But when the first blow came, from Timmy, it was cautious; and Sasha returned it with a cautious blow of his own. *They're testing each other*, I thought to myself, and it was at that point that Buster pulled his wrist free. I had done what Timmy and Sasha were doing, when I wanted to hurt someone bad and wanted to make sure it was done absolutely right. No mistakes, no missed opportunities.

Timmy hit Sasha *Pow-Pow-Pow,!* sounding almost like that and looking a lot worse. She had hit him overhand across the face, throat, and shoulder. I heard a sizzling noise, and I thought, *His blood, burning up before it can splatter.* Incredibly, he was still standing after that, and he hit her back just as hard, twice, undercuts to her face and throat. That's *hatred* ladies and gentlemen, going for someone's face like that. I would understand exactly what that was like, later, but even that day I knew. That's when I decided I would never, ever become a lectrowhipper.

They circled, letting their whips build their charges back up. I didn't really want to watch anymore at that point, but I couldn't help myself. My eyes were riveted, just like everyone else's, on two people who were about to try to elegantly and viciously kill each other. The whips lashed faster and faster as the charges built up, until they must have been almost impossible to control. Sasha struck at Timmy, and she struck at the same moment. He had aimed at her ankle, trying to flip Timmy off her feet so he could hit her when she couldn't hit back. Sasha succeeded, but Timmy hit him right across the eyes at the same moment, then flipped backward, and landed right on her feet again, striking Sasha over the eyes again the second she landed. He staggered back, and there was a growl from the Aesopian section, an angry, hate-filled sound.

Sasha was blind.

Timmy had him now, and she took full advantage of the situation. She had the Lyrri smile back now, the same sweet, almost angelic expression I had grown used to seeing on those doll faces, and now I understood what those smiles really meant. Sasha could do nothing but wait for Timmy's next blow, standing there with his shoulder straight and blood dripping over his frozen snarl. I would have been lashing out in every direction if I had been him, trying to get her at least once more; but Sasha did something better. He switched off his whip.

Now only hers was making noise, and he went right for it, putting everything he had into a flying tackle. She hit him once more before he connected, but he ignored the blow. He grabbed her whip hand with his left hand and her throat with his right, and they went over with her on the bottom. The crowd cheered and started screaming advice to both of them in every language. He wasted no time in sinking his fangs into her neck, and I expected to see it end there with a victory for Sasha—but it didn't.

Lyrri have very tough skin.

So the two of them wriggled around for quite a while, and though she was only half his size, she was a match for him. That really scared me. I wasn't sure why then. Anyway, what eventually happened was Sasha managed to get the whip out of her hand, and with both of them disarmed, the fight was over.

"A draw," said the announcer. "All bets are off."

The crowd was cheering and chanting Sasha's name as he got up. Timmy walked immediately from the pit, leaving him there to accept his applause. I couldn't tell if she was mad about it or not. I didn't cheer with the others. I couldn't stop looking at that ruined face. I felt sick—not pity exactly, he was too good a warrior for that—maybe sympathy was the word. Maybe empathy. A bear man came out of the fighter's door and escorted Sasha from the field, releasing me from the ordeal of having to stare at his pain.

"How many more games are on the schedule?" I asked Buster. He and Alfred were casually munching peanuts.

"Nine more," he said.

I sat back and had a good long laugh at myself for thinking Hook was a tough place to live.

Chapter 9

Timmy and Sasha had the only lectrowhip match on the schedule that day. Afterward, we saw two mangler matches (how much can you mutilate your opponent within a fifteen-unit-time frame), three wrestling matches between lion men and bear men, and three knife matches. When the knife round started, I was very nervous, thinking they had saved the most impressive fighters for the last. How could I possibly hope to compete against the sort of entertainment I had seen so far?

The first two knife fighters came out and squared off. They were Deadtowners, wrapped just like Alfred and Buster.

"Oh, cool," Alfred said. "There's Gene."

Buster leaned over and whispered in my ear. His breath sent a chill straight up my spine. "You could beat these fools, easy."

I wondered if he was trying to flatter me into trouble. But as soon as Gene and the other one started fighting, I knew he was being truthful. They were clumsy and hesitant. They really didn't want to get into it, and everyone could tell. The Q'rin despise that kind of behavior. They laughed and called insults, which prodded the Deadtowners into more action, but not much more.

When their time was finally up, Gene was announced as the winner (so I never did get the other guy's name) with the pathetic total of ten points. They were booed off the field.

"Shit," Alfred said. "I don't blame them for not

wanting to cut each other up just to make it look good. I mean, what's a knife for, anyway? Not for fun, that's what I say. You have to be really good if you're gonna pit fight without getting hurt bad.''

''Like you,'' Buster whispered to me.

The next two fighters were just as amateurish as the first, but they must have been watching from the wings, because they tried a lot harder. It made me a little uncomfortable to watch them, because they were still getting insults from the Q'rin, but they were also getting encouragement from the Lyrri, who must have seen what a couple of bumblers they were. It made me sick, because the Deadtowners really started to hurt each other when the Lyrri cheered them on.

''You know these two?'' I asked Buster.

''No.''

The announcer hadn't even told their names. Your name isn't announced unless you have some impressive wins. So I started to think of them as Red Hair and Blond Hair. Blond Hair was a vicious little bastard. Red Hair was more graceful, and even had a little talent.

''Hey Red Hair!'' I bellowed. ''Quit throwing your shoulder so far forward! Use your legs, damn it!''

People turned to look at me for that one, but I just ignored them. Red Hair tried to take my advice, and he actually did a little better. At the end of the match, he won. People turned to look at me again, and I got some sharp stares from the Q'rin section.

''You're already making a name for yourself,'' Buster said, smiling stiffly. It was like being smiled at by a mannequin.

The last two fighters were Q'rin pros. ''Makrit and Dorrin,'' the announcer called. ''Fifteen units to place your bets.'' Fifteen units was the maximum time limit, so the outcome of the fight was uncertain. The fighters stood very still and stared at each other for the whole betting time, their rocky faces impassive.

''Yeah,'' Buster said, ''these two are the best. If

you're gonna fight, these are the two who are gonna be the most threat."

Makrit and Dorrin were wearing lightly padded vests, which would take the edge off the cuts to the torso, but which also left their arms and necks bare. They had scars on their exposed skin and on their faces. That gave me pause. I wasn't sure I wanted to collect scars on *my* lovely mug.

"Time," the announcer called, and he left the pit.

Even before they started, I could tell they weren't going to be like the Deadtowners. Their movements were so perfectly timed, I wasn't even sure who attacked first. I think it was Dorrin, but Makrit closed with him instantly, and they punched and slashed each other several times before stepping back to consider their next moves. I could see they both had marks on their vests and new cuts on their arms. Dorrin slashed at Makrit's belly, forcing him to jump back; but he landed lightly on his feet, circled, and closed for another compound attack. He gave Dorrin a new cut over an old scar on his cheek.

They were so good, it was sexy. There was no hesitation, no waste. They only paused for seconds at a time before making simple or compound attacks, cutting each other on the arms, torso, neck, and belly. (Since Q'rin bellies are tougher than Human, that area isn't worth as many points).

Makrit slashed Dorrin across the chest hard enough to bring blood right up through the padding, and Dorrin retaliated by cutting Makrit above his right eyebrow. For the rest of the fight, Makrit was shaking blood out of his eyes. He nailed Dorrin on the neck in a compound attack, but the wounds were barely nicks. So he threw all caution to the winds and closed with Dorrin, making his cuts maybe by sense of smell, since his eyes weren't as reliable. Fists and knives flew as they battered each other.

"Hold!" the announcer called, and the fighters separated. They faced the judges so the cuts made during that last bit of close fighting could be evaluated. The announcer listened to the little microphone at his ear.

"Dorrin has 157 points," he called. "Makrit has 154. Dorrin is the winner."

The crowd was on its feet, cheering. It was the kind of close fight they loved to see. I wondered if I would be able to make them as happy.

It was all over then, so we filed out of the colosseum with the crowd. I had to concentrate on not getting crushed or knocked over. I felt dazed. I had thought I wanted to fight there, but now I wasn't so sure. Buster was pressed right up against my back, as close as a lover, and certainly close enough to slip a knife into me if he wanted to. I half considered doing something about it (if only for the sake of pride), but decided I was stuck with the situation. So out we squished.

"Did you like it?" Buster asked me on the way back to the tran. For a moment I thought he meant the involuntary dry humping we'd just done inside the colosseum.

"Yes," I said when I realized what he was really talking about. I was feeling almost as fired up as I used to feel after a Half-G match. Remembering that gave me a sharp pang. How different things could have been.

"I'd like to see a Deadtowner beat those Q'rin fighters," Buster said.

"I'm not sure I'm that Deadtowner," I said.

"Really?" he shrugged that off, as if it were completely unimportant to him. I wondered what he would have said if I had told him that I really wasn't a Deadtowner at all.

At least, at that point I wasn't. That changed the very next day.

What happened was that the bank lost my account. I had gone in that morning to make a withdrawal, scrubbed, pressed, my head high, for all the world like a bodyguard of a rich, important person. I went to the same clerk I had always done business with, the one who always smiled and called me by name. But she wasn't smiling this time, and I didn't see a glimmer of recognition.

"May I have your bank disc?" she asked me. I handed it to her, and she ran it through her scanner. "We have no record of your account," she said as she handed it back to me.

"What?" I couldn't process what she was saying to me. She had to say it three more times.

"I have forty-five hundred credits in this bank!" I said. "You can't just lose forty-five hundred credits!"

"We have no record of your account."

"Then why do I have a bank disc? Look, the bank president's signature is on it and everything!"

"It must be from an old account."

"You can't be serious! Couldn't you just run it through again? Maybe your computer made a mistake."

She took the disc from me and appeared to be running it through the machine. But then she just turned back to the window and stared right through me. She didn't give me back my disc.

"Well?" I demanded.

I felt the pressure of large hands on my arms. I looked up to find two bouncer types flanking me. I looked at the clerk again just in time to catch the shadow of a smile on her lips before she returned to her blank expression. In that moment, I understood.

"Don't touch me," I told the bouncers. "I'll walk out on my own."

They let me go. I walked out with my shoulders straight. I didn't stop until I was in Midtown. Then I turned around and took the back-alley route to the bank. I waited patiently in the underground tran lot until closing time. I was lucky. The clerk was by herself when she came down.

She was very surprised to see me. I punched her hard, in the nose, then dragged her out and through several alleys. She didn't resist, and when I finally stopped and propped her up against a wall, she was calm.

"You can't get your money back," she said.

"Why not?"

"They've been watching you. They know you don't work for Cliff Goldbar anymore, and you haven't found another rich patron. You have no way to defend yourself, you can't even afford the lawyer to make an inquiry. You are powerless, so they simply appropriated your account. They do it a hundred times a year."

Again I saw that ghost of a smile. I slammed her head against the wall.

"They," I said. "You mean *you*. *You're* the one who always handled my account. *You're* the one who's been watching."

"No."

I slammed her head again. Her eyes fluttered, but she was still calm.

"You took the money for yourself. Isn't that true?"

"No."

"I could go to your bosses about this."

She laughed. Something in her tone kept me from slamming her again.

"I'm just an employee," she said. "Yes, I can get commissions for scouting out pigeons. I got a commission for you. But if you try to take this any further, those two big goons who escorted you out of the bank today will take you to Outskirts and put a force bolt through your head. Believe me."

I did, but I was madder than ever.

"You have Automatic Teller Machines in Midtown," I said. "You're going to walk with me there."

She laughed again. "I told you, you can't get your money back."

"I'm not talking about my money."

Her smile died. "You must be joking."

I slammed her again, five times. I waited for her eyes to stop fluttering, then pushed my face into hers. "I'm not joking. Right now I'm very tempted to kill you. I could kill you. Any second now I'm going to do it."

That was true. I wouldn't have felt good about it later, but I would have done it if she hadn't cooperated. She must have realized that.

"I'll take you," she said. "But I don't have much in my account. I can only withdraw two hundred at a time."

"Let's go see," I said.

I expected her to call for help on the way to Midtown, but she didn't. She came along quite passively. No one took a second look at the blood running down her face and caking the back of her head.

We found an ATM near the fast-food stalls. Someone had smashed the hidden camera, but I doubted that would do me much good. I was sure they had pictures of me from my trips inside the bank.

She punched in her account code, but before she could push in the amount, I stopped her hand. I punched in one thousand. Her hand turned into a claw.

"You can't do that!" she screeched. "It won't pay out that much!"

But a moment later, it did. I stuffed it into my pockets and grinned at her.

"That should take care of your commission and then some," I said.

She had already composed herself. "You realize you'll never be able to go into the Spacer Sector again," she said. "The dogs will be out looking for you within the hour."

It was my turn to laugh. "For *your* sake? I don't think so, clerk. I think you're just like me. What was it you said? Powerless."

"Don't bet on it," she said.

"I am betting on it. I'm betting your bosses don't like to be annoyed, by people like me *or* you. I don't think they're going to mind that you paid me some money. Now stop complaining. You lost a lot less money than I did."

I turned my back and walked away from her. "You bitch!" she screamed after me. "You dyke!"

This was reassuring. I don't think she would have been screaming names at me if I hadn't been right.

I went back to my Deadtown apartment and sat on the edge of my mattress. I had just bullied that clerk and robbed her, but I was the one who felt abused and robbed. She had taken my beating without batting an eyelash. Maybe she considered it part of her job.

Someone knocked on my door.

"Who is it?"

"Buster! Let me in."

"I don't feel like having company now, Buster."

"I was at the fast-food stalls, Larissa. I saw you with Miz Money."

I let him in, though I'm not sure why. I was even more nervous with him than usual, because I was feeling mad and vulnerable. He gave me his usual vacant grin and sat down on my mattress. "That was quite a show you put on," he said. "I'd like to know what led up to it."

I shrugged, thinking I wouldn't tell him. But after a few minutes of silence, I broke down and told him the whole story.

"So how much money do you have now?" he asked me.

"A thousand."

He got up and went to my closet. He pulled some of my clothes out and started tearing them into strips. I jumped up and tackled him. "Hey!" I shrieked. "I don't have the money to replace those!"

"You're a Deadtowner now," he said calmly.

"I'm not! I have a thousand credits!"

"So do I."

I don't know how long I stood there and gaped at him. "You've got a thousand credits," I said numbly.

"That's right. Alfred's got six hundred. He's not as ambitious as I am. But it doesn't matter anyway, Larissa. What can you do with it besides buy lunch? You can't pay rent with it, not for long. You can't get off the planet. It may cost one thousand credits to get here, but it takes almost *four* thousand to leave. So what does that mean?''

I dropped my hands. He went back to his shredding. Soon I was helping him. Then Buster broke a dead-towner taboo and showed me how to wrap myself.

I learned very quickly how to hunt the fast-food stalls, but I never liked it. I felt conspicuous there, hunting with the kids. My first day I pushed a female government worker out of her seat to get at her sandwich. But though Deadtowners applauded this, I never used that tactic again.

''Don't be stupid,'' Buster told me. ''Forget about manners. You want to eat?''

''Look,'' I said. ''If I keep picking on small women like that, the male G-workers and the tinkers are going to turn Galahad and come to the rescue. I don't want them ganging up on me.''

He conceded that this was probably true, and I went on with my modified swoop-and-snatch method. Occasionally I broke down and bought food from a store, just to give myself a break. Since I didn't use drugs, food was the only thing I had to spend money on, if you don't count the few books I bought back then. In fact, there was only one other thing I could have possibly spent money on: gambling.

Which led me back to the pits.

I don't mean that I started betting there. I just started thinking about the place. Alfred and Buster asked me about it from time to time. ''When are you gonna fight?'' they would ask. I never answered, because I didn't know. But I did get them to take me back to watch a couple more times; and in the meantime I hunted the stalls, watched other Deadtowners drug themselves into a stupor, tried to avoid the riots, and flat out refused to go with Buster and Alfred on mugging forays. The bank clerk was my one and only.

One day as I sat finishing somebody's meatball

sandwich and black coffee at the stalls, Buster came over and sat down across from me. He had a big black eye from the night before, when he and Alfred were almost mugged on the way home from robbing someone else. If I had been along, they might not have been attacked at all, and I thought he had come over to gripe at me about that. He politely averted his eyes from my food until I was finished eating.

"You don't belong here," he said finally.

I didn't answer. I felt like walking away.

"I'm saying this for your own good," he said.

"You're mad at me? I don't owe you a damn thing, Buster. I'm not going to make my living as a bully and a thief."

"That's what I'm trying to tell you," he said. "I thought you could live this way, but it's not right for you. You can do better."

All of this was coming out of his mannequin's face in a dead serious tone, making it all sound like a very dry joke. I knew that if I were him, I would still be mad at me for kicking his ass, and I might be thinking about getting even. But I wasn't him, and I couldn't even begin to guess what his motives were; so I had to take him seriously until I knew otherwise.

"That's very un-Deadtowner-ish of you," I said. "Why do you care? You aren't even sleeping with me."

"I don't know why I care. Does it matter?"

I shrugged. "Well, since we're being honest, how about you? If you're so smart, why are you still here?"

"Don't you think I intend to get out? Once I have enough to get off planet, I'll probably join the naval service. I know I can pass their entrance exams. So I do have a plan. What's yours?"

"I'm not particularly worried. Maybe I'll fight at the pits and you can win some money on me."

"Good. When?"

I sighed. "Soon. It'll be soon."

He nodded and went off to hunt some more. I went

home and lay on my mattress, thinking. After an hour or so, I got up and started to stretch. If I was going to fight, I needed to get in shape again. I knew it wouldn't take me long.

Chapter 10

Alfred was the one who escorted me down to the pits to enter myself as a fighter. He was the one who had the fighting experience, not Buster—which upset my theory about what Buster had done before he became a Deadtowner. Alfred was big and lean, very graceful for his size, and generally kept a cool hand in fights unless you punched him anywhere near his eyes. But I had never seen him fight with a knife. Yet it was as a knife fighter that he had fought in the pits.

"How did you do?" I asked him.

"Not bad. I didn't get booed too much."

"I see you more as a boxer. Maybe a wrestler."

"Yeah, well, I think they ought to have boxers, too, 'cause that's what I do best. But *they* don't like it. You know, the Q'rin. They think it's tame." He laughed at that. "And wrestling, that's dominated by the Aesopians. Can you imagine wrestling with one of those guys? I did once, just for laughs. It was over in half a minute."

"That took guts!" I said.

"No. This guy, Rorra—he's a bear man—he's got a sense of humor. He was just kidding around. I liked him. But I had a stiff neck, afterward." He laughed again.

I was enjoying having him along. Alfred comes off as a little stupid sometimes, mostly I think because of his size and his long silences. But he's the sort of man I'd want to have on my side in a fire fight, someone who can stay calm and think on his feet. Having him with me as I walked up to the pits made me feel more confident.

"You have to walk through a lot of drill rooms before you get to the assignment window," Alfred said. "It's cool, you'll like it." He pointed to an unmarked door about a hundred feet to the right of the south entrance. "There's our entrance."

He just pulled the door open and walked right in. There were no guards, which surprised me until I noticed that the entrance hall led straight down and into a maze. Alfred was walking down a flight of stairs, and I hurried to follow him.

It was dim, and about thirty degrees cooler down there. The halls and rooms looked like they'd been blasted out of solid granite, probably one of the few dry, solid areas of Capital besides the Hill. It was spooky going down there. Made me think of ancient gladiators and the Minotaur.

Underneath the sound of fighters sparring, exercising, or just plain talking, I could hear the sound of a pump—I think it worked the ventilation system. Alfred stopped outside the open archway leading into one of the drill rooms and waited for me to catch up. I heard a loud cracking noise coming from the room, and his face was intermittently lit with a blue glow. "Take a look," he said.

I joined him and looked into the room. Two lectro-whippers were sparring with their whips down to about one-eighth charge, just enough to keep the whips moving. I couldn't tell who they were, because they were wearing protective gear that covered their entire bodies, sort of like fencing gear. They still hit each other hard enough to bruise right through the gear, but Alfred said, "If that were the way they played the game all the time, I might be willing to give it a try."

I withheld comment. He turned away from the room and led me down another hall, seeming perfectly sure of himself.

"This place is a maze," I said as we entered another gym. This one was brightly lit, and seemed more for general use, with bars and weights and that sort of thing being used by both Q'rin and Human fighters. They eyed both of us as we passed through, sizing us up.

"Once you've been here a few times, you'll figure it out," Alfred assured me. But there were lots of dim tunnels leading away from the main hall we were taking, and I didn't think it was likely I'd ever know where they all led—or would ever want to.

We turned down another large hall and came to a small window. Behind it was a Q'rin clerk.

"Name?" he asked me in a bored tone.

"Larissa—" I was wondering if I should make up a last name, but he didn't give me the chance.

"Specialty?"

"Knife," I said.

He glanced up at me. "Not another Deadtowner," he said mockingly.

"Knife," I repeated. He sneered at me a little longer, then wrote it down.

"Is tomorrow soon enough?" he asked casually.

"How about today?"

He was surprised at that. Anyone who didn't know the Q'rin would have said *fine*, but I knew how cowardly it would sound to want to put a fight off until later.

"I can schedule you as early as an hour from now."

"That's better than I had hoped for."

He was looking at me harder now, as if he were trying to recall where he might have seen me before. "You'll be fighting another Deadtowner, of course. I assume you have your own knives."

"I do."

"Good. You'll be called in an hour."

I made to walk back down the hall again, but Alfred took my elbow and pointed me in the opposite direction. "This way," he said. "I know a gym where the Aesopians work out."

So I went with him to the wrestler's room. That's what I always called it, anyway, once I had seen it;

even though lots of other fighters worked out there, too. It's just that when we walked in, some Aesopian bear men were throwing each other around, and that definitely commanded my attention. They were wearing what I had come to think of as Aesopian fighter's kilts.

"That's Rorra," Alfred said, indicating the bear man who was doing the most throwing. At that moment, Rorra had the other bear man hoisted above his head. He threw the other guy into a corner, where he landed with a resounding *wham,* then got up and ran back into the fray. Rorra grinned and met him head-on. They appeared to be having a lot of fun.

I watched them for several minutes before I noticed Mr. Red Hair, from the other day's knife fight, sitting on one of the hardwood benches that lined the walls. I wondered if he was the one I was scheduled to fight. Alfred and I went over to introduce ourselves.

"I'm Ted," he said. "Yeah, I remember you. You fighting in an hour?"

"Yeah."

"Me, too. Guess it's you and me."

I just nodded. I was wondering how I was going to be able to make this fight look good.

"Look," I said finally. "Remember what I told you the other day, okay? About using your legs more?"

"I remember," he said warily. I could only hope that he would stick it out. I didn't say anything more about it.

In an hour, we were called.

We went straight through a large archway into a hall big enough to admit elephants and up to another archway. This one let us out into the pit, under the hot sunlight and the eyes of several thousand spectators. For a moment, I felt a sharp pang of stage fright; but it was over instantly, and I strode out onto the sand. The Q'rin announcer stared at me. Up close I could see he was missing an eye, and he had dozens of knife scars.

"Knife fight," he said, then took a slight pause to

size me up. "Ten units to make your bets," he finished.

From where Ted and I stood, the buzz of the crowd seemed threatening. I looked at Ted, trying only to see and think of him. He returned my gaze with his face relaxed into an admirably neutral expression.

"Time," the announcer said, and left the pit.

Ted and I didn't move for a minute, and everyone got very quiet. I could feel their eyes on me like a solid weight, but it was exhilarating. I moved closer, just to see how he would react. He tensed, and I decided to close in.

I hit him twice, cutting lose some of the rag-wraps on his belly. He was a little slow reacting, and only managed to nick my knife arm as I pulled back again. He ignored the flapping rags, letting them fall to the ground as he circled me.

I was wishing for my left hand knife, but since Ted only fought with one knife, I was under the same constraint.

He came at me, going straight for the wraps over my breasts, perhaps hoping that I would be humiliated if he cut some holes there, but it wasn't even a consideration for me. I struck his hand away and hit him twice more, cutting his wraps instead and making two long red streaks on his chest. He tried to kick my legs out from under me, but I was already lunging forward again, and he went down instead. I danced away.

He was up again instantly, and circling. His face was beginning to take on a hopeless expression, but his mouth was firm, and I admired that. I attacked him again, and he managed to get in a couple of decent hits on my arms, but I got him on the arms and the belly again, then clipped his cheek on the way out. I dodged his next two strikes, landing a good punch on the side of his head the second time, then slashing him twice in the ribs while he was disoriented.

We both stopped, watching each other. He was breathing hard, looking cornered. I knew it would be a bad idea to go for him just then, when he was the most desperate. I could feel him getting ready to make his move just before he did it, so I was ready. In he came, aiming straight for my face.

He never even got close to my face. I grabbed his wrist and pulled him right off his feet, which won me a cheer from the crowd. I punched him in the kidneys as he went down. In a street fight, I would have stabbed him there. He rolled and pushed out with his foot, catching me in the belly and knocking me on my butt. He threw himself on top of me then, but I was still rolling, and I took him with me. I was on my feet again in half a second, and so was he.

We kicked and slashed each other twice more. Then I lunged in and marked his neck just over his jugular. His face got very white, and he backed off.

"Hold!" the announcer called, making me jump. "Larissa is the winner, with ninety-eight points. Ted has seventy-nine points."

I think I heard cheering at that point, and I remember looking up into the Q'rins section. They were staring at me intently, leaning forward in their seats. I looked up higher and saw an elephant man dressed in ragged fatigues. I was so dazed, I wondered if I was imagining him. Next to him sat a skinny girl in ragwraps and dark glasses. Shade. She gave me the thumbs-up. I nodded to them and turned away.

On the way out, the announcer clapped me on the shoulder.

"We could use you again tomorrow," he said.

"I'll be here."

"Just tell the man at the window."

I did, with great relish.

I admit I drank a little more than usual at the party my housemates threw for me that night. I had fun, even with all the younger kids running around acting like hyperactive lunatics. Alfred gave everyone a blow-by-blow description of my victory.

"And you should have seen the look on that registrar's face when she told him she'd been invited back.

Man! That was a good feeling, seeing that. Respect. Now we got someone who can beat them at their own game."

"Don't be too sure," I said. "I can hold my own, but I've never beaten a Q'rin at his own game." If I hadn't been drinking, I probably wouldn't have admitted that.

Buster took a heavy swig of vodka and twisted his face into a parody of a scowl. "Knife fighting is *our* game," he said. The kids cheered and danced around some more at that. They whipped out their knives and started making feints at each other. I prepared myself to kick if one of them got too close.

"That Dorrin guy won with a score of 157 the other day," I said. "My score today was only 98." I didn't add that my percentage of the take was only 100 credits.

"But you only got to fight for ten units," Alfred said. "They got fifteen. And if you had been fighting someone better, your points would have been higher."

"Maybe."

"No maybe about it," Buster said. "I fought you once. I know what I'm talking about."

He didn't look at me when he said that, and in fact, he hadn't looked at me all evening. I was uncomfortable about being reminded of what I had done to him, and also uncomfortable about watching him drink when he usually just smoked loki. I could feel something building between us like a storm. I wanted to ask him what it was, but that would have been against the rules. So I waited.

An hour later I left, weary of the gibbering and hooting of the maniacs. I was lying on my mattress, trying to remember what exactly had happened during my fight that day, when I heard the soft rap on my door. I knew it was Buster.

When I opened the door, he stood there with his blank face on and looked at me. The light from downstairs was shining on half his face, making him look ugly. I felt guilty for thinking that.

"May I come in?" he said.

"Yes." I stepped aside, and he walked past me, to the mattress. I watched the way his shoulders moved as he walked, and decided that now he was beautiful. He sat down and rested his elbows on his knees.

"I'd like to talk to you," he said.

"All right." I sat down next to him.

"I can make love to you better than anyone you've ever met," he said.

"Really?"

"Yes."

"Why's that?"

"I used to do it for a living."

This knocked me flat. I shut my mouth before I could stutter or say something insensitive. I looked at his profile, another good angle, and saw how beautiful his skull was, how graceful the curve of his neck. I imagined him with long, dark hair, and then it all made sense.

"Let me make love to you," he said.

"Why do you want to, Buster?"

He looked at me with a genuine expression of surprise, not his usual stiff parody of emotion. "Because you're beautiful," he said.

"That's the only reason?"

He shrugged. "I don't know. Maybe. Do you need another one? I could tell you all sorts of lovely things, and you'd believe 'em, too. I might even believe 'em. You want me to?"

"Maybe not. Let me think about it."

I have to admit, I was a little disappointed that Buster could be swayed by someone's physical appearance. Now it all seems rather romantic, the jaded "scarbaby" falling for beauty just like anyone else.

"I can make you hot just by looking at you," he said.

"That's a little hard to believe. Your face is usually so, um—I mean—"

"Let me show you," he said. "Just watch."

And then his face changed. Heat and color poured into the wax of his skin, his pupils became larger, his mouth moist, his lips slightly parted. I had always been too disturbed by his face to look at it so closely before, but now I couldn't look away. It was beautiful.

"Keep watching," he said. And just by changing the tilt of his head, lowering his lids, licking his lips, he made my heart pound faster.

"Come here," he said.

My nipples got very hard. I resisted a minute longer, just to see what would happen. He put his hand on my knee, and heat poured into my thigh. Before I knew it, I was leaning toward him and licking my lips. He met me halfway.

I opened my eyes and saw his scarred head up close. I shuddered, but it was from pleasure more than revulsion. His mouth felt good. He tasted like alcohol and sex, and now his hands were moving. I made myself keep my eyes open. I didn't want to miss anything.

I wonder if anyone ever thought to make a porno vid about two Deadtowners. Imagine them slowly unwrapping each other, exposing hungry skin inch by inch.

Buster's body was perfect, but scarred in odd places, erotic places. He was proud of these scars, so I paid them loving attention. I was almost disappointed when he entered me, because I thought it would all be over soon. But it wasn't. It took a long, long time.

Afterward he lay next to me and whispered love poetry to me until I was trembling. I'm such a fool, I can't remember a word of it, just that it was sweet and hot, and made me feel like Helen of Troy.

"That's lovely, Buster," I said. "You speak it as if you wrote it."

He was quiet for a long moment, simply stroking me and giving me soft kisses.

"I did write it," he said.

"And you call yourself a Deadtowner."

He laughed. "There are worse things. Besides, my goddess is a Deadtowner. Tomorrow you're going to win another fight. May I send Alfred to bet on you?"

"Why don't you come yourself."

"No," he said firmly. His hands tensed, then relaxed again. "Don't ask me why. I don't think I could bear it."

To see me fight, I wondered, *or simply to be asked why*? I thought he would get up and leave then, since his last words made a perfect cue for that sort of exit. But instead he pulled me close and went to sleep. I stayed awake as long as I could, to savor what was left of the night.

Buster kissed me once in the morning and was gone. He had serious breakfast hunting to do at the stalls. He didn't even look hung over.

I lingered in bed awhile, then lingered in the shower, then took twice as long as usual to get through my daily workout. By the time Alfred called for me, we had to run. We barely made the tran.

I was feeling very calm, which made me wonder if there wasn't something wrong with me. Maybe I was in love, or just on the verge of being in love, or maybe even just enjoying being loved. I don't know. Snatches of Buster's poetry kept whispering through my mind, but I wasn't distracted. I was completely alert. People seemed to be moving in slow motion.

"I'll meet you out here after the games," Alfred said when we got to the pit. "I'd like to sit all the way through, okay? Rorra is fighting today."

"That's fine," I said, and sauntered in through the fighter's entrance. I had decided to pretend that I knew exactly where I was going, and this miraculously seemed to work. I found my way to the registrar's window and checked in. He didn't look up. "Your fight is in half an hour," he told me.

Half an hour, I thought to myself as I went in search of Rorra the wrestler. *Twenty units.* I liked Q'rin time better.

I found Rorra with a bunch of other wrestlers, but this time he was just watching. Two lion men were mixing it up. Watching them made my heart pound. I don't think I'll ever be satisfied with watching human wrestlers again.

I had intended to approach Rorra and introduce myself, but he approached me first.

"You're Larissa, aren't you?" he boomed. "I saw you fight yesterday. You're a good fighter." He patted me on the shoulder and grinned with a mouth full of fangs.

"I'm glad you think so," I said, straining to make myself heard over the shouts and growls of the Aesopians. I swear, their language would hurt a human throat.

"Will you watch me fight today?" he said.

"I plan to."

"Good. Perhaps afterward we can go out for a drink."

"I'd love to," I said, somewhat taken aback. It seemed so unreal to be standing there with this seven-foot (eight-foot?) creature, planning to go out for a drink. Why was he being so friendly? "Would you mind if I brought my friend, Alfred? I'm sure he'd love to talk with you."

"Yes, I remember Alfred. It's a date then. Come, let me introduce you to Ousa—*The second best wrestler on Z'taruh!*"

A lion man looked up from the book he was reading in the corner and yawned. "What?" he said. "Is there a mosquito in here? What was that annoying whine?"

"Come meet Larissa, a most excellent knife fighter."

"Oh yes." Ousa gave me a hard look. "I lost money because of you yesterday. Rorra told me I was wrong, but I wouldn't listen."

I was trying to get a look at the title of his book, but it was written in Aesopian hieroglyphics. I would love to own an Aesopian book—though I doubt I'd ever be able to read it—just so I could gaze at the beautiful characters.

"Today you fight Makrit," Rorra told me. "So the outcome will not be so easy to predict."

My heart jumped. A moment later I was angry. Just when had the Q'rin planned to tell me that? When Makrit and I were facing each other? Then I felt proud. Then grateful to Rorra for warning me.

"This is good news," I said, and he grinned again, gripping both my shoulders with his huge hands.

When they called my name, I was proud. Makrit and I met in the main hall and walked out into the light together. He reminded me of my old friend Abriin, though he didn't look much like him. Makrit was taller and thinner, and his hair was cut almost as short as mine. His bony face was cold, his eyes hard. But I felt that same anticipation of a good fight. It made my limbs feel like they were made of air.

"Makrit and Larissa," the announcer said. "Fifteen units to make your bets."

The time flew by. I stared at him and tried to remember how he had fought the three times I had seen him. From what I could remember, he had been almost flawless. He was standing there, absolutely motionless, his weight perfectly balanced. I really wanted him bad.

"Time," the announcer said. I felt him walk behind me and out of the playing area. Makrit was already moving. I waited a little longer, so he would think I was intimidated, then I danced away and got ready for the attack.

We moved in at the same moment and went at it like a couple of surgeons. I felt his cuts, made my own, danced in and out, cut cut, feint, cut—it was as if we were thinking with the same brain. Every move his eyes made spoke volumes to me. We were both smiling.

We were moving almost every second we were out there, pausing only two or three times to look at each other and think, then move again. I knew I was making as many points as he was. If we had been cutting to kill, it would have been much different. The shock and pain would have slowed us both down, and I'm not sure I could have been his equal. I would have had to fight more desperately, take more chances. But as it was, I wasn't ready for it to end when it did.

"Hold!" the announcer shouted, and we froze. Makrit looked as frustrated as I was.

The announcer took more time than usual to announce the winner. I had a small premonition about who it would be half a second before he said it.

"Larissa, 158 points," he said. "Makrit, 159. Makrit is the winner."

We got a good round of cheering as we walked out of the pit. I didn't waste my time feeling disappointed. "When can we do it again?" I asked Makrit.

"Soon," he promised, and went his own way.

Rorra was waiting for me at the end of the hall. "Excellent," he said. "Excellent! Now let me show you where you can watch the rest of the games." He led me down another hall, his huge, furry arm around my shoulders. "You have inspired me," he said. It made me feel better than the cheers had.

The fighters have a special box just off the Q'rin section, where they have one of the best views available, and to which they can go via a secret door under the stands. That's where Rorra led me. He sat me down, patted my shoulder, said, "Enjoy yourself," and descended again to the bowels of the pit.

I took a good look around. I saw an elephant man sitting in front, down a few rows and to the left of me. I didn't look at the special boxes to my right, because I knew the Q'rin nobles who sat there were checking me out. I sat up straight.

After a few moments, Makrit emerged and sat next to me. He said nothing for the next two fights, but I could tell that he meant to eventually, so I didn't let myself become too distracted by the view. I saw another knife fight, this one between two very good

Deadtown fighters whom I didn't recognize, and one mangler fight between a couple of female Q'rin fighters. That was a new one on me.

"Rorra is up next," Makrit said. My neck tingled at the sound of his voice, an odd feeling on that warm, damp afternoon.

"Who is he fighting?" I asked casually.

"His mate, Winna."

That sounded intriguing. I'd never seen a female Aesopian. At least, I thought I hadn't. When the two of them came out of the pit door, I realized that Winna looked pretty much like Rorra, except that her fur had more of a reddish tinge to it. They were even the same size.

"How can you tell them apart?" I said, more to myself than anyone else; but Makrit answered me.

"Don't you have a nose?" he said.

I almost laughed at that. His nose was as big as any Q'rin's, what Humans would have called an *eagle beak*. I was sure it was a lot more sensitive than mine, and, in fact, I thought he could probably smell me more thoroughly than a Human man, smell my deodorant, my—well everything. I started to sweat at that thought, and I was sure he could smell that, too.

"Rorra and Winna," the announcer called. "Wrestling. Ten units to place your bets."

I was glad I don't bet, because I couldn't have picked a winner in that fight. I could pick a winning knife fighter if I wanted to, but that's not allowed. That would be like insider trading. I could only watch other knife fighters and try to measure my own chances against them. And that was enough.

"Time," the announcer said, and left the pit.

Rorra and Winna got into it immediately, colliding like a couple of small planetoids and then grappling almost like sumo wrestlers. There were a few minutes when they just seemed to be frozen there, embracing like the loving couple they really are; but they were really struggling to unbalance each other. Finally Rorra got the upper hand, and toppled Winna sideways. He tried to pin her as soon as they hit the ground, but she was up again in a flash. Then it was grappling time again.

"They know each other too well," Makrit said softly. "When you know your opponent's moves so intimately, you can only dance with her."

"She could always surprise you," I said, noting his use of the female pronoun and wondering if he was only referring to Winna.

Rorra finished the contest fairly soon, though Winna put up a good fight. When it was over, I half expected to see them embrace, but they simply walked off the field. If I hadn't known already that they were mates, I wouldn't have guessed.

"Do a lot of—mates—fight each other here?" I asked Makrit.

"No. Most find it too distracting."

"I don't know about that. It seems like a good way to work out marital problems."

I had been joking, but he gave no sign he was amused. "Would you kill your mate in a fight?" he asked.

"No!"

He gave me a long look, and I began to wonder where this was leading. He wasn't exactly checking me out in the usual way, as if he were attracted to me. But I don't know if Makrit could anyway, he'd been a fighter for so long. I began to worry that he might come on to me, which would be awkward considering our profession (yes, I already thought of myself as a professional fighter). Privately, I agreed that it would be too distracting to fight someone I was emotionally involved with.

A paranoid little corner of my mind pointed out to me that he might think dating me would eliminate me from the competition.

I barely saw the last fights, I was so caught up with wondering what he would do next. My experience with John Lovelock simply hadn't prepared me well enough for a subtle man like Makrit. When the last fight was over, he just sat still, and since he was between me and the aisle, with his long Q'rin legs stretched out in front of him, I couldn't leave without asking him to move. I watched the crowd moving past our box for about fifteen minutes before I finally worked up the resolve to move.

"I have to go now," I said, standing up. He got up, too, but didn't get out of the way just yet.

"Have supper with me," he said.

"I can't," I almost stuttered. "I promised to meet a friend afterward."

"Break your promise," he said.

I shook my head. "It's Rorra I'm meeting. I want to keep that date."

I waited in vain for him to say that it was all right and that he understood, and I certainly should have known better than to expect that from a Q'rin, even a modern-thinking Q'rin from Z'taruh. Of course, he never did, and I had to move past him without another word. He let me go; this was all within the proper protocol. But it still made me a little uncomfortable.

Alfred was pleased to see me emerge with Rorra, Winna, and Ousa, who had decided to come along at the last minute.

"Oh, cool," he said, which was only what I had expected. We went to one of the shacks on the edge of the field, right across from another field called Packrat's Plot. Naturally, the shack was called Packrat's Shack. It was mostly frequented by fighters. I was a little embarrassed when we walked in and I saw Makrit sitting with Dorrin and another man. Makrit threw me hot-cold looks, but didn't come over to our table.

Since Rorra had won eight hundred credits that day, he was buying. I ordered a rum and Coke, and the others had brainbusters, even Alfred. I hoped I wouldn't have to carry him home.

"Now, my dear," Rorra said as he took my hands, "before we get too drunk, we should talk about something serious. I'm sure that one of the lords will approach you soon. What do you think about that?''

I shrugged. "I'm not sure. I've made some good money so far on my own.''

"Personally, I prefer being independent,'' said Winna. Her voice was quite feminine; beautiful, in fact. "You don't make as much money, but you have absolute freedom.''

"This is true,'' said Rorra, "but we are Aesopians, and our situation is different.''

"How is it different?'' I asked.

He let go of my hands, and lifted his glass of brainbuster. It was fascinating to watch him lift it to his mouth, which, after all, was at the end of a muzzle. But he drank it without spilling a drop, and when he put the glass down again, it was half-empty.

"Ah,'' he said. "That is a good question. It has partly to do with the Ragnir war, Larissa. As you know, we were on the losing side.''

"With us,'' I said.

"Yes, but that is not all. We have a long relationship with the Q'rin, for good or ill. Under some circumstances we can accept their patronage, under some we cannot. It is *cultural*.''

"All right,'' I said neutrally.

The three of them gazed at me, measuringly, but I kept my neutrality in place. I felt like goldilocks being confronted by the three bears. Well, two bears and a lion.

"We mean no dishonor,'' Ousa said. "It would not necessarily be bad for you to accept a patron. Not only will you earn much more money, but you will attain power within their society if you choose. Perhaps this is important to you.''

"Well.'' I sipped my own drink. "What if it is?''

"Then get a contract,'' he said.

I blinked at him. "A contract?''

"And when you do, bring it to us. We will have our best mind go over it. If you like.''

Alfred nudged me. "Do it,'' he said.

"Huh?"

"Girl, this is a once in a lifetime deal. I would grab it in a minute."

He really didn't have to tell me that. Even if I didn't trust the Aesopians, I would be curious to see what they had to say. And there is no way in hell I would accept a contract without having a good lawyer go over it.

"I would be very happy to have your man look at my contract—assuming I'm offered one," I said. "Thank you."

"You're welcome," said Rorra. "Now, let's get drunk."

And they did, but it didn't make a lot of difference. They got a little louder and more playful, an intimidating sight. I caught glimpses of Makrit watching us, so I nursed my drink for as long as I could. Rorra must have seen me doing it. He leaned over and put his huge arm around my shoulders. His fur was silky and clean, and his breath smelled like minty alcohol.

"One more thing," he whispered under the noise of Winna and Ousa laughing. "Remember that it is easier to gain a patron than to get rid of one."

"I will," I said, resolving on the spot that I would say no to the lords. It just sounded too complicated.

When we got home from that second fight, Buster wasn't around. He stayed away for three days, then came home with a new smile glued on his face, a maniac's smile. I made him get rid of it when we made love a few nights later. He had some new cuts on his body.

"What's going on?" I asked him.

"Nothing. Just a relapse."

"What's that supposed to mean? You're working as a scarbaby again?"

"No."

"Then what?"

He turned on his side, facing me, and gave me the sexy face. "You think you're to blame?" he asked.

"Am I?"

"The beautiful Larissa has stirred up my old passions and my old pain. Is that it?"

"Sure looks that way."

His face drained of expression, until I had trouble keeping my eyes on it. "Do you think I'm in love with you?" he asked.

Actually, I did. I immediately felt stupid, And disappointed.

"Didn't I tell you I could make you believe it?" he said.

"Yes." I lay down, too, with my face up, because it's harder for me to cry in that position, and I could feel the tears building. Crying has always made me feel helpless.

"I do love you, Larissa."

"Stop it."

"All right." He stroked my forehead, kissed my cheek, soothing me. "I love making love to you. You believe that, don't you? Sperm doesn't lie."

That made me laugh.

"Making love is the only truly honest thing I can do," he said. "Especially fucking and having an orgasm. If you watch my face when I'm doing that, you'll see me as I really am. When I'm with you, fucking is almost the only thing I think about."

"What else, then?" I asked.

"I can't tell you."

I brooded about that. He was taming me with his hands, and I knew it. He was distracting me with his double-talk, leading me away from the subject of his new scars and that awful smile. But then suddenly he brought up the subject himself.

"I cut my own scalp off, you know," he said.

"No. I didn't know."

"He loved my hair. In fact, he was obsessed with it, liked to ejaculate into it. He sometimes even wanted me to choke him with it."

"He wanted you to kill him?"

He laughed like a barking dog. "No! Haven't you

ever heard of autoerotic strangulation? You know, masturbating while you choke yourself? You're not supposed to kill yourself doing it; though some people end up that way, which is why it's better to do it with a partner—''

And then he launched into a description of strangulation during sex, stroking my breasts and kissing me all over every few breaths, really working himself into a frenzy. Seeing him that excited got me excited, too, though I didn't like the idea of being choked. He didn't try that, but once he bit me.

''Don't!'' I screamed, and he apologized.

''I won't do it again,'' he promised.

''And no choking,'' I said.

''No choking.''

Then he came like a freight train.

Chapter 11

My next several fights were with Deadtowners, all of them very good fighters. I won every fight, but two people pushed my limits, Lynn Kwan and Oscar X.

Lynn Kwan was as tall as I was, but much thinner—what you might call willowy. Her face was unspectacular, but I always thought of her as beautiful, maybe because of the way she moved, literally like a willow in the wind. I think I even felt a little jealous of her.

Oscar X was actually a lectrowhipper, but he liked to knife fight for variety. We had a drink or two together once in a while, and he told me silly jokes. He had an accent that he described as warped Australian. "It's what we spoke on Colony 2," he told me. "I doubt they'd recognize it back in the Mother Country."

I laughed, and reminded myself that Oscar X was the only Human fighter who could face Timmy the Lyrri and live. Out of the pits, he was so relaxed and witty, and though I wasn't romantically inclined toward him, he helped me forget about my troubles with Buster, at least for a little while.

Buster disappeared for two weeks, just a few days after our conversation about choking. When he came back, he had no new scars, and he seemed more like his old self—which only made me more suspicious. I even went to Alfred about it. I stopped him in the hallway of our building on his way to the stalls.

"Look," I said, "who's this guy Buster cut his scalp off for? Mr. Choke Me."

"Oh shit," Alfred said, turning white. He really looked upset. "He's dead. Buster told me he was dead."

"Who was he?"

"A Lyrri. His name was Allaa—"

"*Allah*? As in *God*?"

"Huh? I said Alla-*a*. You pronounce the *a* twice. Anyway, this was all before I knew him, but I think he was kind of tied up in knots about this guy. Wrote him poetry and everything. He's really good—you ever hear his stuff?"

"Yes. Go on."

"That's all I know, except for what I saw the night I met him."

Alfred looked both ways down the hall to make sure Buster wasn't around before he continued. "I found him in the alley behind the Baby School. I was supposed to score some loki, you know? And I saw this miserable bundle of rags. I went to check it out, and Buster lifted his head. It was all bloody; he had just cut his scalp off. His face was twisted in this expression like you wouldn't believe, like the way you would look if your mom died or something, and he said, 'I sent him my hair, he loves my hair!'

"He was so pathetic, I just couldn't stand it. I knew he was a scar—oh, shit."

"Don't worry," I said. "I knew."

"I never could stand to see that. It's bad enough to see kids being sold for sex, but that other thing is just too much. So I took him home, and in a couple days he was like you see him now, one of the best damn Deadtowners I ever knew. And smart. He's helping me study for the naval entrance exams."

"So how did Allaa die?" I asked when it looked like he had lost track of the story.

Alfred turned pale again. "He choked himself while he was jacking off."

"Let me guess," I said. "He was using Buster's hair as a noose."

"That's what his relatives said. They came to talk

to Buster, and when they had left—you know, smiling like they always do—Buster told me all about it. He seemed kind of relieved. That's what I thought, anyway."

"Could Buster have lied? Maybe Allaa is still alive? Or Allaa's relatives were lying, and now Buster knows it?"

He thought about that for a moment, and it was my turn to look up and down the hall. I felt like a character in an old mystery vid.

"I don't know," he decided. "I kind of wish you hadn't said that, because now *I'm* wondering."

He went away looking depressed and confused, but I felt better for knowing more of the story. I didn't much want to follow Buster around to see if he was meeting his old Lyrri lover—that was his business. But I did pursue my inquiry a bit farther, this time at another source.

I went down to the pits on one of my off days in search of Rorra. He works out there every day. I found him in the wrestling room, as usual, mixing it up with Ousa and another bear man I didn't know. I watched them until they were finished.

"Could I buy a drink for you?" I asked him.

"Of course," he said as he dried himself vigorously with a towel. (Aesopian's sweat almost as much as humans do, but they don't stink, at least as far as my nose can tell.) "Do you want to see me alone, or may I invite Ousa and Radra?"

"They can come, too," I said.

The four of us retired to Packrat's Shack, where they ordered brainbusters and I had my usual rum and Coke. "I'm not sure if it's polite to bring this kind of subject up to an Aesopian," I whispered to Rorra, who was sitting next to me. "I want to ask you something about the Lyrri."

"Ask," he said. "It's best that you should know your enemies."

"My enemies?"

"Yes. I mean *enemy* in the sense of one who will hurt you if at all possible, one who is dangerous."

"Uh-*huh*. Well, this is about a friend of mine." And I told him the story of Buster. Ousa and Radra listened, too.

"You say this Allaa choked himself to death on your friend's hair?" asked Ousa when I was done.

"Yes."

"Not possible." Ousa gulped the rest of his brain-buster. "Did you see Sasha the wolf man fight Timmy a few weeks back? He tried to take her throat out. Wolf men have very powerful jaws, but he was unable to do it. Your friend's hair would have given out before Allaa's neck."

I glanced at Rorra, who was rubbing his furry chin and staring at the table. "Radra," he said, "will you fetch us another round of drinks?"

When Radra had gone, Rorra turned to me. "I didn't want to say this in front of the young one," he said. "But I wonder if this Allaa wasn't in love with your friend."

"Why wouldn't you want Radra to hear that?"

"It's a perverse idea."

"I agree!" Ousa said emphatically, then patted Rorra on the shoulder. "But speak freely, my friend."

"Thank you," said Rorra. "What makes me think so is that he wanted your friend to choke him, not the other way around. And also, I think there is strong evidence that Allaa is dead."

"Why? On both points."

"Usually, the Lyrri torture their Human lovers, not the other way around. It is a tradition with them. But if they fall in love, they take the passive role. This is an extreme rarity, and is considered contemptible. Allaa's relatives might easily have murdered him if they found out about this relationship. Then they would have told your friend he was to blame, in order to enjoy his pain. That is what I think."

"But why do you think Allaa is dead?"

"Because if he weren't, your friend would have seen him again. Lyrri are also tenacious. They don't let go of what has caught their interest."

Radra came back then, so we dropped the subject. I had a different picture of Buster's love affair now. Allaa almost seemed tragic. It was a strange notion.

"You fight tomorrow?" Rorra asked me, nudging me away from that line of thought.

"Yeah. Lynn Kwan. Then Makrit again."

"Two fights in one day?" he asked, his brows rising. "Interesting."

"That's rare?"

"Yes. I think someone may be getting ready to make you an offer."

"One of the lords?"

"Yes, almost certainly."

This prospect drove Buster and his dead lover completely out of my head for the rest of the day. I felt very smug and very nervous, a combination that set my stomach churning. I spent the next several hours composing rejections to imagined propositions, none of which came close to fitting the situation that actually unfolded the very next day.

Did you ever know one of those girls who, without even trying, can make you feel like a clumsy, graceless clod when you're standing next to her? That was Lynn Kwan. Her every move was so graceful, every expression so charming, it just was impossible not to feel a little jealous, even for me.

She was sitting quietly in the wrestler's room when I came in late and a little out of breath. "We fight in five minutes," she said, nonchalantly.

"We do if you ever wake up from your nap," I said, just as casually.

"Don't worry, I'm awake." She didn't get up, just sat there with her long legs stretched out in front of her, lightly slapping the wooden bench with her open hands. I stayed on my feet and let my breathing get back to normal, fixing her with my best Nefertiti expression. She never showed it, but I suspected she felt the same way about me as I did about her. After all, I had beaten her six times in a row.

"You have to show me how you put on those rag-wraps someday," she said, smiling. "They're so sexy. Don't you think I would look sexy wrapped up?"

"Ask one of the guys," I said. "But you aren't ever going to wear rag-wraps, Lynn. You like your pretty clothes too much."

"That's true," she admitted. She liked to dress up like a Ninja, even though she was Chinese, not Japanese. She loved to tie her long, silky black hair at the shoulder blades and let it swing with her every movement. The girl knew what she had.

By that time we had all the men watching us, except for the Aesopians (I guess we don't smell right to them). Makrit had come in just after me and was leaning against the far wall.

Lynn asked me, "What's it like having tits that big?"

"It's just like having little tits," I said, "only much, much better."

She winked at me and jumped to her feet. I let her brush past me and precede me out the door. As I followed Lynn, I met Makrit's eyes. "One woman fighting is a pleasure to watch," he said. "Two women fighting is a feast." I was out the door before I could think of anything to say back.

I know a lot of men like to watch the women fighters just to see us move our bodies. That's okay with me, because I feel that way when I watch the men, too. Kind of adds spice to the job. And to think I could have been peeling latex off my body in nightclubs, instead. If I'm going to shake it, I'm going to do it with a weapon in my hands.

When we emerged onto the sand, the Humans started whistling and calling, "Cat fight! Cat fight!" in gleeful tones. One guy screamed, "Cut her tits off, Lynn!" which made me a little mad. I don't like remarks like that. But I saved my energy for Lynn, because I knew she was going to try to save face that day. She had lost by a larger margin every successive time we fought, and if she didn't rally today, we wouldn't be fighting each other again. That would place her on the second string. I think that's why she decided to fight me two-handed that day, instead of using her usual one-handed method. I'll admit, the change made me nervous.

Lynn and I faced each other while the announcer paced back and forth. "Larissa and Lynn Kwan," he called. "Ten units to place your bets. This is a fifteen-unit fight."

That was a little irregular, and a bit of an insult to Lynn. Ten units to bet meant everyone already had a pretty good idea who would win. Her face didn't show it, though. She had the inscrutable look down pat.

"You'd better kill that ugly black bitch, Lynn!" my heckler called, and then I heard an "Oomp!" I looked up to see a commotion in the stands. I saw arms flailing, and then Alfred stood up, triumphant, from the melee. He waved at me with blood on his hands and yelled, "Knock her dead, beautiful!"

I felt better after that, and promised myself I would give Alfred a big kiss later.

"Time," the announcer called, and made to walk out of the pit. But he paused next to me first and gave me a hard stare from his one good eye. "Fight well," he said, and then left the pit.

Lynn was staring at me with her black eyes one moment, then moving with the breeze in another, and the fight was on. Two knives appeared in her hands, like magic. I always admired her ability to draw so smoothly. I drew mine and kept moving.

So far, Lynn was the only fighter who had been willing to fight me two-handed—which is the way I like—and she was the only *woman* I had fought, which made me wonder if fighting two-handed was something only women could do. You know, sort of a right-brain, left-brain thing. Women's hemispheres are supposed to be better integrated. But Lynn actually might have done better sticking with the one-handed style. When she swooshed in and out of range for the first few cuts, her left hand wasn't very strong. She made some neat little slashes with it, but no serious cuts. I, on the other hand, cut deep and hard with both hands, marking her arms, belly, and face. She kept moving like she couldn't even feel it.

In the first five units, she was her normal self, moving as gracefully as a ballet dancer and fearlessly attacking me again and again, much faster than any of the male fighters could have moved. But that left hand held her back, and I was making two hits for every one of hers. She was bleeding more than me, and seriously lagging behind in points.

In the second five units, things seemed to slow down, at least from my point of view. I knew Lynn was going to lose, and that she was being humiliated. I took no pleasure in that, but I didn't show any mercy. I cut her again and again, as efficiently and emotionlessly as I could; but I must have gotten cocky, because she surprised me. She slammed into me and bashed my nose with her forehead, then cut me over several vital spots on her way out. I staggered back, dizzy, knowing that she would be flying past me with another attack, and guessing that she would do it on my right side because of her weak left hand. I kicked out in that direction and got her with a good solid *thud,* sending her flying.

We were both dazed for a moment, and I felt damn lucky. If she had succeeded with her tactic, she would have caught up to me in points. My ego reeled at that notion.

Blood poured out of my nose for a unit or so after that, then stopped. Lynn was moving more cautiously—I think I may have bruised some of her ribs. Her eyes were glittering now, and I knew it was because of tears unshed; but my eyes felt wet, too, from pain and anger. She aimed a few cuts at my face and neck, knowing I would be sensitive about that area, and I cut her over her wounded ribs. I'd like to say it was nothing personal, but I'm really not sure it wasn't.

"Time!" the announcer called. "Larissa has 207 points, Lynn Kwan has 170. Larissa is the winner."

We got cheers, cat calls, and invitations. Lynn was breathing hard, and it looked like one of those tears might flow onto her cheek at any moment; but her face was calm.

"I should never have picked the two-handed style," she told me. "I might have beat you one-handed."

"You might have," I admitted.

I let her precede me off the field. On the way out, the announcer clapped me on the shoulder and smiled. I know my Nefertiti mask was in place, and he couldn't have seen how bad I felt for Lynn, or how happy I was for myself. All those emotions couldn't fit on one face, anyway.

I had an hour to rest and clean up before my fight with Makrit. I went to the surgeon's office, as I usually did after a heavy fight. I didn't really want knife scars, though many knife fighters consider them badges of honor. To me, a knife scar is a road map to how many times you got hit when you shouldn't have. Sometimes you can tell where a fighter is weak by looking at the scar patterns.

Besides, I'm proud of my velvet skin.

Lynn was there, too, which didn't surprise me. She was as vain as me. She didn't say anything to me until she was about to leave. "Are you going to fight Makrit today, too?" she asked.

"Yes."

"I envy you," she said, and walked out.

The surgeon, who was a Lyrri instead of the Q'rin doctor I was used to, said, "How glorious your skin is. I've never seen such a deep color. Have you considered getting some sort of ritual scarification?"

"No," I said uneasily.

"You should. Your ancestors used to do it. The females made scars on their breasts and bellies, which, when stroked, evoked considerable pleasure."

"You say that as if you were there to see it," I said.

"I wish I had been."

I was nervous for the rest of the time I was at his mercy, but he closed up every wound with amazing finesse, leaving the barest hint of a seam, which I knew would be gone in a day or so. It did seem to hurt a little more than usual. I wondered if I was imagining that.

My nose wasn't seriously damaged, and required only a few minutes attention. Then I hit the showers and got ready for my fight with Makrit. I wrapped myself in record time and hustled into the wrestler's room. He wasn't there, but I knew he would be on time.

I had thought my fight with Makrit would be pretty much like it was the last time, only this time I might win. But he came on a lot stronger from the word go. The first thing he did was to knock me flat with a punch from his free hand (he didn't have Lynn's problem with weakness) and then come after me like a mad butcher when I was down. I was amazed to find myself falling back on my Half-G experience in order to keep my bones from being broken. After that, he didn't connect another solid blow.

If I wanted to score any points at all, I had to go on the offensive, otherwise I'd spend the whole time running, which wouldn't look too good. I had the advantage of being lighter and faster, so I just braced myself for a new batch of wounds and went for his face with the nails of my left hand while cutting him with my right. That caused him to jerk his face aside, reflexively, and I nailed him under the ribs and on his neck.

Unfortunately, the next time I tried that, he tackled me; and I almost killed him accidently, because my knife was between us, facing him. As it was, he got a deep gash in his side. He reared up and made to slash my face, now that he had me pinned, but something stopped him. He paused for what seemed like a long time.

"Hold!" the announcer shouted. "Makrit forfeits. Larissa is the winner."

He dropped his hand and got off me. He helped me to my feet. Some people were cheering, but most were talking. I have a feeling there were some heavy bets riding on us, and no one expected a forfeit.

Makrit was just staring into my face the same way he had when he found he couldn't cut me there. He was swaying a little, but maybe that was from blood loss.

"You should get to the doctor," I said gently.

He nodded, and walked off the field. I made to follow him, but someone was waiting for me just inside the tunnel.

He was a young Q'rin warrior, very tall and dressed formally. I thought his features were rather fine for a Q'rin. "I am Hazaar," he told me. "Lord Oshrii would like to see you in his box now. You may watch the rest of the fights from there."

This was not the way I had imagined I would be approached. This wasn't even a request; it sounded more like an order. "I ought to go to the surgeon first," I said.

"You're barely wounded."

I took stock. He was right. Now I was embarrassed, which weakened my position even more. He took my arm, and escorted me down the tunnel. He moved almost as gracefully as a Lyrri, which made me watch him suspiciously from the corner of my eyes; but his skin was dark copper, and though his features tended slightly toward the Human, they couldn't be called Lyrri-like by any stretch of the imagination.

He took me down one of those tunnels I had thought I'd never explore. My stomach tightened as I lost my sense of direction.

"I don't blame you for seeing the surgeon every time you get a scratch," Hazaar said as we walked. "Beautiful skin like yours shouldn't be marred."

We turned another corner in the maze and walked down an empty corridor. The lights were dimmer here, and I was beginning to feel nervous about Hazaar. How did I know he was really from Lord Oshrii? I prepared myself to draw my knives, but didn't feel hopeful about the tactic. Hazaar had a force gun strapped to his hip, one of the real fancy ones you only see on an elite guardsman.

We came to a locked door at the end of the corridor, and he turned to look into my face before he opened it, maybe to see if I was nervous or frightened. I'm pretty sure I had my face on straight. He opened the door, and we climbed up into the light.

We emerged near a box full of Q'rin warriors, all of whom were staring at me with no sign of curiosity or warmth in their faces. I wasn't sure which of them was Oshrii, and no one spoke to alleviate my ignorance. I stood there for some time, feeling Hazaar at my side, waiting in vain for a sign.

Finally I said, "If no one is going to speak to me, I'm leaving."

"Really?" said one man. He was perhaps thirty, not the oldest man there, and he was dressed no more formally than the others. He had classical, rocky Q'rin features.

"Yes," I said firmly.

"I'm Oshrii," he said, then stared some more, until my heart started to pound. I knew better than to tell him my name, because he already knew it, and I couldn't think of anything else to say. He waited until just one moment before I would have worked up the courage to walk away, and said, "Please sit down."

Hazaar directed me to my seat. Once again, I felt I was being ordered instead of invited, but I was too intrigued and intimidated to protest. Hazaar sat next to me and looked at me as if he were thinking of engaging me in conversation. He looked at me that way the whole time I was there, but never spoke. I looked back and tried to figure out what he was trying to tell me with his eyes.

There were three more fights scheduled that day, and I probably heard Oshrii and his entourage speak only half a dozen words to each other during that time, all in the Q'rin language. I could barely make myself pay attention to the fighters, only noticing what their weapons were before I went back to my silent conversation with Hazaar. Belatedly, I remembered that females aren't supposed to stare directly at Q'rin males, at least on Hook, unless they're flirting. That proved how flustered I was. But I kept staring, since I had already done whatever damage might have been done.

When the fights were over, we sat quietly and watched the people crowd out of the colosseum. I looked to see if Alfred was around, but couldn't see him. I felt Hazaar's eyes still on me. When the stands were almost empty, I heard Oshrii say, "I have an excellent stable of fighters."

It took me a moment to realize he was speaking Earth Standard, and was therefore speaking to me. "*Stable?*" I said, feeling heat rise to my face. I was grateful my coloring would hide it.

"You find that word offensive?" he asked.

"I do when it's applied to people."

"You would never belong to a *stable*, then."

I was surprised that he had offered me such a perfect opportunity to turn him down. "No," I said firmly.

He laughed in that brief, abrupt way they have of laughing, "Hah." It was a sound that could have been ironic or could have been contemptuous. Whichever it was, I didn't want any part of it.

"I don't think it's an inappropriate word," he continued in a reasonable tone. "Why do you?"

"Because stables are where people keep animals," I said.

"Exactly." He smiled. "So?"

His men laughed, not quite as briefly as he had before. My face was practically radiating heat now. I got up and tried to leave, tripping over Hazaar's foot, which may or may not have been deliberately thrust in my way. I grabbed the edge of the box and turned to glare at Hazaar. He met my eyes for a moment, then dropped his gaze to my breasts.

Oshrii was still smiling. "If you want me to believe you're better than an animal, you have to prove it to me," he said.

"I don't have to prove it," I snapped. "I won't be one of your fighters, and I don't give a damn what you think of me."

His smile changed instantly into an enraged snarl. "You do have something to prove to me, and you'd damn well better care what I think!"

"Go to hell," I told him.

He jumped to his feet. "How dare you speak to me this way!" Then he was laughing again, his anger evaporating so quickly that I knew it had all been an act, maybe even a joke. "Perhaps you're not good enough to be one of my fighters, after all," he said, then turned his back on me.

So that was it. He had guessed that I would turn him down, and wanted to be the one to turn *me* down.

"Maybe you're right," I said to his back. "I really don't care. I'll never fight for you." And I left the box.

It wasn't until I was almost to the north exit of the colosseum that I realized I had done exactly the right thing. At least I had in terms of saving face. If I had wanted to discourage Oshrii's interest in me, I had done exactly the *wrong* thing.

I spent the rest of the day in a daze. I wasn't sure whether to feel triumphant or scared or embarrassed, and I had to ask everyone who spoke to me to repeat everything.

"What happened to you today, anyway?" Alfred asked me on the way home from the pits. I hadn't even wanted to stop for drinks at Packrat's Shack. Too many Q'rin in there.

"I turned one of the lords down today," I said.

"Oh. Cool," he said, and didn't ask me about it again. I almost wished he had, so I would have an excuse to talk about it, but I also had the feeling I should sleep on it and give myself a chance to cool down.

So I went to bed. But instead of the restful sleep I needed, I had a nightmare. It was the kind where you don't realize at first that you've fallen asleep. I was fighting with Makrit at the pits. The entire audience was made up of men, and my rag-wraps kept flapping loose. Makrit slashed at my chest, and I felt more of my wraps give way. When I glanced down, I noticed my breasts were exposed.

He kept cutting off my wraps until I was completely naked. I wasn't embarrassed, just mad that the announcer hadn't stopped the fight when it had obviously dragged on past the maximum time limit. He probably just wanted to see me humiliated, like all the men in those stands who were staring and grinning at me. Finally Oshrii stood up and cried, "Time! Makrit is the winner, Larissa forfeits!" and everyone cheered.

I felt Makrit's hand on my shoulder. I noticed his side was bleeding. "Because you did so poorly today," he told me, "you'll have to fight The Butcher."

He backed away from me, out of the light and into the tunnel. I stared at the doorway in that helpless way you feel in nightmares. Someone was coming up the stairs. There aren't any stairs in that tunnel, but there were now.

The Butcher was naked, and just as young and powerful as I remembered him. His face was just as ordinary, and his dick was just as big.

"Hello sweetheart," he said. "Remember me?"

As he advanced, I retreated, until I felt the pit incline behind me. But when I looked, the rods were gone, so I ran up the incline and started to scramble up the wall. I was almost to the top when a head appeared above me. It belonged to Rorra, the bear man.

"Larissa," he asked, "is this really the way you want to do this?"

I woke up then, which infuriated me. That certainly

wasn't the way I wanted to do it. I knew I could have beaten The Butcher in a fair fight. I'd done it a million times in my fantasies.

Evidently, I just couldn't do it in my nightmares.

Chapter 12

I was out the next day buying a strongbox. Over the past few months I had earned about ten thousand credits at the pits, and since I certainly couldn't trust the banks, I needed a more secure place than my mattress. I was more practical than my dad had been, though. I bought a stasis pad to put it on, so no one would be able to pick it up unless they had the proper code. Theoretically, I suppose someone could saw all the way around the field and just steal the floor along with the box, but that would take a lot of time. I felt secure with my choice.

I was on my way home from the safe shop when I spotted Buster with a Lyrri. I don't know why, but my heart stopped. They were standing together on a corner, too close to be casual, but not close enough to be exactly intimate. I hadn't seen Buster in a few days, and though his life was certainly none of my business, I missed him in my bed. I wanted to know who this Lyrri was, so I walked right up to them.

"Hi Buster," I said. "Who's your friend?"

Buster didn't look surprised to see me, not that I had gotten much better at interpreting his expressions. The Lyrri smiled at me and extended his hand.

"My name is Chaz," he said. "And you are Larissa. I've seen you fight."

I took his hand, expecting him to shake with me and let me go. But he held on. His hand was like warm marble, and it felt like he could crush my bones without any effort at all.

"How soft your skin is," he said. "Like velvet. Are you and Buster lovers?"

I didn't answer, but Buster said, "Yes."

"I envy you," Chaz told me. Or he told Buster, I'm not sure. His eyes were so black, I couldn't distinguish his irises from his pupils. They seemed to want to swallow me up.

"I was just asking Buster about someone you may know," Chaz said. "A girl named Shade. Do you know her?"

"No," I said, half truthfully.

"But you've seen her."

"Yes."

"Do you know where she is now?"

"No," I said, happy to have an absolute truth to tell.

Chaz sighed. "I've been trying so hard to find her. I don't know why I've failed. I don't want to hurt her, you know. I only want to do business with her. Will you tell her that if you see her?"

He seemed so gentle and sincere, if he hadn't been holding my hand that way, I might have wanted to help him. He was probably the most beautiful being I've ever seen in my life, and I have to admit he was fascinating. But when I said, "Yes, of course I will," I didn't really mean it.

He released my hand, and turned his eyes back to Buster. "Will I see you tonight?" he asked.

"Not tonight," Buster said.

"Ah," Chaz said sadly, and he walked away. He moved like a powerful cat. Belatedly, I started to shake.

"Look what he's done to your wrist," Buster said. I looked. I now had a bracelet of finger-shaped bruises. They were darkening even as I watched. They didn't hurt yet, but I was glad I wasn't scheduled to fight for two more days.

"Don't fall for the handshake trick again," said Buster. "Don't let him touch you at all, if you can help it."

"Do you let him touch you, Buster?"

"Not yet."

Buster and I started to walk toward home. I looked at him from the corner of my eyes and tried to decide what he might be feeling. It was no good. He was even stiffer than usual.

"What do you suppose he wants with Shade?" I asked.

"He wants to eat her alive."

"Why?"

"He's fascinated with her."

"I thought he was fascinated with you."

His mouth jerked into a smile. "No, he's only titillated by me."

"Are you titillated by him?" I asked, averting my eyes from his face.

"He looks like someone I used to know."

I figured that had to be Allaa, but I didn't have the guts to ask. Not when he was smiling that way.

"So what has Shade done to fascinate him that way?"

"I don't know. He keeps talking about her eyes, and about his losses at the pits. He seems to think she can help him win big."

At the mention of Shade's eyes, I got a little chill. I had never seen them—they were always hidden behind her dark glasses—but I could feel them looking at me. She reminded me of Mattie M'Benga, only more so. I didn't really believe in telepaths; but theoretically, if Shade were some kind of telepath, she and that elephant man, Knossos, probably had quite a racket going.

"I see you got a strongbox," said Buster. "Pretty soon, you're going to have to move on, Larissa."

"Where?" I said, my throat closing up at the thought. "I have a lot of money, but it wouldn't last long if I actually had bills to pay."

"Pretty soon you'll be earning enough to live wherever you want to. You could work for a year and make a fortune, then leave Z'taruh. Hell, you could join the navy with Alfred and me. Some pipe dream, eh?"

"I'm not sure I want to leave Z'taruh."

He gave me a jerky shrug. "Then rent a fancy apartment. Invest your money, play politics, buy yourself a bunch of dogs, sponsor your own fighters—hell, anything! Don't be such a coward, Larissa."

I didn't speak to him the whole rest of the way back to our building because I was so mad at him. He just walked along with his mannequin's face, as if he didn't give a damn. I supposed what really bugged me was that he was right on target.

"Let me know if you need any help with your box," he said when I left him in the hall. I slammed my door, resolving never to give him the time of day again.

But when he knocked on my door that night, I let him in.

I was fighting for the next seven days in a row at the pits, and even fought Makrit again, twice. He was back to his own style, and beat me once. Both times we fought, our points were very close. Afterward, I would go with Alfred to Packrat's Shack to drink with Rorra and the others. Sometimes I saw Makrit there, but he wouldn't look at me.

The most interesting thing that happened was I finally got to fight Dorrin. I had seen him fight many times before, and thought his style was very much like Makrit's, so I assumed he would be the same sort of challenge. But I forgot that I'd never seen him fight a woman before, and I quickly found out that Dorrin was an old-fashioned guy.

The first ten units were like a bad dream. In fact, they were exactly like the bad dream I had had about Makrit and The Butcher. Dorrin kept aiming cuts at my chest, trying to cut the wraps there, and he did actually succeed in half exposing my breasts, much to the delight of the crowd. But I was very careful in those days to wrap myself securely, adding many extra layers to my vulnerable zones.

"You don't belong here," he kept saying. "I'm going to make you wish you'd never picked up a knife."

He really seemed to mean it, too. He honestly thought if he managed to humiliate me by reminding me and everyone else that I was a woman, I'd hang my head and go home. It was disappointing. For the first ten units, I fought him like I always fought Makrit, hoping he would realize he was facing a pro, and I suppose I was being just as pigheaded as he was. But in the last five units, I gave it up and really went for him.

In fact, I went for his eyes. If he hadn't been such a good fighter, I might have blinded him; as it was, I managed to nick him in his right eye, which must have stung like hell. Tears streamed down the right side of his face, and he kept trying to blink away the irritation. He was furious about it, and really wanted to hurt me then, but it was much easier to avoid him now that he couldn't see me as clearly. I just went to it and meticulously gathered my points, cool as a cucumber.

"Hold!" the announcer shouted when our time was up. "Larissa has 204 points, Dorrin has 195. Larissa is the winner."

I got my cheers, but I barely heard them. He was still crouched like he wanted to go after me, still holding his knife in the attack position, and still snarling with those big, sharp teeth.

"Dorrin," the announcer said.

Dorrin didn't move.

The announcer snapped something in Q'rin Standard, and Dorrin straightened, but didn't lower his knife. I looked him right in the eye and prepared myself, sincerely believing he would attack me. He just couldn't seem to believe I had beaten him, and a storm was raging in his eyes—even the bad one.

Two armed guards stepped between us. "Go to the showers," one of them told me, and I went. I was very nervous while I was in there, though. I kept thinking about Korry Vather and his failed ambush.

* * *

Later, when I was in Packrat's Shack with Rorra and the usual crowd, Makrit stopped by the table. "May I sit down?" he asked me.

"Sure," I said, scooting over for him. He nodded to the Aesopians, ignored Alfred, and sat next to me.

"I wanted to congratulate you on a good fight," he said.

"Thank you."

"Dorrin is one of Lord Oshrii's fighters," he said.

I hadn't known that. I took a sip of my rum and Coke, keeping my eyes on his. Now that I had run into a real Q'rin sexist, namely Dorrin, I was beginning to appreciate what a rebel Makrit was. He was staring back at me just like Hazaar had, but there was no implication of obligation on my part. I appreciated that, too.

He stayed for one drink and then excused himself. We both knew our relationship could never go farther than it already had, not if we were to continue fighting each other professionally. But I sometimes wonder what would have happened if we had become lovers. He was quite a man.

"Oshrii plans to approach you again," Rorra told me when Makrit was gone. "I'm sure of it."

"Why do you say that?"

"Dorrin is his best knife fighter."

"Well," I said, perhaps too loudly, "then I'll just have to tell Oshrii *no* again, because I'm looking forward to beating Dorrin as many times as I—"

Rorra grabbed my arm and pulled me closer. My butt slid along the bench, and I came to a halt with a resounding *slap*. Winna and Ousa leaned over the table, until the three of them were looming over me, all muscle and fur and fangs. "My *dear,*" Rorra said, "I can't believe you could be so oblivious. Don't you realize how close you're coming to starting a feud? Not only with Dorrin, who—you must know—wanted to kill you today, but with Oshrii. Don't waste your time with childish bragging."

"I wasn't bragging!" I protested.

"All right," Winna said, patting Rorra's arm,

"don't be so hard on her. She's young." But then she pointed her clawed finger right at my nose. "Dorrin is a sexist. You wounded his pride and gave him a nasty surprise. Now he wants to hurt you, understand? Maybe on the field—maybe *off*."

"I doubt he'd make a move while Oshrii is interested in her, though," Ousa said. "He wouldn't deliberately sabotage his patron."

"He wouldn't if he were *reasonable*," said Winna.

The three of them stared at me to see if the implication was sinking in. It was. I shrugged. "What am I supposed to do then? Apologize?"

"Never," said Winna. "Not even when you're joking."

"I don't think you've handled things so badly, Larissa," said Ousa. "Of course, I am a lion man, and we are known for our—ah—*pride*."

Winna snorted at that, raising a cloud of dust from the table.

"But seriously," he continued, "you have been the best fighter you can be. You have looked after your own interests, and you haven't allowed Oshrii to intimidate you into accepting his offer. You just need to understand Q'rin male pride a little better. Rorra is right, you mustn't make loud comments about how you can beat this one and that one."

I was already feeling embarrassed about that. "All right," I said. "Anything else?"

"Yes," said Winna. "Watch your back. A force gun could render you unrecognizable."

Just what I needed. More paranoia.

The Aesopians relaxed again, and Rorra kept his huge arm around my shoulders, patting me gently as if I were a child. That's what I felt like when I was near him; he and the others were so *big*. All three of them were over eight feet tall, I'm sure. And when Rorra hugged me or touched me, I never felt any kind of sexual intention from him—or any other Aesopian male, for that matter. It must have been a matter of pheromones, because (clinically speaking), if you just looked at their bodies, they were like very large, furry versions of the male Human or Q'rin body.

"Are you busy tonight, you and Alfred?" Rorra said, interrupting my perverse musings.

"I'm not," Alfred said eagerly. He had kept quiet during most of the conversation, greedily drinking in every word.

"I'd like to invite you to a private wrestling match," said Rorra.

"At the pits?" I asked. "I didn't know they had special—"

"They do," said Rorra, "but you wouldn't like them, and that's not where we're going. I can't tell you where, we'll have to blindfold you."

"Oh," I said uneasily.

"Oh, don't be so paranoid," Ousa said. He gulped the rest of his brainbuster and delicately wiped his muzzle. "We are your friends. We just have to be careful."

"Come on." Alfred poked me. "Don't blow it."

So we all got up and wandered outside to the public tran stop, where we got on the Midtown line. We sat near the front, and some of the government workers who would have been sitting next to us moved to the back. I think they had meant to do it discreetly, but when they all got up at once, it was pretty obvious. The Aesopians ignored them, perhaps because they're used to people being frightened of them. I wondered why *I* wasn't frightened of them, why Alfred wasn't. What did we know that wasn't obvious to them, too?

When we got to the center of Midtown, we got off the tran and went into an alley. Seven other Aesopians were waiting there, two wolf men, two lion men, and three bear men. I got the impression that they were expecting us, so maybe Rorra's invitation had not been as spontaneous as it looked.

Alfred and I looked tiny standing among ten Aesopians in that narrow alley, literally caged in by muscle and fur and fangs.

"Still willing?" Rorra asked me. I started to turn

and look at him, and stumbled. A lion man reached out a hand to steady me. I glanced up into his calm, dangerous eyes, and I still wasn't afraid.

"Yes," I said. For better or worse, I trusted him completely, and if my instincts were so wrong, I was better off dead anyway.

They blindfolded us. I could only see thin slivers of light coming through the bottom. I admit, I tried to see as much from these narrow openings as I could. I heard footsteps going away from us.

"Hey," I said.

"Alfred is going separately," said Winna. "We'll take a different route. Come on." She took my arm and gently began to lead me into the unknown.

We walked for a long time, got on another tran (which may have been a private one), and then walked some more. I would have gotten pretty claustrophobic walking blindfolded for so long if anyone but Winna had been leading me around. She talked to me in quiet tones from time to time, easing my isolation. I admit, I felt a little bored, though. I was happy when I heard distant voices.

"Sounds like a crowd," I said.

"We're almost there," Winna told me. "Be patient."

Several minutes later I could tell I was right in the middle of them, and my heart was fluttering excitedly. My blindfold was removed, and I was staring straight up into the face of a wolf man. He was blind, his eyes completely gone, and he was holding a huge staff which was carved all over with totems and hieroglyphics and topped with an iron cobra's head. After being blindfolded so long, my eyes filled up at the sight of him and overflowed.

"Larissa, this is Sasha," said Winna.

"I'm pleased to meet you," I said, happy with myself for not stuttering.

"The pleasure is mine," said Sasha. He turned slowly and walked into the crowd. The cobra's eyes on the top of his staff were glowing, as if they could see for him.

"Let's see who we can find," said Winna. She nudged me, then peered into my face. "Are you crying?"

"No," I said, wiping my face. "My eyes just need to get used to the light. I blinked as I took a good look around me, as dazzled by the sights and colors as I had been that first day at the pits.

We were standing in a clearing of sorts, among some ruins that could have been in the Outskirts or in the deepest heart of Deadtown. The stones and metal looked shattered, just like the old mines on Hook. About two hundred Aesopians were gathered there, many of them carrying staffs. I fell into an awed silence, feeling the pressure of their collected presence.

"There's Alfred," Winna said. Alfred waved to us from a group of Aesopians near a low wall. I was startled to see two Q'rin warriors with them.

"Let's go over," Winna said, taking my hand. I stumbled along after her, while everyone stared at me hard enough to make me feel like it was my bones and guts that were being looked at.

"Where are Rorra and Ousa?" I asked. "Didn't they come with us?"

"They're here," said Winna. "You'll see them soon."

Alfred nodded to us when we came up. One of the lion men had his arm draped lightly over Alfred's shoulder, and Winna kept hold of my hand. I think that was to tell everyone who was staring, *They're with us*.

"This is Sakros," Alfred said, indicating the lion man.

"You're Larissa," Sakros said before I could say my how-do-you-dos. "I've seen you fight."

I noticed the Q'rin men moving discreetly closer, and I tried not to look at them. "Do you fight at the pits?" I asked Sakros.

"No!" He shook his mane and laughed, extravagantly. "I lose my temper too easily. But I love to watch. You're a good fighter."

"Thank you."

"Why don't we sit here," Winna said when the silence had stretched too long. She nudged me toward the wall and the two of us sat. The men remained standing, all looking very proud and warrior-like.

"Male pride," Winna whispered to me. "Personally, I like to rest my feet from time to time."

"Me, too," I said, feeling much more relaxed. Standing at attention for so long had made me feel like I was about to fight, and that didn't seem like an appropriate reaction.

"I'm glad you invited Alfred, too," I whispered to Winna. Alfred had such a solemn look on his face, he looked ten years older.

Winna squeezed my hand. "Hear that?" she asked me.

I listened, and could only hear the sound of voices. But after a while, I felt a pulse in my breastbone, then became conscious of a low drum. But was it a drum at all, or the beating of all those huge hearts?

"Why all this secrecy?" I whispered to Winna. "I feel like a—I don't know—conspirator or something."

"You should," she said. "It's a crime for so many Aesopians to gather together in Q'rin territory."

"I didn't know that." And now was a fine time to be telling me. It was beginning to occur to me to wonder just what they wanted from me. But all I asked was "Why is it a crime?"

"Child, haven't you heard of the Ragnir war? You Humans were on the losing side with us, remember?"

"Yeah, but *we* can congregate as much as we want. Why can't you?"

"Because we went on fighting after you surrendered."

Heat built up in my face until I almost felt like fanning myself. But I was too proud to give in to that urge. "What's the penalty if you're caught?" I asked.

"Slow dismemberment."

Well, that was just wonderful. This was what I got for trusting my almost nonexistent instincts. Now I had committed a capital crime.

"Oh, well," I said.

"Are you sorry for taking the risk?" Winna asked me.

I didn't know how to answer that.

"I'm sorry," she sighed. "We thought you knew the law, Larissa. I promise you, if we are attacked, I will make it my personal duty to get you away safely."

I was really confused now, so I just said, "Thank you," and pretended to be interested in the crowd.

Those two Q'rin men were watching us, and they may have overheard some of our conversation. I wondered about them, and about the three-dozen or so other Q'rin I saw wandering around. If my punishment would be slow dismemberment, how would their own people punish them? With something worse? I finally decided it was just more weird Z'taruhn politics, and left it at that.

The drumming was audible to me now, though I still couldn't tell where it was coming from. The voices died down to a low rumble, and shortly thereafter an elephant man stepped into the clearing. He was Shade's partner, Knossos. He wore ragged fatigues, which were even plainer than what some of the other Aesopians were wearing; but it was obvious he was someone of importance, from the way he carried himself and from the way the voices instantly quieted when he came into sight.

When Knossos spoke, his voice was deep enough to drown out the drum, but I couldn't understand what he was saying. He was speaking the Aesopian language, but not in the growly, sibilant way I was used to hearing it spoken by the bear and lion men. His dialect had a deeper, drumlike quality to it. I was able to make out two names from his speech: Azren and Hassos.

At the sound of their names, two more elephant men approached through the crowd. The elephant men all stood about two feet taller than the other Aesopians. They were like walking trees. When Azren and Hassos were standing with Knossos, I could see how much older he was than them; their gray skin was smooth, while his was a map of wrinkles. But the muscles under his skin were rock hard, and of the three, he was easily the most imposing.

Azren and Hassos faced each other, and Knossos spoke again. This time, all of the Aesopians carrying staffs answered him, plus one older Q'rin warrior and a Human woman who looked like a bag lady; these two were also carrying staffs. Knossos walked from the clearing and joined the audience.

For a few long moments, there was just the sound of the heartbeat drum. The elephant men gazed into each other's eyes, and I held my breath.

Then suddenly they were shifting their weight, raising their arms, and crashing together like a couple of mountains. If we had been at the pits, people would have been cheering and yelling advice at this point, but none of that went on here. This wasn't just a simple contest of strength. It seemed more like a religious ceremony.

Azren and Hassos struggled together for several minutes, then broke free and started to throw powerhouse punches at each other, making sounds like sledgehammers pounding slabs of meat (with the bones still inside). My fists balled up in sympathy, and my body got as tight as a plucked wire. I caught a glimpse of their eyes, which were now red, and I shivered.

Azren connected a blow to the side of Hassos's jaw, which sent him reeling to one side, and he hit the ground. I felt the vibration roll under my feet.

Hassos was up in an instant and moving across the clearing toward Azren, as light as a butterfly. They clashed again and locked arms. For several moments they froze in that position, and I watched their muscles bunch and strain. They locked tusks, scoring each other's faces in the process. Their eyes were locked in the same fashion, and I prayed to God that I should never be on the receiving end of a glare like that.

Hassos's muscles bulged out like boulders, and Azren began to rise into the air. With one great surge, Hassos threw Azren across the clearing. He hit with a resounding *thud* (and another vibration rolled under my feet). Azren got up very calmly and ran back to Hassos. This time they locked arms for only a moment, and then Azren connected two good blows to Hassos's jaw. Hassos went down on one knee, raised an arm to protect himself from two more blows, and struggled to his feet again.

I expected them to grapple, but they just stood and stared at each other for a moment. Then Hassos held out his hand, and they gripped forearms. The light was already fading from their eyes.

The crowd gave one great shout (making me jump about three feet), and it was over. Hassos walked directly from the clearing, but Azren stayed put. He was staring at Knossos. I expected that Knossos would come out and declare him the winner or something, but I finally realized I was watching a challenge.

Knossos drove his staff into the hard ground and walked into the clearing. He stopped about four feet from Azren and gazed into Azren's eyes. From where I was sitting, I could see both of their faces. Azren's eyes still glowed with some red, but Knossos's eyes were a deep, calm brown.

Azren slowly lifted his right hand and made a fist. He crossed his arm and placed his fist right about where his heart would be if he were Human. He bowed to Knossos, and when he lifted his head again, his eyes were blue. I heard Winna sigh, and let out my own breath.

A moment later, people were moving and talking again. Knossos put his arm around Azren's shoulders, and they walked from the clearing. Knossos was talking to Azren, and Azren was nodding. I wished I knew what they were saying.

I felt Winna's eyes on me, and turned to look at her.

"I thought you should see this just once in your life," she said.

"Thank you," I answered. But I wondered why she cared.

Chapter 13

Oshrii approached me again, just as Rorra had predicted. He did it about a week after I had seen the elephant men wrestle, but he didn't come personally. He sent his second, Hazaar.

I was sitting at a table at the fast-food stalls and nibbling at a turkey-and-avocado sub, just relaxing and feeling pleased with myself. I didn't hunt the stalls anymore, like the other Deadtowners, because I didn't have to. Any Deadtowner who thought I was a coward for it could just come and tell me so to my face, but no one did. Life was looking good.

I saw Hazaar approaching with two other Q'rin warriors, but they sat at another table while he continued on to mine. I had seen him around since my confrontation with Oshrii, and he quite often stared the way he was doing now, but usually he would end up turning his back and going his own way. This time was different.

He sat down across from me. I munched my sandwich in a leisurely fashion, and gave him stare for stare.

"Shouldn't you be stealing your food like a proper Deadtowner?" he asked me.

"Shouldn't you be running errands for Oshrii like a proper errand boy?"

That didn't dent his confidence a bit. He just grinned at me and leaned closer. I let myself notice the lean muscles in his arms as he rested his elbows on the table.

"Dorrin sends his regards," he said.

"Really?"

"Yes, but they're not warm regards."

I shrugged. "I won't let it ruin my day. Maybe we'll get a chance to fight again, and he can get even."

"Personally, I think you'd beat him again."

For the next five minutes or so I just worked on my sandwich, letting that sink in. I looked everywhere but at Hazaar.

"What does Oshrii think?" I asked him when I was done with my sub.

"He thinks you might be willing to consider his offer again."

"He's wrong."

"You haven't even heard it, you stubborn woman. Shut up and listen."

I did, just because I couldn't think of anything else to say.

"You would earn five thousand credits a month. You would be housed in Oshrii's private compound, provided with the best medical care, and fed extremely well. Lord Oshrii has been known to give generous gifts to his favorite fighters. I'm sure you would become one of these."

"I'd have to *live* with him?" I asked. I wasn't considering the offer seriously, but I still felt nervous at the idea.

"Not with him, in his compound. I live there, too."

"Oh." I took a long sip of decaf and let my eyes wander around. When I looked at Hazaar again, he wasn't grinning anymore.

"I like being independent," I said.

"Don't be stupid." He put one of his big, warm hands on mine. It felt good there, and I found myself wondering how long I could draw out this conversation. "You can't earn half as much as an independent," he was saying. "What are you taking in now—five percent of the pot? Not bad for a Deadtowner, but you can do better."

I leaned closer, too, until my breast was almost

touching his hand. "I don't like Oshrii's attitude," I said.

"I understand." He moved his hand slightly, brushing my nipple. "This matter needs to be settled in such a way as to save face on both sides. You deserve respect."

"Is that so?"

"Yes."

"Hmmn." I gave him a little smile that had nothing to do with our conversation.

"Let me negotiate for you. Oshrii is a powerful lord. You don't have to be satisfied with just being a fighter. There's room for advancement."

"I don't want to talk about that stuff right now," I said, feeling myself being maneuvered in the wrong direction. "Don't you ever have anything else on your mind?"

His hand started to radiate heat. Bingo.

"Stubborn woman," he said. "Maybe I should get you drunk."

"Maybe you should."

He was giving me that really intense male-on-the-prowl stare. It was great. "If that's what you want," he said, "that's what you'll get."

He stood up and made a sharp gesture to his men. They got up and went away. He turned to me and held out his hand. I took it and pretended I really needed help getting to my feet. On the way up I checked out his long, hard body and wondered what kind of surprise he had for me between his legs.

"Do you mind riding on the tran?" he asked.

"No."

"I know some nice places in the Spacer Sector."

That raised my eyebrows. He was telling me that he was one of those Q'rin who didn't mind mixing with other races, even when he didn't have to.

"Sounds great," I said, taking his arm, and we strolled away from the stalls.

Hazaar matched his movements to mine so smoothly as we walked together, we were like one machine.

Later we moved together in another way, but for the time being, it was fun to play the game. Buster hadn't been in my bed for days, and I was hungry.

We went to Medusa's, a place I hadn't been since Rodney the rat's short-lived fighting days. We sat near a wall so he would have something solid to put his back to, because his men weren't there to look after it. I sat a foot or so farther away from him than I really wanted to, just to make a point.

A waiter hustled over to us before we had been sitting there for more than half a second. "Whiskey for me and a rum and Coke for the lady," Hazaar said. The guy practically ran to obey.

Hazaar had his eagle eyes turned away from me while he looked at the crowd, a mixture of dogs, government workers, offworlders, Skids, even Deadtowners. Medusa's is considered neutral ground, inasmuch as any ground on Z'taruh could be called neutral.

"See any friends in here?" I asked him. "Or enemies? It's hard to picture you with friends."

"I thought you were my friend." He gave me a sideways look.

The waiter plunked our drinks down on the table. Hazaar tossed him the credits without even looking at him, and shoved my drink toward me. He drained half of his without even blinking. I sipped mine.

"How do you expect to get drunk that way?" he laughed.

"Don't worry about it."

He grabbed the back of my chair and pulled me right up next to him. "Try some of this," he said, putting his arm around me and holding his brainbuster up to my mouth. For one horrible moment, I thought he was going to force it on me, but he just waited for me to accept his offer. He wasn't smiling, and I realized that if I didn't take it, I might hurt his pride.

"Just a sip," I said. "I'm not used to it."

He gave me a sip and watched while I got it down. "That's not so bad, is it?" he asked.

"Not if you just take a little."

"Have some more."

So I took another sip. And another and another. He administered the drink like a doctor coaxing a reluctant child.

"Do you feel it now?" he asked.

I almost said no, but then the room took a slight lurch to the left. He grinned at me, and I watched his tongue slide over the edges of his teeth. "One more sip," he said.

"No. I can't."

"All right." He put the drink down and stroked my cheek. "You look so sleepy."

"I'm not."

"Good," he said, and he kissed me right in front of all those people. He was a lot gentler than I had expected him to be. Heat poured from his mouth and into my body, pooling in all the right places.

From that point on, all I saw or heard was him. He drank another brainbuster, giving me a few sips when I felt I could handle it again. My rum and Coke was completely forgotten. I leaned into him, giggled, licked his ear, and said, "How can you drink those things without falling over?"

"I'm sober," he said. "My system is stronger than yours."

He was acting really arrogant and horny, so I could tell I was tickling his pride properly. I wanted to tell him to hurry up and take me to a hotel, but I still had enough judgment left to wait and see what he would do. After he finished his second drink, he got up and pulled me to my feet.

"Let's get out of here," he said.

I took his arm and did my best not to fall over. The room kept taking little jerks to the left (I guess I'm inclined to that direction), but I managed to look steady, even if I couldn't walk that way.

"I'm getting sleepy," I told him.

"Do you want to lie down?" he asked.

"Yeah, but I'm not really sleepy."

I got another kiss for saying that, out in the street where it's not at all neutral. I loved it, but I was glad he was wearing his force gun.

We walked to a hotel that had a mostly Q'rin- and Lyrri-dog clientele, a one-hour kind of place, if you catch my meaning. The building obviously wasn't constructed by Q'rin architects, but it had a sort of fortified look to it. When we went into the lobby, everything was kind of dark and secretive. Hazaar tucked me into a corner and said, "Wait here. Don't talk to anyone. Call me if you're approached, don't worry about looking chicken."

I just nodded. Normally, I would have made some joke about his warning (or taken heed of it), but I was really beginning to feel the brainbuster by then, and I felt like I was trapped inside a Surrealist painting, all exaggerated lights and darks. I lost all track of time, and once he had disappeared to arrange for the room rental, I couldn't decide if he had been gone for five minutes or an hour. I forgot his advice, and wandered farther into the lobby.

I was very surprised when I noticed there were other people in there, and that they were watching me. I wandered closer, to see them better. I made out some Lyrri- and Q'rin-dogs standing in a group. To my altered consciousness, they seemed fascinating and very remote. But, of course, they weren't remote at all, and when I got too close, one of the Q'rin-dogs came after me.

He seized me by the wrists and said, "Whose pet are you?"

With my wrists immobilized and my legs so wobbly, I was helpless. I wasn't used to feeling that way, and I didn't know what to do.

"What a beautiful thing she is," one of the Lyrri-dogs said in Human Standard, obviously for my benefit. "What does she taste like, Orrit?"

"I'll find out," said Orrit, pulling me closer, and at that moment I remembered Hazaar's directions.

"Hazaar!" I screamed.

I heard the sound of running, and Orrit looked over my shoulder, a snarl on his face. Then I was pulled away from him. Orrit went immediately into a defensive stance, but before he could get his arms up, Hazaar punched him in the jaw harder than I've ever seen anyone punched in my life. The sound was just like the exaggerated sound effects you hear in vids. No kidding. Orrit was out cold.

Hazaar cast one threatening glance at Orrit's friends, but no one took him up on the challenge. He turned his back on them and offered me his arm. I took it, and we went in search of the elevator.

I got another kiss in the elevator, so I'm not sure what floor we ended up on. I let him lead me to our room. Once inside, I sat down on the bed and started to unwrap myself. He watched, fascinated.

"I've never had a Human woman before," he said.

"Really?" I said neutrally.

"To be honest, I'm not even sure it's possible. I'm not sure our—parts—are compatible."

"From what I've heard," I said as I unwrapped my hips, "they are. You've talked to other men, right?"

"Men exaggerate to make themselves look good," he said.

"Well, let me see yours, and I'll tell you if I can—um—handle it."

He took off his clothes, and I got a sample of the thrills men feel when they watch women do that. His penis was erect before he even got his pants off. He walked over to the bed and stood before me. "Well?" he demanded.

I touched it gently. "Hmmn. It's larger than I'm used to (no lie!), and it's shaped a little differently. Almost like a barb on top."

His breathing got heavier as I stroked him, pretending I'd never seen a Q'rin penis before. "I haven't seen what you've got," he panted.

I giggled. "It's in an awkward place," I said.

"Perhaps we can find a position that will give us both a good view," he said.

From there, things just got better and better.

Hazaar and I spent the entire night together in that hotel, and breakfasted together in the morning. I fully expected him to bring up business again, but all he said was "Order whatever you want. The pancakes are especially good here."

So we both ate like horses, made love again, and walked to the tran together when it was almost noon. We parted there, and he gave me another public kiss. "Don't feel you have to talk about business to call on me," I told him.

"I won't," he said. I watched him walk away and wondered if I was ever going to see him again. I hoped I was, because I was hooked.

I would have liked to enjoy myself with memories of the evening before while I rode back to Deadtown on the tran, but the closer I got to home, the more disturbed I felt. I found myself thinking about Buster, and actually feeling guilty. This was ridiculous. He had made me no promises, and he wasn't even around most of the time. I wondered if I should stop making love to him, since I was involved with Hazaar now—but was I really involved with Hazaar? The whole thing was terribly annoying.

By the time the tran let me off in Deadtown, I was in a really rotten mood. I wasn't scheduled to fight again until the next day, and I didn't know what to do with myself. I needed something to occupy my mind so that it would stop bouncing back and forth between Buster and Hazaar.

I stomped up the stair of my building with vague plans to work out all afternoon. Buster and Alfred met me halfway up. "Hey, cool," Buster said. "We were hoping you'd show up. Want to go to a party?"

"A party?"

"Yeah, at Blackie's house. You ever met her?"

"No."

"Have you got other plans?" Buster asked, smiling

his mannequin smile. I felt a pang from the center of my chest all the way up to my throat.

"No. I'd like to come."

"Well, good." Buster took my arm. I noticed a new series of bruises on his throat. They trailed down under his rag-wraps, mingling with some scabbed-over scratches at the edges. "Let's escort this lady to the soiree," he said.

Alfred took my other arm, and we stomped down the street together. They were both grinning, but I was beginning to feel vaguely worried.

Art slut, is what I said to myself the first moment I laid eyes on Blackie. I didn't know where I had heard that term before—certainly not on Hook, where there isn't any art—but it fit her perfectly. She came traipsing into her Deadtown condo with her pale olive skin just like Solange's and her hair seven shades darker, her eyes crazed with stims and her red mouth looking ready to eat anything that came too close. "Buster!" she squealed. "*Al*-fred! You sexy monsters! Where have you been? Why have you, like, been ignoring the vibes I've been sending you?"

"Huh?" said Alfred. "Blackie, this is—"

"*No.*" I jabbed him in the ribs before he could say my name. Blackie was already sailing across the room to another group of Deadtowners. I didn't exist for her, and I wanted it to stay that way. A witch should never know your name.

Now I must confess, what had just happened between Blackie and me is what you might call a *female thing*. Sometimes we take an instant disliking to each other. I suppose it's all based on subliminal signals and value judgments concerning figure, dress, makeup, the manner in which we speak, and God knows what else. Once this dislike is established, it's very rarely changed. What I usually do in this situation is ignore the other woman, but in this case it was impossible. Blackie was everywhere, touching, screeching, inciting all those drunk, mean Deadtowners into a higher pitch of chaos. She was the center of a tornado.

I felt an odd touch of nostalgia in the midst of that craziness, something that was reminding me of Hook. I finally decided it was the angry body odor that hung in the room almost as palpably as steam. It was like being crowded into an overheated classroom with a bunch of miner and military brats. I had almost forgotten it.

Alfred, Buster, and I formed a wedge and made our way to the booze. There was plenty of it, so we didn't have to fight to get some. Alfred hooked a bottle of whiskey, and we planted ourselves near a door in case things got too hot. A moment later, two Deadtowners got into a fight-to-the-death knife fight and started flailing around. Alfred and I kicked them away with our long legs whenever they lurched over in our direction, while Buster watched nonchalantly and drank the whiskey. Finally one of them stabbed the other in the neck, and it was over. They threw the guy's body out the window. I don't know if he was dead or not.

"Fun party," I commented to Buster.

"Yeah," he said. "Gets your mind off things."

While I wondered about that, a tall, redheaded Deadtowner wandered over. "You guys're hogging the whiskey," he said.

"Hey, Jake," Alfred said.

Jake nodded to him and looked at me. His hair was the same color as Korry Vather's, but his face was completely different. It was the face of a kid who'd had to fight for everything. "Who's this?" he asked Alfred.

"Larissa," said Alfred.

Jake and I exchanged nods, and he took a pull from the whiskey bottle. Alfred took one, too, and I had a very small one. I was still a little dizzy from the day before, and I wanted to stay sober. Jake found a space against the wall next to Buster and leaned there. "That Lyrri-dog's been around here," he said to Buster.

"Yeah?"

"Uh-huh. He and Blackie hang out a lot. She likes him."

"Likes him?" Buster gave an artificial laugh. "She fucking solicits for him."

"Yeah," said Jake. "Except he's the one who pays."

"Depends on how you look at it," said Buster. His fingers drifted to the bruises on his neck.

"He's asked about you, Buster."

"We've been in touch."

Jake took another pull of the whiskey and offered it to me again. I turned it down, so he passed it to Alfred. He surveyed the room for a long moment, then said, "Yeah, he's been asking about that bitch, Shade."

"Shade's not a bitch," said Alfred.

Jake snorted. "Fuck, she doesn't even have tits, man."

"So? She's got nice eyes."

"You can't fuck eyes."

Buster laughed again, raising the hairs on the back of my neck. "Some people can," he said.

"Yeah." Jake sucked down the whiskey. "Shade is a bitch, but I wouldn't turn her over to that fucker. Blackie would, though, in a minute. She's fucking *cold*."

"Oh?" said Buster. "You still sleeping with Blackie?"

Jake shrugged. "Just because she's cold doesn't mean she don't have beautiful tits." His eyes wandered over to mine. I got the message, but ignored it.

Blackie chose that moment to walk up. She gave Jake a forlorn look, then put her arms around Buster. "Guess who's coming tonight?" she giggled.

"Me, I hope," he said.

"Chaz!"

Buster's face froze into its artificial smile. She continued to grin at him, her face inches from his. At that moment I went from disliking her to hating her.

"I think he's got a thing for you, Buster," Blackie said.

"Really?"

"Yes. He asked if you would be here tonight."

"I thought he was looking for Shade."

Her smile died. "Don't talk about her. I'm still mad at her."

"Is that why you're giving me to Chaz, then? To distract him?"

Blackie backed away from Buster. "Like, don't be such a shit head, okay? Just don't start hating me, Buster, because that hurts me more than anything."

Jake snorted, spitting whiskey everywhere. "How many times am I going to hear you say that tonight?"

Blackie gave him a stricken look, then turned on her heels and fled.

"She's full of shit," Jake said. But a moment later, he followed her.

I took Buster's hand. It felt dead in mine. "We don't have to stay, you know," I said. "We can get out of here before the monster comes."

His hand suddenly caught warmth as he squeezed mine. "Larissa," he said softly. "Do I scold you about your affairs? I thought we cared for each other more than that."

I let his hand go.

About an hour later, Chaz drifted through the door. He and Buster immediately locked eyes, but he didn't approach for a while. He just stared.

Alfred started drinking more at that point. Buster stopped altogether. Alfred hooked another bottle, and because I wasn't drinking at all, he drank a good deal of it himself. He kept looking at Buster, but he wouldn't say anything. Not until Chaz finally came up.

"Let's get out of here," Chaz said to Buster.

Buster just nodded.

"Man," Alfred made to grab Buster's arm. "Don't go—"

Buster moved to avoid Alfred's hand. Chaz put his arm around him, and the two of them strolled away like a couple of lovebirds. Alfred slumped against the wall and took another drink of whiskey. ''He can't help it,'' he told me. ''That's just the way it goes.''

A little while later, we left together. Alfred was so drunk, I had to support him. He was acting very cheerful and energetic, you know, the way drunks do when they're about to have some kind of explosion. We staggered down the alleyways together, in the general direction of home. Suddenly Alfred stopped dead in his tracks, almost pulling me off my feet.

''Why didn't we stop him?'' he said.

''We couldn't,'' I said.

''We're never going to see him again.''

''What do you mean?''

Alfred started to cry. It wasn't a drunk, blubbery sort of crying. It was harsh. Heartbroken. I put my arms around him while he shook. I'd never done that before. He slowed down, started up again, then finally wound down. He leaned against me, and his weight pushed me against the wall. I think he almost kissed me then, but he didn't quite make it.

''He's going to kill Buster,'' he whispered.

''Alfred, what could we do? Buster wants him.''

''He was helping me study for the entrance exams. We were going to join the navy together.''

''I'm sorry.''

''Me, too,'' he said. He leaned against me awhile longer, and I let him, because it was the only thing I could give him to make it even a little better.

After that he let me help him home. We didn't say anything more about Buster, but I felt a weight on my heart that seemed to get heavier with every step. I knew Alfred was right. I wasn't ever going to hear Buster's poems again.

By the time we got home, we were both crying.

I don't know if Buster was dead then, but I never saw him again. Alfred waited around for a couple of days, then he disappeared, too. I suppose he went to confront Chaz. That would mean that he died. But sometimes I like to imagine that he ran off and joined the navy like he said he wanted to.

I was left in the building with the younger ones. One or two of them were in their early teens, and they became top dogs. They treated me with respect, so I just ignored them. I didn't really feel like I was *home* anymore. Alfred and Buster had been good friends, for Deadtowners. I really missed those two thugs.

Chapter 14

For several days after the disappearance of my friends, I was kept busy at the pits. In fact, I was scheduled every day for almost two weeks. This suited me fine, because it kept me too busy to think; and since I didn't have to think, I didn't have to wonder if I shouldn't try to find them.

In my defense, it was very unlikely that I could have done anything about the situation. Rorra asked me why Alfred hadn't been around lately, and when I told him what I suspected, he patted me on the shoulder. "I'm so sorry," he said. "Your friends are gone."

So I got on with my life.

I got my chance to fight Dorrin again, about ten days into the schedule. I was glad it happened then, because I had had a chance to warm up on some excellent fighters, including Makrit. Makrit had been more aggressive with me this time around, so I felt I was ready.

When Dorrin and I stepped out onto the sand together, I expected him to glare at me or say something vicious. But he was perfectly neutral. He reminded me of Makrit when he acted that way, and I wondered if this wasn't a ploy to make me misjudge him. I meant to keep my eyes on him for the whole pregame period, but something made me look up into the stands.

Hazaar was sitting in Oshrii's box, next to Oshrii. I looked into Hazaar's eyes, then quickly looked away. I hadn't seen him since that hot night we spent together, and I didn't want to start this match feeling nervous.

"Fifteen units," the announcer called, and when

the bets were in, he left the field. Dorrin and I took a breath.

He started out slow, which put me on edge. He circled to my right, moving about half a beat behind where he usually was. When he lunged in for a single thrust at my belly, he seemed to be favoring his right leg. I hadn't seen him injured there lately—perhaps he'd been in a bar fight.

When I pressed in for a compound attack, he responded the way he normally would, cutting me as many times as I cut him, so I danced back again to consider things for a moment. He moved back, too, from his left leg to his right, and he stumbled. Instantly I was after him, but I realized I'd been tricked even as I was moving. He put his weight firmly on his right leg and decked me with a left cross, sending me tumbling.

Somehow, through all the chaos of stars and sand, I caught a glimpse of him coming after me as I fell, and I knew he was going to try to pin me the same way Makrit had once, only he wouldn't hesitate to carve my face. I struck out blindly with my knife, and—quite by accident—struck him in the throat. My knife cut deep.

He went to his knees, clutching the wound. A lot of blood was pouring out between his fingers, but it wasn't going *spurt spurt*. I wondered if that was a good sign.

The medics came and got him, taking a little longer than they should have. I didn't like Dorrin, but that made me angry. I had his blood all over my arm, and the whole time he knelt there, waiting for the medics, he seemed to be trying to say something to me. Probably, "Fuck you, bitch!" The crowd was screaming or cheering, but I don't know if they were giving us our due or just excited by the blood.

The announcer tapped me on the shoulder. I was shocked to see his scarred face so close to mine. "Didn't you hear me?" he said. "You're the winner. Now hit the showers."

By the time I had cleaned up, I felt much calmer. I headed to the wrestler's room, hoping to hook one of my Aesopian friends for a drink, which I felt I could really use at that point. When I walked in, Rorra and Ousa were practicing in their wrestler's kilts, to a large audience of idle fighters. I was about to take a seat in the corner when I noticed Sasha, the wolf man. He was sitting off to one side, listening, dark fluid running from the corners of his ruined eyes.

"Sasha," I said to him, "may I sit next to you?"

"Please do, Larissa."

So he remembered my voice, and maybe my smell, too. I sat and watched Ousa and Rorra throwing each other around for the next several minutes. Once or twice I let my eyes wander to Sasha, but even though I knew he couldn't see me, I felt funny about staring. His hands kept clenching and unclenching around his staff, which wasn't the fancy warrior's staff I had seen him carrying at the elephant match, but a plain blind man's staff. I imagined the cobra-headed staff thrust into the ground in the abandoned clearing next to all the other staffs. A warrior's graveyard.

Rorra and Ousa finished their match, and everyone went back to their own business. I sat uncomfortably with Sasha, wishing Rorra or Ousa would come over and say something. I couldn't think of anything to say myself. Finally Sasha broke the silence.

"I'm sorry I never had the chance to see you fight, Larissa. I've heard good things about you."

"Oh"—cough, cough—"really? I mean, thanks. I saw you—I mean"—Oh, hell!—"I saw your fight with Timmy."

"Ah."

Rorra disappeared through the fighter's door, and Ousa sat in the far corner with one of his books. I was stuck.

"Were you old enough to fight in the Ragnir war?" Sasha asked me.

"Oh, no. That was before I was born."

He slapped his knee. "Of course it was. I keep forgetting the difference between our life spans. I am sixty years old, just coming into my prime."

"Wow."

He nodded. "It's just that you remind me of someone I knew on Ragnir. A Human soldier-woman. That's what she called herself."

"Really?" I was starting to get interested. "She had a voice like mine?"

"Yes. And her—presence—was like yours. She was my commander."

"What was her name?"

"Captain Carol Stahmer. I served under her for two years. We saw action together on Ragnir, and after The Recall, she refused to abandon the Aesopians in her division."

"The Recall?"

"You've never heard of it?" He cocked his head, and when I didn't answer, he said, "Well, I suppose such a shameful episode has been expunged from your history books."

"I guess so." I hadn't the heart to tell him what a lazy bum I'd been in school.

"She received orders to leave us on Ragnir, so the Q'rin could 'mop us up.' But she refused. She and a few others. They shuttled as many Aesopians back to the mother ship as they could, under fire, then came back for more. She and I searched together, and we rescued many—but we had to face the Silver Bullets as well as Q'rin warriors."

"What are the Silver Bullets?"

"That's what the wolf-man hunters called themselves. The Human soldiers who hunted my kind because they thought we were werewolves."

"Werewolves?"

"Yes. Men who metamorphose into wolves. These Silver Bullets had never seen Aesopians before, and they had never fought alongside us. They were new recruits, who came in when the war was almost over. They were animals. They considered themselves brave warriors if they could kill a wolf man and wear his head as a helmet. I killed as many of the Silver Bullets as I could, before I left Ragnir. But I never wore their heads.''

I had to sit and digest that for a while. Finally I asked, ''What happened to Captain Stahmer?''

''She died trying to get the last shuttle of Aesopians back to the mother ship. I had gone on the shuttle just before hers. It was a cruel fate.''

''I'm sorry,'' I said.

Rorra came back in then and saw us. He came over and touched Sasha's shoulder. ''Stories of the war, my friend?'' he asked.

''Just a few.''

''Well, best she hear them from a reliable source.''

''That's what I thought,'' agreed Sasha.

Sasha came with us to Packrat's Shack, but he didn't tell me any more war stories. He just sat and listened to everyone else talk.

''I hear Dorrin will recover,'' said Rorra. ''You had a bit of luck there, Larissa, catching him under the throat that way. No insult intended.''

I shrugged. ''You're right. It was luck. Now I expect he hates me more than ever.''

Rorra didn't answer. He was looking over my shoulder. The others were looking, too, and Sasha had his head cocked. I turned and saw Oshrii standing there. Hazaar was with him.

''I'd like to speak with you,'' Oshrii told me.

I looked at Rorra, who nodded. I got up and went with Oshrii and Hazaar to another table. The three of us sat in silence for a moment, until I said, ''This better not be a replay of last time, because I just haven't got the patience.''

''Last time?'' said Oshrii. ''You mean your last time with me, or your last time with Hazaar?''

I glanced at Hazaar, who actually dropped his gaze.

''You're losing me,'' I said to Oshrii.

He laughed. ''Don't start fighting with me so soon.

I just want to talk. The last time I hurt your pride, and I'm sorry for it."

"All right," I said.

"Good. I know your defeat of Dorrin today was more luck than skill, but luck is a virtue, too. I'm prepared to make you another offer."

He nodded to Hazaar, who produced a folder. Oshrii took it from him, regarded me for a moment, and then handed it to me.

"What's this?" I said.

"A contract."

I looked inside. It was all written in Q'rin Standard. "Oh, great," I said.

"The duplicate is in Earth Standard. Besides, your Aesopian friends read Q'rin, don't they? And I know you're going to show it to them."

"I may show it to them, but that doesn't mean I'll sign it."

He shrugged. "Let me buy you a drink."

When I didn't say anything, he called the server over. I gave Hazaar another look, and this time he returned it steadily. "Brainbuster?" he said softly, and smiled.

"No way," I whispered back.

Oshrii ordered me a rum and Coke, and the usual for them. He kept looking at me with this almost-amused expression on his face, as if he thought I couldn't possibly turn him down. I wondered how much Hazaar had told him about our night together.

"You're a good fighter, Larissa; on and off the field. I think you could go far with me." Oshrii glanced over at the Aesopian table, and nodded toward Sasha. "The blind one used to be a good fighter. But he was an independent. If he had had a sponsor, he could have had his eyes fixed."

"You mean by the Lyrri surgeon? He would never have allowed it."

"But he was wrong, that's my point. Better to have eyes and make one small concession. A blind man is useless."

"You're losing me again."

He grinned at me. "I know. The Aesopians are a noble race, it's hard to think ill of them. I don't blame you for that. As long as you don't spend *too* much time with them."

I might have thought of something to say back, but at that point I felt Hazaar's hand on my knee, burning a trail. So I just took a deep breath and gulped my drink.

"Have your—lawyer—go over the contract," said Oshrii, "and tell me what you think. Here's my personal card." He handed me a three-sided disk. "It will let you into my compound. Feel free to visit, for business or pleasure. I'm sure Hazaar will welcome you anytime."

They got to their feet, and turned to leave. Hazaar threw a look at me over his shoulder and licked some brainbuster from the corner of his mouth. At least, that's what I think he was doing.

I took the folder back to Rorra, half expecting him to be mad at me for talking with Oshrii. But he just said, "Is that your contract? Good. Let's have a look at it."

Rorra set up an appointment for me with his expert, someone who was presumably the best on Z'taruh. "In the meantime," he told me, "I think it's time you started to learn Q'rin Standard."

"What?" My heart sank. "I'm no good at languages. Besides, I don't even think I want to sign the damned contract."

"All the more reason to learn the language. If you're going to depend on the pits for your livelihood, you'd better learn the language of the people who own the place."

"But I'm a dummy about language!"

He waved away my objections. "Don't be silly. Just get yourself some sleep-tapes. How do you think I've learned my languages?" He tapped me in the chest with one clawed finger. "I'm just as lazy and stubborn as you are."

So he took me to a language shop, and I bought six weeks worth of tapes, including a few on slang. "Those may be the most important of all!" Rorra said.

Every day for the next six weeks, whether I had a fight scheduled or not, I slept with those tapes hooked up to my ears. In the morning, I would wake up speaking that night's language lesson. I listened to all the basic grammar tapes first. Q'rin Standard grammar is a lot like Japanese Colonial grammar (I've slept with a lot of language courses since then), much more logically structured than Earth Standard, which is based on English.

Two weeks after I received Oshrii's contract, I had my meeting with the expert, at our favorite table in Packrat's Shack. I was astonished to find out that the expert was Knossos, the elephant man. He was sitting alone when I came in, his huge body dwarfing the table. He had my contract in his big hands, and seemed absorbed in it. He only looked at me when I had been sitting at the table for about fifteen minutes.

"Ah," he said, with a voice like the bass section of an orchestra. "You're Larissa. I am Knossos, resident expert in contracts. I've examined this contract thoroughly, and I've made quite a few changes. I'd like to go over them with you, step-by-step."

"All right," I said, eyeing his tusks. "I'm ready."

"Well. First, this is a five-year contract, which simply won't do. I've changed the term to one year. He should renegotiate with you every year, or he'll own you. Understand?"

"Absolutely."

"Next, the payment. Five thousand credits per month isn't bad, but he could earn that much on you in a week. So I've upped it to seventy-five hundred."

"Sounds great. Think he'll go for it?"

"Yes. Now, for the insurance. He wants to cut out seventeen percent of your income to pay for your medical and dental expenses. I've cut it to thirteen."

"Ah."

"And here's an interesting little section. It concerns the Triad."

"Uh-oh." I hadn't thought about the Triad until that moment, not in connection with me, anyway. The Triad fights are only fought once a year or so, and they're always fought to the death. That's not my cup of tea. Knossos's brown eyes studied me from deep folds of gray flesh, and I thought he nodded.

"Yes," he said. "I thought that would interest you. The way this is written, Oshrii can enter you in the Triad without your consent. You would literally be bound by law to fight. I've changed it so that he required both your written consent and your *oral* consent to the contest officials before he can enter you. This ought to apply to special fights, too, but I must warn you. Some lords are not above arranging *special* special fights, and what goes on in the lower pit is not always remembered. You'll have to decide whether Oshrii is a man you can trust."

I'd never heard of the *lower* pit before. I assumed it was at the other end of one of those mysterious side tunnels in the maze.

Knossos went on to talk about a lot of other details, mostly minor, and most of which I didn't hear because I was busy thinking about his warning. Finally, he said, "That winds it up. Before you sign this, make sure he initials every major change. Then bring it back to me, and I will witness your signature, then sign it myself. Any questions?"

"Yes," I said. "Do you think I ought to accept Oshrii as my patron?"

He stared at me for a long moment, his giant hands folded on the table in front of him. "How much are you earning per month?" he asked me.

"Right now, between three and five thousand."

"Are you simply trying to gain passage off this planet, or is fighting your career?"

"I consider it a career," I decided.

Those old, sharp eyes examined me, and I thought

I caught a glimpse of red in them. "Are you afraid?" he asked.

"Sometimes. Is that what you mean? I like being able to do what I want, but I don't want to get a little older and find out that I've lost my edge. Maybe I should build a little security for myself."

"Well," he sighed, "if that's what you're planning, by the gods, don't put your money in a Z'taruhn bank. I can understand your need. A one-year contract shouldn't bind your freedom too much. But I would plan an escape route, in case of emergencies, if I were you."

I nodded, and he stared at me some more, so forcefully I almost squirmed. "Have you considered joining the military?" he asked.

"Not really. I grew up a military brat, but I'm really an athlete."

"Ah. Well, perhaps one day you'll change your mind. I must go now." He stood. Even sitting, he had towered above me, but now I had to crane my neck to look him in the eye. "Rorra will arrange another meeting if you'd like to go through with the signing. I wish you luck, but you are a talented young woman, and I think you'll do well, whatever you decide."

"Thank you," I said. "Thanks very much. How much do I owe you?"

"If you sign, fifteen percent of your first paycheck. If you don't sign, simply give Rorra five hundred credits. He'll pass the payment on to me."

"Great," I said. "Glad to have met you."

"I, too." He gave me a slight bow, and turned away.

Once he was gone, I wondered if I had acted as clumsily and gracelessly as I thought I had. He had treated me like an equal, but I felt outclassed. Rorra came up and patted me on the shoulder. "How'd it go?" he asked.

"Fine," I said. "I think."

I had a surprise visitor a few days later, right after a match with Oscar X. Oscar had cut me pretty nastily on the cheek, a mark I wasn't about to put up with, and I had gone to the Lyrri surgeon to get it fixed. I was sitting there, trying not to wince, wondering for the hundredth time if the doctor was hurting me delib-eratley, when Chaz the Lyrri walked in.

"Don't move," the Lyrri doctor warned me. "Now I'll have to fix this spot again."

"I can't have visitors now," I told Chaz, then winced at my own foolishness. He could have been there to talk to the doctor.

"I have special privileges," said Chaz, smiling gently. "And I use them. I thought it was such a shame when that nasty man cut your beautiful face, I just had to make sure the doctor was setting it to rights."

"She won't let me give her any ritual scars," chided the doctor.

"This isn't funny," I said. They didn't react at all to that.

"I've decided to bet on you from now on," Chaz told me. "You always seem to win."

"Not always."

"Almost always. I suppose they'll be giving you point handicaps soon."

I mumbled something noncommittal.

"I was wondering, do you have a patron?" He came closer and laid a hand on my knee. My muscles jumped under his hand.

"I'm negotiating with one."

"Of course you are. Someone with your talents must be in great demand. But I'm going to give you my card, anyway. Perhaps you'll come over for a drink."

His face was so beautiful, so earnest, it really gave me the creeps. I found a secret corner of my mind wishing that he could be as wonderful as he looked—or even half as wonderful. I also felt a strong urge to ask him about Buster. But he and the doctor had me outnumbered.

"I don't think so," I said when he tried to hand me his card.

His smile faded. "My dear," he said, "you're going to hurt my feelings. At least take the card." He pried my hand open and placed it in my palm. "You don't have to do anything with it."

He closed my fingers over the card and patted them. I decided I'd better humor him.

"Now I'll let you get back to your doctoring," he said, walking backward toward the door. "Do call me sometime." He turned as gracefully as a dancer and made his exit. I looked at his card, wanting very badly to throw it on the floor. But the doctor was watching me. He shook a finger at me, smiling playfully.

"He's after you!" he said. "You've got an admirer. I envy you. Chaz is such a beautiful man."

"You know him?" I asked.

"He's my cousin."

Wonderful. And now it was my turn to be the object of his titillation. Did that mean Shade was dead, or was he just passing the time until he could get his hooks in her? Or maybe he was always chasing people, like a serial killer, always looking for opportunities.

I got away from the doctor as quickly as I could and headed for Packrat's Plot, hoping to talk to Rorra about it. I thought he might be able to clue me in as to where I might get a force gun. It was a big favor to ask, but there was no way I would be able to defend myself against Chaz with a knife. I wasn't even sure that marble skin could be cut.

But on the way over, I literally ran into Hazaar. I stumbled off balance, and he steadied me. "Into the brainbuster already?" he asked. I was happy to see he was alone.

"No," I said. "I was just preoccupied."

"I hope you were thinking about the contract," he said. I was steady on my feet now, but he didn't remove his hands.

"In a way," I said.

"You've been taking a long time to think it over. Are there some details you want to discuss with me?"

With him standing so close, I realized I wanted to do a lot more than "discuss" things with him. I put my hands on his shoulders. "No," I said. "I've decided to sign the contract."

He didn't say anything or move a muscle in his face, but his hands tightened around my waist.

"Before I do, though," I said, "Oshrii has to initial some changes. I won't sign unless *all* the changes are initialed."

"Where is the contract?" he asked.

"At my place."

"Let's go get it. I'll have a look."

By that evening, all of the changes were initialed except for a few of the minor ones. I found Rorra, and asked him to arrange another meeting with Knossos.

A week later, I met Knossos at the Salvation Army dining room, which is Skid heaven. I had a hard time picturing him in the company of so many run-down bums, until I noticed that a lot of those "bums" had on ragged uniforms. More Ragnir vets. Knossos was sitting at a table on the far side of the room, near the exit. When I went over to his table, the lion man and wolf man who had been sitting with him nodded to me and left.

"Don't let me interrupt your lunch," I said to Knossos, who was working on a bowl of vegetable soup.

"Don't concern yourself about it," he said graciously. "I'll look at it while I eat. I promise not to get soup on it."

So I watched him as he perused my contract and spooned soup behind that trunk of his without spilling a drop. I couldn't help but stare, and when he raised his eyes to me again, I almost jumped.

"I'm surprised he approved so many of the changes," he said. "I thought he might object to more of the minor changes, if only for the sake of pride."

"Me, too," I said. "But he was actually rather cordial."

"Well, he knows he's getting a prize. You should

remember that, too, young woman. The Q'rin are sometimes too selfish with their praise."

"I will," I promised. "I grew up on a Q'rin-dominated planet, so I'm used to them."

"That's an advantage," he said. "Now, before I sign, I should warn you of a new development. I have a debt that I have been paying off for the last several years; and I am within a few months of eliminating it. Like most creditors, mine are not happy with that prospect. Since they are Q'rin, and this is a Q'rin-dominated planet, the political climate is becoming rather hot for me. My signature on your contract could conceivably cause problems for you in the future."

He took one last spoonful of his soup and pushed it aside. "To cut to the chase—would you rather have someone else be the cosign for you? I can even arrange a meeting with a reputable Q'rin lawyer."

"No," I said, without thinking about it very much. I admit I was a little overwhelmed by the elephant man, and probably should have listened to his advice. But to tell him I wanted someone else to sign with me was like saying I had no respect for him. I couldn't have done it without hanging my head.

He nodded, and produced a pen from his worn breast pocket. I wondered how those big hands would be able to manipulate something so slender, but his signature was crisp and beautifully written. Next to it, mine looked a little sloppy.

"Thank you," I said.

"You're welcome." His brown eyes were warm. "Good luck, Larissa."

I ran home and took 1125 credits out of my strongbox. I didn't want to wait to pay Knossos until my first check came. If he really had a debt to pay, I wanted to make sure *my* debt was paid, too.

Chapter 15

The day after I signed the contract, I moved into the Q'rin complex.

I was able to fit everything that was important to me into a small suitcase (which was mostly taken up by my strongbox and stasis pad). The rest I left for the kids in my building, who accepted it gleefully and without thanks, which was only proper. I hopped on the Midtown tran line, which I rode to the pits; and from there I got on the Scorpion line, which let me off right in the steel heart of the Q'rin Sector, outside the front gate of the fortress.

I was taking a risk by wearing my Deadtown rag-wraps so far into Q'rin territory. I would have been conspicuous enough in regular clothes, Human faces were so rare there. But when I got off the tran, a lot of people seemed to recognize me from the pits. My name was spoken a few times, and I got some polite nods along with the glares.

I walked straight up to the heavily guarded front gate, feeling the eyes of the wall sentries a couple of hundred feet above me. The fortress loomed over me like some vast, metal blue monster, ready to pounce. A two-man flier buzzed over the wall and flew off in the direction of the Spacer Sector. I stopped to watch it disappear, admiring its red and black colors, then took a deep breath and marched right up to the gate sentries. They were waiting for me.

The captain looked at my card, then at me, then gave me a short nod and waved me in the direction of the gate. It was standing open for the day, and a wide road passed through it. Personal trans drove along the center of it, forcing me to the side.

Hazaar had told me to follow the main road all the way past the third gate. "From there you can ask directions to Oshrii's compound. It should be another forty-five-unit walk from there, if you move briskly."

"Can't you just send a tran for me?"

He had laughed at that. "I don't even ride in one of those, unless I have pressing business. You can walk, like all the other fighters, and most of the warriors, for that matter. It's good for your legs."

So in that respect, the Z'taruhn Q'rin were just like those of Hook. But there were some differences, which I discovered as I took the long walk to the second gate. The thick-walled buildings were clumped together to form rows, which were laid out in a maze-like pattern. On the roofs were force cannons—and some other equipment so sophisticated I didn't even know what they were. Most of the guns were aimed toward the sky, and some were aimed at the walkways, including the one I was on. All of that was the same. But between those rows of buildings were lush gardens, which seemed obscenely overgrown. Flowers of every imaginable color pulled at my eyes and clogged my nose with their perfumes. I saw Q'rin warriors stopping to sniff them, looks of blatant satisfaction on their rocky faces. It embarrassed me at first.

The second gate was set deeply into a row of buildings that formed an inner wall of sorts that ran parallel to the outer wall of the fortress. This inner wall had three other gates as well as the south gate, which was the one I took. It was less heavily guarded, and the guards there were relaxed enough to attempt to flirt with me. "Come and see me when you get tired of Oshrii," one of them told me. He was very young, about my age, so I gave him a little smile.

As I was walking away, another one said, "I'd like to have a couple of super-units alone with that one," in Q'rin Standard. I gave no indication that I had understood him. I was almost fluent by then, with only another week of language sleep-tapes to go. They were in my suitcase next to my strongbox.

As I made my way farther into the complex, flyers passed overhead at regular intervals, and I saw many personal trans on the road. This put Hazaar's assertion that Q'rin warriors all walk somewhat more in the light of a joke. I hadn't really believed him to begin with—I knew he spent most days traveling back and forth inside Capital, even if he did ride the public trans from time to time.

But I did pass many warriors on the walkways, including several lady-dogs, who checked me out even more thoroughly than the men did. The traffic got thicker as I approached the third gate, which was set in a wall of buildings that were at least a story taller than the ones surrounding the second gate. I could see the buildings of the inner fortress looming even higher, some of them higher than the fortress walls themselves. I wondered if Oshrii lived inside of one of those high buildings, which all seemed to have personal landing pads for the fliers that were coming and going. Just as I was thinking of Oshrii, I saw him. He was waiting for me outside the gate, with his personal guard. Hazaar wasn't with him.

Oshrii gave me a little smile as I walked up to him. "I'm on my way out," he said, lest I think he had come down specifically to greet *me*. His tran was standing nearby. "Keep on this road until you find the Landing Field Road. You can't miss it. Turn right up that, and take it almost to the end. From there, I'm sure you can find someone to direct you."

"All right," I said. He gave me the once-over, taking in my rag-wraps. I glanced at his men and thought they looked disapproving. But Oshrii said, "I think you should continue to wear those when you fight. It's a good gimmick."

"I hadn't thought of that," I said. "But it sounds like a good idea."

"You've been studying Q'rin Standard?" he asked me.

"Yes."

"Good," he said in Standard. "We'll speak that from now on. I hope you'll be as successful as you promise to be, Larissa."

He turned on his heels and went back to his tran, his men following at a respectful distance. I passed through the third gate, wondering if I had just been welcomed or warned. Or both.

Landing Field Road was indeed easy to find, since it was even wider than Center Road, and since there was a landing field at the end of it. Oshrii's compound was about halfway down the road. I would have missed it if I hadn't run into Hazaar along the way.

"If you really want to see the landing field before you see your apartment, I'll take you," he said. "It's just for scouts and fliers. There's a much larger field outside the fortress for bigger craft, and of course you know about the one in the Spacer Sector—"

"I have my own apartment?" I interrupted him. I had thought I would be in a barracks or something.

"Of course, what did you think? This way."

He took my suitcase and led me down a side path through another one of those extravagant gardens, toward one of the large buildings with a landing field and some large cannons on its roof. "Oshrii's place," Hazaar said. Nearby were some smaller buildings with more guns and whatnot on the roof, and across another large garden were some even smaller buildings with nothing at all on the roofs. I guessed my apartment was in there somewhere, and I was right.

Close in, I noticed that the buildings had reflective windows that were almost the same color as the walls around them. If I hadn't seen smoky images of Hazaar and myself in them, I wouldn't have noticed them as quickly. Whoever was on the other side of those windows could see us clearly, though we couldn't see them at all. I became a little paranoid about reflective surfaces after that, even the regular mirrors in my own apartment.

We crossed the garden and walked up to a door on the end of the row. Hazaar produced a triangular card and stuck it into a slot near the door. It was spat back out at us, and the door opened. Hazaar ushered me in.

When I said that the buildings across the garden were smaller, I only meant in relation to Oshrii's house. My apartment was as spacious as a high-priced apartment in the Spacer Sector. The people on the Hill weren't the only ones with money on Capital, that's for sure.

"Is it to your liking?" Hazaar asked me, courteously.

I thought he was being rather formal with me, but I just couldn't believe my eyes. We were standing in the audience room, what Humans would call a living room. It was furnished in the sparse, Q'rin style, but what was there was made of fine woods, metal, and imported Zorin leather. I wandered over to the conversation area and ran my hand over the back of a chair.

"Yes," I said finally. "It's beautiful. I didn't know you people had such a sense of—I mean, it's more beautiful than any apartment I've ever seen."

"I haven't seen the inside of many Human dwellings, so I'll have to take your word for that. Let me show you the rest."

So I wandered after him through a huge dining and kitchen area, peeked into the guest bath, almost got lost in the private bath and dressing room, and finally walked into the bedroom. Hazaar put my bag on the bed and turned his back to it, his face unreadable.

"If you want a tour of the landing field and outbuildings now, I'm free for a little longer. We could have lunch afterward."

"All right," I said, wondering what the hell was wrong with him.

Hazaar's formality lasted through the tour of the field, where he introduced me to the guards in case I ever had to travel from there in the future. We wandered down some more rows of buildings that were somehow connected to Oshrii—I wasn't sure exactly how at that point. We finally ended up in his apartment, which was in the heavily armed buildings closest to Oshrii's house.

"I have offices in the main house," he said, "but this is my place."

I nodded, feeling very shy. He seemed a little more relaxed in his own apartment. He kept staring at me and then looking aside, as if preoccupied. We sat down at his dining table and ate lunch in silence. I was thinking to myself that the Q'rin are angular people who live in angular houses, sit on hard, angular furniture, and eat off of angular dishes. I was trying not to think of anything else.

"I won't see you tonight," he told me when we were finished. "But I'd like to have supper with you tomorrow."

I was feeling a bit miffed at that point, but I said, "Okay."

He grabbed me and gave me a long kiss. Now I was really confused.

The next morning I was awakened at dawn by my personal com. Hazaar was on the other end. "Get dressed and run out to the drilling field," he told me. "You'll work out with the warriors every morning. From there, you can ask one of the other knife fighters where your drilling area is. Work out a schedule with them."

He hung up before I could ask him anything.

So I threw some regular clothes on and gave my face and teeth a quick scrub. Then I was out the door and running, trying to remember where the drilling field was. It turned out to be a little farther down Landing Field Road. I followed a bunch of warriors who were jogging in the same direction.

I did calisthenics with them for a couple of superunits. It was the toughest workout I'd ever had, but I got through it. Afterward, a young Q'rin woman walked up to me and gave me a friendly slap on the arm. The sides of her head were shaved, but her hair was long in back.

"You're the new knife fighter, right? They told me you were Human. I'm Tilli. I'll be your drill partner for today, if you want."

"Sounds great," I said, pleased that I could understand every word of her Q'rin Standard and respond in kind. "I'm Larissa."

"That almost sounds like a Q'rin name," she said, and grinned. We walked together back down Landing Field Road and headed into Oshrii's compound toward the knife fighter's court.

I think Tilli was considered a little plain by Q'rin standards, but her body was lean and graceful, and she had an easy smile. I was surprised she was so friendly. The other Q'rin women I had seen so far had been a little cold, especially the civilians.

"I've seen you fight at the pits," she told me. "I'll have to fight to keep up with you."

But she was good. I was breathing hard by the end of our drill. I worked a couple of rounds with another fighter, too, a man named Kallis, who looked me over like a sex-starved fiend when he met me, but then fought coldly and emotionlessly.

"Where's Dorrin?" I asked Tilli. I wasn't looking forward to working out with him.

"He works out in the afternoon," she said. "He doesn't like to work out with women."

I thought that was for the best.

In the evening, I had supper with Hazaar at my place. My kitchen was full of ready-made suppers, and even had a few Human items in it. I made steak and mushrooms. Mushrooms are happily abundant on Z'taruh.

He spoke very little during supper, except to say that he was very busy trying to find a contractor for some work Oshrii wanted done.

"Another landing field?" I asked him, half-expecting him to tell me to mind my own business. But he answered immediately.

"We're cramped inside this fortress," he said. "We feel we need a larger one."

"How many people live in here, anyway?"

"Roughly, about twenty thousand warriors. And about five thousand civilians. We have another thirty thousand warriors outside, in the city."

My mind boggled at the thought of a bigger fortress, but I didn't pursue the thought very long. I was wondering if Hazaar was planning to spend the night with me.

He wasn't. He got up after supper and said, "I have something important to attend to tonight. I'll call you in the morning."

"All right," I said, courteously. I decided I wasn't going to ask him about it.

But if he did it to me one more time, he was history.

I had hoped, maybe even assumed, that Hazaar and I would be lovers when I moved in. But I was beginning to suspect that he had simply been used to tempt me into signing the contract, and now that I was in, he would drop me. It was a painful thought.

But as it turned out, Hazaar had another woman before me, and she was not thrilled to see me come into the picture. Her name was Katta. I met her while I was walking through the garden, on my way to knife practice. She had two male warriors with her.

"So this is what it looks like," she said, using the Q'rin neuter quite deliberately. The warriors chuckled in that brief way they have, and the three of them stared at me.

"Who the hell are you?" I asked. *Hell* was the only Human word I used.

"I am Hazaar's lady," she replied.

I was suddenly very, very angry, and about twice as humiliated. I hardly knew what to do with the emotion—it was my first real taste of jealousy. I looked her over, just as she was doing to me, and found her very beautiful. Her body was a lot like mine, and she had a luxurious growth of black hair. It had copperish highlights, like her skin.

"So," she said, her musical voice dripping with venom, "I see he has developed a taste for *bald* women."

I liked my hair the way it was, but I felt like strangling her at that moment. The two warriors were grinning now, which pissed me off even more. But I controlled myself, keeping my Nefertiti mask firmly in place, and turned my back on them. I walked away with my shoulders square and my head high. I heard her laughter behind me, and it cut deep.

That afternoon I was a lot meaner at knife practice than usual. Tilli noticed right away. "I see you've met Katta," she said when we were done, ruefully wiping the blood from a cut on her brow.

This embarrassed me even more. Now everyone knew my business.

"Don't let the ladies make you angry," she said. "They resent female fighters because we can share something with the men they cannot." She slapped me on the back. "Eh? cheer up. You can have any man you want in this compound." She lowered her voice. "Even Oshrii. He has six children by six different women."

There was admiration in her voice when she said that. Q'rin men outnumber the women about three to one—you really have to be powerful to attract that many females. I supposed it said something about Hazaar, too. But I'm Human, and I was still angry enough with him to punch his lights out.

"Come on," Tilli said. "To the showers. Cool off, woman." She walked away without looking to see if I followed. I thought about going back to my apartment to shower, but decided I didn't feel like spending the rest of the morning alone. So I ran after her, and we walked together.

The bathhouses were for general use, so they lay between the compounds, not really in any particular lord's territory. Consequently, they were not as carefully watched. Not by cameras, anyway. Tilli and I passed the last surveillance camera on the edge of Oshrii's compound and walked in a disciplined, dignified manner until we were sure it couldn't see us anymore. Then we walked like normal people.

A two-man flier buzzed over our heads and flew out over the fortress wall. I recognized Oshrii's ID number. So either he was inside, or Hazaar was, or both of them. Thinking about Hazaar made me mad again, so I tried to think of other things. I did feel some fleeting amusement when I thought about how jealous Cliff Goldbar would have been of Oshrii's rooftop landing pad; not to mention his flier, which wasn't like the clumsy, expensive helicraft Cliff had fancied. Q'rin fliers can go from horizontal movement to vertical in half a sub-unit, dropping to the ground as lightly as birds. They have more firepower, too.

The women's bathhouse was guarded by lady-dogs (or else who would guard the guards?), who nodded to us in a friendly fashion as we walked in. The female warriors liked us because we were fighters. Once we were inside, though, I got a nasty surprise.

Katta was there with some of her lady friends. They were all naked, and they were waiting to see what I had. Tilli ignored them, scrubbing herself vigorously at the pump and soap in preparation to immersing herself in the communal bath. I stripped off my clothes and did the same. Katta could just get a good look at my beautiful self for all I cared.

"Look at that *skin*," she hissed. "It's as if she were burned all over!"

"And that face," another one added. "Half-formed."

"I don't know," said a third. "I think she's rather attractive."

They splashed water at her, and there was laughter. Tilli threw me a mischievous look. "Is that the best you can do, Katta?" Tilli said. "How pathetic. Why don't you just fight it out, like the men do when they're jealous?"

Katta's face darkened, but the third lady, the one who had come to my defense, laughed. "She's right. Imagine fighting over a man. What woman ever stays with one man all her life, anyway?"

Tilli and I got into the water and regarded the other women across the way. Katta was still looking hateful—and I was still pretty mad myself—but the others were giving me curious looks.

"My name is Alian," said the third lady. She was older than the other two, perhaps in her thirties. The second lady never told me her name, which I don't regret at all. "I've won some money on you," Alian said.

"I'm glad" was all I could come up with.

Other women had come in by then, and they all seemed fascinated with my body. Most Q'rin women were as tall as me, and from the neck down I wasn't very different from them—perhaps that's what they found so interesting—but it was true that next to theirs, my face looked almost childish. They had the same bony faces as the men. But I had grown up seeing faces like theirs, so I could see the beauty in them.

When I had soaked until my fingers were wrinkled, I got out and dressed myself, ignoring the stares. I knew I would have to get used to them. I walked back to my apartment and waited for Hazaar. I hoped he would come for supper, because I wanted to tell him something.

He showed up an hour later. I invited him in, and sat down with him in the living room. I avoided his touch. He frowned at that.

"I met Katta today," I told him.

I thought a look of pride flickered across his face. "I see," he said, waiting for me to continue.

"If you already have a lady, I won't have anything to do with you, Hazaar. I am not going to spend the next year waging war with that woman. And besides, I'm not the sort of woman who likes to share."

I had thought he would be angry with me, but he

seemed pleased. ''You want me for yourself?'' he asked.

''Yes.''

''I told Katta she was free last night. That's why she came to you today. Q'rin females are not used to being rejected.'' He smiled, relishing the memory. ''So,'' he continued, ''by Human custom, that would mean you are *mine*, alone.''

I hadn't quite thought of it that way, but it was true. ''Yes.''

''Then let's seal the bargain.'' He picked me up and carried me into the bedroom. It was nice to have a man who could do that.

We had supper two hours late.

Chapter 16

I was lucky that Q'rin days of the week also number seven, and that they have practical names like First-day, Seconday, etc. But I had forgotten that Q'rin months differ slightly from the Earth schedule Humans tend to follow, even on planets that don't have 365-day years. The Q'rin are more practical. So my nineteenth birthday almost passed without my noticing it. Fortunately, I had mentioned the date to Rorra.

So I went into Packrat's Shack, thinking my birthday was another week off, and Winna came up to me before I could get to the table.

"Say, Larissa," she said, "aren't surprise birthday parties a Human tradition?"

"Yes—"

"Well—*surprise!*" She stepped aside, and I saw a table laden with punch and birthday cake. All my Aesopian friends were there, and a lot of my pit friends stopped in to congratulate me.

"May you be at the top of your field for another fifty years at least," Winna toasted me, then guzzled her punch. Everyone applauded. It was probably the best birthday party I'd ever had.

Hazaar wasn't there. He didn't share the free time I spent with the Aesopians, and, in fact, I had received several hints from both him and Oshrii that I should give up that company. But I wasn't about to. I continued to drink with them and watch them wrestle up until almost the very end.

About two Q'rin months into my contract, Oshrii

decided to ask me about Knossos's signature on my contract.

He summoned me to his office in the big house. I'd never been there before, so I was surprised when the only one who met me at the door was a stern young clerk. He led me down an entrance hall that had a lot of suspicious reflective surfaces, and into Oshrii's office.

His office was very plain. It contained one large desk with a personal terminal on it and two chairs. Oshrii sat behind the desk, and a giant of a Q'rin-dog stood by the other chair.

"Larissa," said Oshrii, "this is Special Agent Donokh. He's here to interrogate you concerning the elephant man."

Donokh had my contract in his hand. "Sit down," he instructed.

I sat. I was comforted that at least he didn't seem to have any electrical devices with him.

"This is very incriminating evidence," Donokh said, poking the contract under my nose. "What is the extent of your relationship with the Aesopians?"

"I see the wrestlers at the pits every day," I said. "I have a drink with them a couple of times a week. Rorra the bear man made an appointment with Knossos the elephant man for me, to go over my contract. I think Knossos did a great job. I've only seen him twice in my life, both times for business. That's about it."

"Would you say your feelings toward the Aesopians are friendly?" Donokh's tone was almost casual. He was standing at ease, but I'd seen that stance at the pits, and I wasn't fooled by it.

"The wrestlers are my friends, yes. We work at the same joint, and they have a sense of humor. They're good fighters." I shut up, hearing myself talk too much. Oshrii was smiling gently, but I wasn't fooled by that, either.

"Will you see Knossos again soon?"

"No. If Oshrii wants to negotiate another contract

with me next year, I'll try to locate Knossos. If I can't, I'll find someone else."

I had thought I was doing pretty well at that point, but Donokh was very annoyed with that answer. His mouth tightened to a thin line and his breathing became harsher. I thought he would slap me, but instead he seized my chin and said, "We have laws, here. We don't like to see them broken. Just so you know, if you're caught at an Aesopian assembly, your automatic punishment will be slow dismemberment. We usually start with the fingers and toes, then go on from there. No one is exempt."

"That's my property you're handling there," Oshrii said.

I finally lost my temper. "That's *my* property he's handling!" I snapped, and knocked Donokh's hand away.

They both stared at me a moment, then suddenly laughed. Donokh took a step back. "Just so you know the rules," he said.

"I do."

"Of course you do," Oshrii said. "You're stubborn, but you're not stupid. There won't be any more interrogations of this sort—from Special Agent Donokh."

Donokh turned to look at Oshrii, a little more slowly and deliberately than was natural. "I have the emperor's authority in these matters," he said.

"I concede that. But the emperor was schooled in an Aesopian university. So were you, Donokh—if my sources are accurate."

"Meaning?" Donokh didn't put his hand on the big force gun that was strapped to his hip, but his hands hung loosely at his sides, close enough to draw quickly. Oshrii leaned back in his chair and rested his hands on its arms.

"Meaning exactly that," said Oshrii. "Nothing more."

Up until that point I had thought it was them against me. Now I wasn't sure what was going on.

"Are you finished with her?" asked Oshrii.

"Yes." Donokh took his eyes off Oshrii long enough to nod to me, then stalked from the room. But I didn't let my breath out just yet. Oshrii was giving me such a hard look, his eyes were twitching.

"That should not have happened," he said.

"I don't understand."

He got up and walked around his desk, until he was standing over me like Donokh had. "I want you to stop seeing the Aesopians."

I'll admit he had me scared. But I said, "No."

More eyeball twitching. "You take a lot of chances," he said.

"I won't get involved in politics—"

"You are involved in politics!" he shouted.

"Not the kind you're thinking of. I haven't broken any laws, Oshrii." That lie went past my lips, smoothly. "I don't intend to. I have some drinking buddies. That's all."

He turned his back on me. "Get out of my office," he said. "I don't think I'd better see you for a while."

I went. But I knew I had won a victory of sorts. No one was going to tell me who I could and could not see, not even the man who could order me dead if he wanted to. It was a freedom I just couldn't give up.

Outside, I ran into Donokh again. He motioned to me from the garden wall. I thought about walking away, but I finally went over.

"Keep your voice down," he told me. "My jammer has limited abilities."

"Uh," I said.

"I want to speak with the elephant man. Can you set up a meeting?"

"Maybe," I said, "but you could do it just as easily yourself. Just ask Rorra. That's what I did."

He shook his head. "I've tried that." He rubbed his chin and looked away from me, then looked back. "Some advice for you, Larissa. Don't break any laws. Because if you do, it won't be me you have to fear, but Oshrii."

"Okay," I said, wondering if he was about to come

onto me. He was actually very attractive, but I didn't want that complication. "I'll take that advice," I whispered.

"Good," he said. "I'd hate to see a good knife fighter go to waste."

He turned and stalked away without another word. After a few minutes, I did the same, taking another route from the one he had chosen. I didn't want to see a good knife fighter go to waste either.

I didn't see Oshrii for another month after that, and then it was at supper. Hazaar came to collect me after knife practice. "We are dining with Oshrii tonight," he said.

"Uh-oh" was my reply.

He raised an eyebrow, but waited until we were in my apartment before saying what we were both thinking. "You shouldn't have defied him, Larissa. Not about *that*. In fact, I'm surprised you got away with it. If you had been Q'rin, he would have shot you on the spot."

I retreated into the shower then, but he just followed me into the bathroom and shouted over the water. "There's still time to change your mind about it," he said.

"No." I was a little surprised at the feelings aroused by that notion.

He didn't say anything else for a while. I lathered up and rinsed, feeling his eyes on me—what he could see of me through the rippled transparency. When I came out, he was sitting on my vanity stool, watching me. His eyes were half-closed, and he was breathing a little harder. That was the way he always looked when he was becoming aroused. I dried myself, wondering how much time we would have before Oshrii's supper.

"You are lovely," he said. "Then, in a harder voice, "I want you to move into my apartment."

"What?" I stopped what I was doing and confronted him with my hands on my hips. "Why?"

"If you're going to meddle in dangerous politics, I want you where I can keep an eye on you."

"Is that supposed to make me feel safer?" I asked.

He gave me an appraising look, quite different from the one he'd been giving me the moment before. "If you were alone in this apartment," he said, "naked, just coming out of the shower as you are now—and you were confronted by two assassins. What would you do?"

My body tensed. My closest knife was on the vanity, and we were both about equal distance from it. We leapt for it at the same moment. I got to it first, but he tackled me and pinned my wrist to the floor. I struggled under his weight for a moment, while he talked.

"Now I can kill you, Larissa," he said. "I can strangle you with this free hand, like so." He put his right hand on my throat. "Or I could put a force bolt through your head, or cut your throat. Many different things."

"I keep my door locked," I said.

"Someone could get the code. I'm in charge of the security for Oshrii's compound; but one of my officers with ambitions, perhaps someone seeking to make points with Oshrii—"

He left that hanging. I was startled that he would come out and say something like that. I had thought my apartment might be bugged. He released me and sat back on his heels. He tapped a little box on his belt. It had a flashing red light. A jammer?

"I told you," he said, "I'm in charge of security for Oshrii's compound. No one knows better than me what sort of dangers you face."

"If Oshrii wants me dead that much, why should you defy him?"

"He doesn't want you dead," he laughed. "He wants you *useful*. And you are useful, and so am I; but why shouldn't we be useful to each other as well?"

Somehow, that still didn't make me feel safer. I got

up and stalked into the bedroom, to get dressed. He followed me, but didn't try to stop me.

"Think it over," he said. "There are a million things you don't know about this place, about *us*. You have to stay alive to learn them."

"I'll think about it," I promised. But I was leaning away from the idea, even after his lesson in my vulnerability. I had always had my own room, if not my own apartment.

"I know something that may influence your decision," he said, tossing my knife on the bed when I started to look around for it.

"What?"

"You'll see it at dinner," was all he would say.

And he was right.

The dinner was in a guest hall in one of those buildings I usually never went to—though I could have been there for years and not seen most of the Q'rin complex. All of Oshrii's fighters were there, including Dorrin, who had shaved his head so that he only had one braid, just like my old nemesis, Abriin. Oshrii wasn't there yet.

"What's going on?" I asked Tilli as she sat down across from me.

"Apparently Oshrii has signed on a new fighter, and we're to meet her tonight," said Tilli. "That's all I know."

"Oh," I said, feeling a little miffed. They hadn't thrown a supper for me when I signed on. Hazaar draped his arm over the back of my chair and stroked my neck, soothingly. Dorrin sat himself to my right and amused himself by seeing how many times he could "accidentally" brush against me. He did some stuff under the table, too. I'd been told by Hazaar that Q'rin tables were so tall that you couldn't see what sort of weapons your dinner guests might be training on you from underneath them, and vice versa, so a sort of trust is established. But I'd been fondled under the table so many times by now, I was beginning to suspect ulterior motives.

While we waited for Oshrii and the mystery guest, I counted the empty chairs. There were four. Hazaar's guards were standing behind us, at attention, and I assumed Oshrii's personal guard would do the same. So who were those two extra chairs for?

I almost fell out of my seat when Oshrii showed up with Timmy the Lyrri on his arm; Timmy the lectro-whipper, whom most pit fighters referred to not-so-jokingly as Timmy the executioner. She was wearing gauzy pale-green wraps around her body instead of her usual lectrowhipper outfit. They made her look like the negative image of a Deadtowner. She moved next to Oshrii like a ballet dancer about to do a grand jeté (or some such thing), smiling graciously, her white skin glowing against the black and copper of his arm. Two Lyrri-dogs came in behind them, and then Oshrii's personal guard.

"These are the rest of my fighters," Oshrii was saying as they came in. He didn't look at any of us as he said it. "I'm sure you know them already."

It was a compliment to us, and we were all careful not to smile about it.

"Of course I do" came the answer, but not from Timmy. The one who answered was walking just behind them, and it was only from her voice that I could tell she was female. She was dressed just like the Lyrri next to her, in skintight black clothes.

Oshrii sat at the head of the table. Timmy sat next to him, and the other two Lyrri sat to his right—the woman who had spoken immediately so.

"Lady Lyanna," Oshrii announced to us. "These are—"

"Oh," she interrupted him gaily, "I know their names!" And she named us all, giving us each a smile as she did so. A chill went up my spine when she got to me. "Larissa the beautiful," she called me, and I was glad when she had passed on to the next.

"And I'm sure you all know Timmy," she told us. "But not my dear brother, Lyadd."

Lyadd grinned. His hair was long and inky black, like his sister's, and coiled at the back of his neck. The two of them were malignant, matching dolls.

I hoped this dinner wasn't going to last too many courses. I wasn't the only one, either. Tilli and a couple of the men seemed as uptight as me. The others either ignored the situation or seemed to enjoy it. There was a lot of laughter and talking during the appetizer course.

Supper was rolled in pretty quickly, and devoured with the usual Q'rin enthusiasm. But the after-dinner drinks lasted forever. I leaned back in my chair, out of Timmy's line of sight, and tried to stay awake.

"Larissa," she suddenly cried—it was the first thing she had said all night. "You and I are the only non-Q'rin fighters in Oshrii's household. Isn't that funny?"

"Hmmn," I murmured.

"It's too bad you're not a lectrowhipper. We could practice together."

"Uh-huh." Oh, my god!

"Would you like to come over to my apartment later, for a drink? You could bring your handsome friend, there."

"Uh—"

"We can't, tonight," Hazaar said. "We have other plans." He didn't say any of the other things a Human would add to soften the rejection, but she didn't seem to mind. I squeezed his knee under the table.

"I'll be so lonely without my Lyrri relatives," Timmy said mournfully. But then she brightened. "I'll have to invite some of them to live with me. And we can have parties! Everyone will be invited."

"A charming idea," said Oshrii. Across the table, I saw Tilli stiffen. A look of fury crossed her face, but she got it firmly under control.

"Well," Oshrii said at last, "those of you who would like to leave now may do so without fear of insult. The rest of us will retire to the conversation room."

Tilli and I got up, but the rest remained seated. I knew Hazaar was compelled to stay, so I didn't wait for him. She and I left the room together, and when we were outside, I asked her, "Are you busy for the next couple of hours?"

"No," she said neutrally.

"Want to go to the pits for a drink? I need to get out and have some fun, tonight."

"I'd be delighted," she said, and we walked through the three security gates and out to the tran stop. We didn't say another word beyond "Nice night, isn't it?" until we were off the tran and walking across the field toward Packrat's Shack.

"So," I said, "do you think Oshrii has lost his mind?"

She sighed. "He hasn't lost his mind, he's changed it."

"Oh?"

She gave me a hard look. "I've never been afraid to speak my mind before, not under the right circumstances, anyway. But now I'm afraid to talk to *anyone* about my feelings. I don't know where anyone stands."

We walked in silence until we got to the Shack. I did a double take when I saw Special Agent Donokh leaving the bar with, of all people, Shade. They were headed toward the animal show that had just moved into Packrat's Plot. She had her hand draped over his arm, and they seemed to be really absorbed with each other. It was kind of cute to see that giant man with that little girl. I wondered how they would—*manage*. At least I knew she was still alive, though I wasn't sure why I cared. I guess I sort of liked her.

Tilli and I found a table next to some Aesopians I didn't recognize. But she seemed more comfortable close to them than she did next to the other Q'rin in the room.

We ordered drinks. I was surprised to find that she

liked rum and Coke, too. "Look," I said when we were both halfway through the first round. "Let me make it a little easier for you. I don't like the Lyrri. I don't trust them. One of them killed a close friend of mine, and part of the reason I accepted Oshrii's offer was to get away from him. Now I find they're moving in next door."

She finished her drink in one large gulp. "Another!" she snapped at the server.

"Me, too," I said, hurrying to catch up.

The server was back in two minutes, with fresh ones. Tilli took a sip and said, "So, Larissa. You thought you could stay away from the Lyrri. I wish that were true. They should not be meddled with. We always used to keep them at arm's length, and I don't really understand why that's changed. Some of the lords—Oshrii—" she stopped and looked around.

"Do you think Oshrii is sleeping with Timmy?" I asked. "Or Lyanna?"

"I doubt it," she said. "I didn't see any bruises on him, and he hardly seems the type. No, it's not that. I think the Lyrri have been tempting some of the lords with"—she lowered her voice until I could barely hear it—"new technology. I think this has only happened in the past few years. Lyrri are suddenly taking over certain Q'rin jobs."

"Like?" I prompted.

"Have you ever heard of the Lords of Torture?"

"No."

"It used to be that the special agents did all the interrogating. And they were not gentle. But now, sometimes, suspects are given to certain Lyrri-dogs, the Lords of Torture. They can cause pain you've never even dreamed of. And they can keep prisoners alive indefinitely. It's not right."

"I agree." I swallowed more rum and Coke, remembering how Oshrii had promised I'd never be interrogated by *Donokh* again.

"And have you noticed," she went on, "that the

Lyrri surgeon at the pits hurts you more than the Q'rin doctor did?"

"I thought I was imagining that."

"Just be grateful you haven't required any serious surgery. That time Dorrin had the cut in his throat, he was with the doctor for hours. And he couldn't scream, because his throat—you see? Did you see how he looked when the Lyrri walked in?"

"No." That was something to be said for him, anyway. "I get the feeling we shouldn't discuss this with anyone else."

"Not if we want to live."

I didn't bother to point out that we had been the only two who had opted to leave the party. I suppose that wasn't necessarily suspicious behavior, but I couldn't help sneaking looks at the other Q'rin in the room, wondering if they weren't trying to listen in.

"Tilli, how long has Oshrii owned your contract?"

"Ten years," she said.

That was spooky. She looked about my age. That meant she had been fighting since she was a child—and also probably since before she was able to negotiate a contract properly. Sounded kind of like slavery.

"Someday I'd like to join the navy," she said, evoking sad memories of Buster and Alfred. I blinked furiously and gulped the rest of my drink.

After a month of watching Lyrri traipse back and forth from Oshrii's office and Timmy's apartment, I moved in with Hazaar. For weeks afterward he was smugly satisfied with himself. Now he *really* had me. But I wasn't unhappy with the arrangement. He was hardly ever home—except in the evenings—and he never took me for granted.

My work at the pits changed, too, because a lot of new fighters came in, and most of these were Deadtowners. Something changed in Deadtown then, something that was shaking Deadtowners loose from their nests and making them take desperate chances. They didn't shave the sides of their heads, but kept the

Deadtowner cut, maybe out of a sense of pride. Timmy started doing her hair just like theirs.

Most of these new fighters were knife fighters, and they changed the game radically. These folks weren't out for points, they wanted blood. I had to kill some of them.

The first one was a kid named Webster. I had watched him fight a few times before, and he had a sort of insane unpredictability that made him one of the crowd's favorites. He was what you might call a berserker.

"Fifteen units to place your bets," the announcer called after he'd looked us over. I took the warning. I can still see Webster's vacant grin. I knew something was about to happen, and I hoped it wasn't going to happen to me.

"Time," the announcer called, and left the pit. He had barely stepped foot off the sand when Webster threw himself at me like a storm. Suddenly I felt like a military brat again, fighting a miner brat back on Hook.

But I regained my cool quickly. He was going straight for the vital spots, not using a lot of finesse, so I knew when to dodge almost before he struck at me. I closed in on him and went for his neck and arms, trying to slash the arteries there and slow him down with blood loss. I hit some of my targets, and the blood poured, but he didn't slow down.

His body leaned in toward mine like a damned pit bull's, and his kicks and punches jarred me to the bone. He slashed at my throat, and grazed me over the artery. When he did that, I struck out desperately for the same spot on his neck, only I hit true. I cut his artery in half. His blood fountained across the sand, spraying me from head to waist, and Webster went over like a slab of cold meat.

The crowd screamed and cheered like some huge, crazed animal.

Oshrii was very happy with me after that fight. He

invited me to supper, a small affair with just him, me, Hazaar, and a couple of officers.

"Today you went from being a good fighter to a great fighter," Oshrii told me.

"Why? Because I killed a man?"

"No. Because you killed a man well."

They toasted me then, and Hazaar's hand burned on my thigh.

I wasn't happy about killing Webster, but I didn't feel guilty about it. I had defended myself. I had fought in the pits for a year without killing anyone; and now these yahoos had come into the game with their berserkergang attitude, and what else was I supposed to do?

The next one who died was some fellow named Alex or Alec. Once again, the announcer gave a fifteen-unit time limit for bets. He didn't wait any longer after the announcer had left to attack me than Webster had.

He was harder to fight, too. He closed with me and stayed there, refusing to back off, making furious jabs at my belly. He was trying to batter me backward, keep me in a retreating position, and I couldn't afford to let him do that.

He was another one of those one-knife fighters, and he used his free hand to grasp at my rag-wraps, trying to pull me close. I did a lot of dodging and dancing, and I gave that free hand of his a deep gash. But he kept trying, and finally he got a good handhold. He pulled me close; before he could sink his knife into my side, I kneed him in the groin so hard that he lifted into the air a couple of inches. He would have fallen forward, but he still had hold of me, and I was leaning into him. He went over backward, pulling me with him. I had almost killed Makrit that way once, and I wasn't about to let it happen to me. I twisted, and his knife just grazed my ribs. Without even thinking about it, I sank my knife into his side, twice, all the way in. He let go of my wraps. When I scrambled to my feet, he was just lying there with a confused expression on his face. He died a couple of hours later.

I saw Makrit in the tunnel on the way out from that fight. He was on his way in. He had some new scars. "These new ones must want to die," he said as we passed.

That night, the Butcher visited my dreams. I was reliving my fight with Alec, seeing it pretty much the way it had been; only I was cutting him more and hurting him worse than I really had. He fell over with me on top of him, and I stabbed him in the side, and then someone behind me said, "That's the way to do it!"

I looked over my shoulder. The Butcher was standing behind me, hunched over with his hands braced on his knees, his dick and his chin thrust forward. I tried to pull loose from Alec, but his hand was still clenched tight around my rag-wraps. I stabbed him again, to try to make him let go.

"That's the way to do it! That's the way to do it!"

Alec just wouldn't let go. I stabbed again and again, until my arm was covered in gore up to the elbow. The last thing I heard The Butcher say before I woke up was, "Here, let me show you how to do it!"

At least that time I had wanted to fight him instead of running away. That was an improvement.

Chapter 17

About six months into my contract with Oshrii, I lost my left ear. That's a day I'll never forget.

It started in the wrestler's room. I was watching Rorra and Winna go a few rounds, and doing some minor stretching of my own, trying to loosen up. I got in all the workout I really needed back at the complex, and by then I was in top condition—even better condition than I'd been in back on Hook. I was feeling great, and ready to go.

A Deadtowner girl came into the room and sat down to watch me. She glared at me, seething with a degree of hatred that seemed unwarranted, even if she and I were going to fight soon. But those new berserkers liked to psych themselves out that way, so I ignored her.

Winna came over and tapped me on the arm. "Have you seen that one fight?" she asked.

"No." I looked at the new girl again. She was about a foot shorter than me, thin, with a red-haired Deadtowner cut. She had buck teeth, and nasty little eyes.

"Watch out for her," Winna said.

I nodded, but I didn't listen as well as I should have. Some things just have to be learned the hard way.

"Hey, military cunt!" the new girl called. "I'm gonna cut your tits off!"

That's when I realized she was a miner brat. God only knows how she escaped from Hook. I supposed there was an interesting story behind it, if I'd ever cared to hear it, which I didn't.

"Save it for the pits, asshole," I laughed. Some of

the other Deadtowners laughed, too; but none of the Aesopians. Their eyes shone with a reddish tinge. Another warning I left unheeded.

All the way out to the pit, she kept up a litany of abuse and threats. I let them roll off me. I wasn't the military brat I used to be, I was a pro, and I intended to go at her like a surgeon when it was appropriate to do so.

"Fucking bald bitch," she hissed at me as we faced each other across the sand. "Fucking whore."

"Shut up," I said lazily. "I'm trying to hear the announcer."

It went right past her. She was so consumed with hate, she couldn't stop spitting it for a second, not until the announcer said, "Time!" and walked from the pit. Then Karen's mouth went slack and her eyes glazed over.

Oh shit, I thought, *not another one*. I was annoyed. Then she came at me like a windmill in a hurricane.

But I dodged her cuts easily. I let her get in close and started calmly collecting my points, taking only minor cuts on my arms, and a few shallow slashes across my rag-reinforced belly. She was collecting damaging cuts all over, and was far behind in points by the first five units. I wondered what the hell she was even doing in the pit with me if she was such a second-rate fighter. Was Oshrii really that eager to see me shed blood?

Then she lunged forward and pierced my ear, right at the bottom near the lobe. With a fierce grin, she sliced upward, and my ear went flying. The crowd shrieked.

For half a second, I felt like crying. Then a red wave rushed over me, and I lost it. I went after her face, and she returned the favor. It was cut, cut, cut, and no dodge, no technique. It was a Deadtowner grudge fight. I had the satisfaction of cutting the tip of her nose off and making her mouth about an inch wider on both sides. I felt her cuts on my cheeks, but could barely find the time to care. I was about to cut her eyes out when someone dropped a net over me. I was yanked backward, and the world went spinning. I heard someone screaming threats nearby, and realized it was me. I slashed at the guards through the net, and they pulled it tighter around me. The last thing I saw before they hauled me off was an upside-down view of the stands—people shaking their fists, or cheering, or laughing, or shaking their heads—and two women, just calmly watching. One of them was the bag lady I had seen at the elephant match, months ago. The other one was a skinny girl wearing dark glasses. Shade.

Karen was mouthing off again as we were carried down the tunnel, and I renewed my struggles. If I couldn't get out and kill her, I at least wanted to kill the men who were carrying me. It only seemed fair.

I was half-blind with blood and tears, and screaming at the top of my lungs when I was dumped onto the floor and cut out of the net. My knives were pried from my hands, and something big and furry fell onto me, almost smothering me. Someone grabbed my chin and said, "Larissa! Larissa!" Until I blinked the gunk out of my eyes and shut up long enough to concentrate on who it was.

It was Rorra. He had me pinned, and he looked mad.

"We have to get you to the surgeon before you lose any more blood," he commanded.

"Okay," I said.

Fortunately, they took me to the Q'rin surgeon instead of the Lyrri. He gave me a sedative before he worked on me.

"That one is beneath you," Rorra said. "Let it go. There will be other fights."

Damned right, I promised myself, *I'm going to kill that bitch next time.*

Then something occurred to me. "My ear! Did they find it? Could they maybe sew it back on?"

"I don't know," said the surgeon. "If they caught it in time, they could put it in stasis. Then you could get it sewn on later. For now, I'll just stop the bleeding there."

He worked on me for a couple of hours, taking care of all the rest of the damage. But the fact that my ear was gone was starting to sink in, and I don't mind admitting that I shed some tears over it. Rorra patted my shoulder and made comforting noises.

When I got home that night, I just sat in the dark for a long time. Hazaar came in after awhile, and looked at me. He looked at the spot where my ear used to be and said, "He patched it up well." Then he kissed me and carried me into the bedroom. I had never seen him so tender before.

When he was asleep, I went into the bathroom and looked in the mirror. It didn't look as bad as I had thought it would. I wondered if I shouldn't let my hair grow long enough to cover it, and cried some more. I thought about the nasty little miner brat who had done it to me, and dreamed again about killing her. It was like having a stomach full of poison.

In the morning, Oshrii called me into his office. He watched me for several moments while I sat motionless, my Nefertiti mask in place, determined not to show the slightest emotion.

"A fighter who loses control like that is useless," he said, finally.

"I agree."

"Really? Does that mean you've learned from the experience?"

"Yes."

He smiled, softly. "That remains to be seen. But I have confidence in you, Larissa. I'm inclined to believe you."

He drummed his fingers on his desk and regarded me for a while longer. "I have some bad news," he said. "You won't be fighting Karen again."

My stomach lurched. Was I on the second string already? Just because of one loss?

"Karen was killed in a bar fight last night," he continued, watching my face. "Apparently, she was doing some bragging to the wrong people. Someone decided to make her prove her claims."

"Who?" I said, thinking of Rorra.

"Makrit."

My stomach returned to its normal position, and peace began to trickle in.

"I see," I said.

"I know you wanted to revenge yourself on her," he said. "If you want to call blood feud on Makrit, I will arrange it for you."

"Oh, no," I said. "I'm pleased he did it. Maybe it's for the best." That was a lot to admit, but I was off balance, and feeling very emotional.

"Very well," said Oshrii. "You may go now—oh, I almost forgot. I have your ear in stasis."

Like hell he almost forgot. "You do?" I said, trying desperately not to sound hopeful.

"Yes. You can have it back when you've earned it. You're dismissed now."

It was quite a slap in the face, and I must have shown it, because his smile filled up with satisfaction. But I didn't let myself hate him, then. I just nodded and walked out.

I knew I was going to get my ear back eventually. I just had to be patient.

I didn't hear as well from the left side after I lost that ear, but that doesn't mean I didn't pick up on rumors. There were a lot of them those last few months. I heard very little from Hazaar; he was gone even more than usual, negotiating a deal with a contractor for some work Oshrii wanted done in Deadtown. Most of what I heard, I heard in bars.

For instance, there was the raid at the Baby School. I had heard about that place before. It was one of Abdul's favorite places to go whoring. I heard two dogs talking about it in Packrat's Shack.

"You were there?" one of them asked the other, and it was his tone of voice that pricked my ear up.

"I'm not proud of it," the other said. "I was under orders." I noticed he had three empty brainbuster glasses sitting next to him, and was working on the fourth.

"Is it true they were all children in there? No Human-dogs at all?"

"None that I saw. But we were ordered to kill everything in sight. We must have burned twenty-five, thirty of them." He took a long pull of brainbuster. "I can still see them. Hear them crying. I think I always will."

"I hear Lord Bronnin countermanded the order—"

"Well, we didn't hear it! Not until it was too late!"

The first guy squeezed the other guy's arm just below the elbow, until he quieted down. "Won't do any good to get yourself in trouble, soldier. What's done is done. We've all done things we're not proud of."

"They called it the Baby School," the other guy said, slurring his words. "Do you know why they called it that? Because it's where children learned to service grown men."

The first guy grunted. "Maybe they're better off dead, then."

"They tried to seduce us when they realized why we were there."

That was the last thing he said about it. I wished he'd talked more, because I wanted to know if it had been Oshrii that had ordered the raid, not to mention why. I knew someone on the Hill had owned the place, and those people on the Hill never invited Q'rin to their side of town—not openly, anyway. They thought that just because they were in charge of some drug farms, they were in charge of the whole planet. Maybe Oshrii wanted to teach them differently.

I never found out who ordered that raid, so I still don't know if Hazaar had been there, helping to kill those children. Now I don't want to know.

After overhearing that conversation, I started to attend some public hearings in the complex. Court was usually held in an outdoor amphitheater near the rear of the complex, where the special agents had their compound. They had a security entrance back there and everything.

The Q'rin judicial process was surprisingly fair—unless there were Aesopians in question. Oshrii sat on the judging council, and he had influence over four of the eight other judges.

I remember the day they brought a bear man in for vagrancy. My heart skipped a beat until I saw it wasn't Rorra or Winna.

"How do you plead?" they asked him.

"How else?" he asked calmly. "I have no money."

They fined him two hundred credits. He laughed when he heard it. "What difference does it make? I can't pay your fine. It may as well be two thousand credits."

So they gave him a thirty-day prison sentence. A lot of people in the crowd growled about that, and Lord Bronnin tried to get the sentence reduced to ten days, but he was outvoted five to four. They took the bear man away.

"It's the Lords of Torture for that one," someone said behind me. "You can bet on it."

Later I heard the bear man died while attacking his guards. The next time I saw Rorra in Packrat's Shack, I was almost afraid to look him in the eye.

"You seem quieter than usual these days," he told me. "Is it—is it your ear? I hope I'm not being insensitive."

"No," I said. "I was just wondering if you, ah, need any money."

He blinked at me for a moment, then rubbed his chin. "Oh. I see what you mean. No, Larissa. I'm—covered." He patted me on the shoulder, and I breathed a sigh of relief.

I didn't see as much of him or Ousa and Winna in those days; or rather, I didn't tend to see them all at once. Usually I saw one or two of them at a time, in the wrestler's room or in Packrat's Shack, and I saw some new bear and lion men coming in, even a few wolf men. They were all good fighters, and I wondered why they hadn't come to the pits before. There was a lot of money to be made, and the Aesopians were all poor as church mice. The funny thing was none of them ever dressed any fancier, and I saw a lot of Aesopians sleeping in alleys around town. So where was the money going?

Meanwhile, more Deadtowners poured in, and the knife fights got even more vicious. Makrit and I stayed at the top of our field, though, as the months went by.

Then one day I was invited to another of Oshrii's suppers. "All the fighters will be there," Hazaar said. "It's a late lunch, at the pits."

"Well!" I said. I had heard there were special dining rooms at the pits—and special rooms for other purposes, too—but I'd never been in one. "Who's this one for?"

"The tinker, Field. Oshrii wants him to build the fortress in Deadtown."

He said the word *fortress* casually, but I knew major information was being passed my way. No wonder the Deadtowners were shaken up.

"Someone else is coming, too, someone you may know. A young woman named Shade."

I must have shown surprise, because he said, "You know her?"

"Sort of," I said. "I met her a couple of times when I was living in Deadtown. What made you think I knew her, though?"

"She is a friend to Knossos, the elephant man. The man whose signature is on your contract."

"I never traded more than a few words with her," I said.

He nodded, and seemed satisfied with that.

When Shade walked into the dining room with the tinker, Field, I hardly recognized her. She had put on a few badly needed pounds, and had long red hair. I assumed it was a wig. The only thing that told me for sure it was her was her dark glasses and that feeling I had of being watched by her hidden eyes.

"How's it going?" she asked me, casually. Oshrii and Hazaar watched us closely.

"Fine," I said back, just as casually.

"I regret that Timmy the lectrowhipper can't be with us today," said Oshrii. "She is with the surgeon."

I sure as hell didn't regret it. I hadn't fought that day, so I hadn't seen Oscar X give her a thrashing (bless his heart!), but I could tell Mr. Field had. He looked a little green at the mention of her name.

Mr. Field sat next to me, so poor Shade was forced to sit next to Dorrin and Kallis. They immediately started coming onto her, and Oshrii didn't do a thing to stop it. I wondered what the hell was going on. Mr. Field was getting angrier by the moment. Did Oshrii want this guy to build his fortress or not?

"Have you ever had sex with a Q'rin," Dorrin asked her in Earth Standard.

"None of your business," she said, stuffing her lunch into her mouth at an appalling rate.

"She hasn't," Kallis said, "or she'd show more respect."

"She wouldn't be sitting down, either," said Dorrin. They laughed, while Shade just went on chewing.

"Why' don't you try it?" Kallis said. His hand disappeared under the table, and Shade stiffened. "You won't know what a real man feels like until you do."

She slapped his hand away. "No," she said.

"She's scared," Dorrin said. "She must have a tiny cunt. She thinks we would tear it wide open."

Privately, I thought so to, but I certainly never would have said it.

She picked up her drink and slurped it, then looked Dorrin in the eye. "I'm not afraid of you," she said. "I just don't want you."

I think that hurt his pride, but he accepted it. Shade went back to inhaling her lunch, and Mr. Field relaxed visibly.

"Are you a lectrowhipper?" he asked me, politely. I could tell he'd never been to the pits before.

"No," I said. "Knife fighter."

"Oh. If you don't mind my saying, you look more like a basketball player."

"Basketball?"

"Yes. It's a little like Half-G ball, only it's played in normal gravity. You have to be tall to be good at it. I played it when I was in high school, but I didn't have the height *or* the talent."

"I used to play Half-G," I said. I wondered if I would be any good at basketball. I was suspicious of any ball game that was played in normal gravity.

Mr. Field and I made polite conversation until the end of the lunch, and then he and Shade said good-bye. Oshrii saw them out, and the rest of us began to disperse. Hazaar took me by the elbow and directed me out of the maze, onto the field toward the Scorpion tran line.

"What do you think?" he asked me.

"About Mr. Field? He seems like an honest man."

"Good. But he's not the one I mean. I'm talking about Shade."

"I didn't even get to talk to her. I'm not sure she remembers me."

"She remembers you, be sure of that. Do you know she won every bet she placed today, except one? And I think she may have lost that one on purpose."

"Really?" I thought back to the first day I ever spoke to Shade, the day she told me I should become a knife fighter. The memory gave me a little shiver.

"Have you seen her with Knossos, lately?"

"I haven't seen either of them lately; and to tell you the truth, Hazaar, I find it hard to believe they spend time with each other. Knossos is—well—"

"He's a nobleman," Hazaar finished for me. "You can say it here, just don't say it in the compound."

"You're the one who said it."

He slapped me on the ass. "I may be drawing up a contract for this Shade girl."

"What? She's not a fighter."

"She can't lose, Larissa. Think about it. She looks at the fighters, and she can tell who's going to win. Do you realize how useful that talent could be, oh, say in a war?"

I tried to keep my face straight over that one. I had been watching the "shake-up" on Z'taruh lately: the restless Deadtowners, the quiet feuding inside the Q'rin complex, the busy Aesopians. Now I had a name for it.

And I didn't like it one bit.

Chapter 18

Tilli came to me one day and said, "Have you noticed for the last several months that a barnyard odor has been wafting across the field from the animal show on Packrat's Plot—"

"I sure have." I wrinkled my nose.

"Yes, and all kinds of people have been coming and going from there, and strange music can be heard over all the sounds of all those exotic animals, hmmnnn?"

"You want to go?" I didn't have any fights scheduled that day, and she was already done with hers. Why not?

"Just let me clean up," she said happily. I wondered if it would do any good to shower, considering where we were going, but I didn't say so.

We rode the Scorpion line down to the pits, and walked across to Packrat's Plot. I thought I was going to choke on the methane fumes before we even got up to the front gate of the animal show, but after fifteen minutes or so, I actually got used to the smell. I guess Tilli did, too, or else with that sensitive Q'rin sniffer of hers, she would have turned right around and marched back to the tran stop.

We strolled through the entrance and into the crowd. By then I could hear that strange music she had spoken of earlier, but it was so mixed with bleats and roars and hoots, it was hard to tell where it was coming from.

"I want to see the scorpion woman first!" Tilli insisted. "I've been hearing about her for weeks!" So off we went to look at the scorpion woman.

She was Q'rin, a very attractive woman if you didn't count the fact that she had poisonous bugs crawling all over her. There were scorpions of all sizes, colors, and origins; some that even had two tails. They marched up and down her body while she posed and undulated and eyed every Q'rin male in sight. They all stared back, absolutely mesmerized.

"What's she doing?" I whispered to Tilli.

"I don't know," she whispered back. "She wants something."

At that moment, the biggest Human being I have ever seen walked up to the scorpion woman. He was holding a leash, and at the other end of the leash was a scorpion the size of a small cow. The scorpion woman patted it on its green and turquoise carapace, telling it what a good beastie it was in Q'rin. The big man chucked her under her chin, and she batted his hand away. He slapped her on the butt, ignoring the scorpions who scuttled onto his hands and stung him.

Tilli elbowed me in the ribs. "That's him!" she hissed. "That's the man who eats live lizards! I've been hearing all about him—"

"—For weeks. Me, too. You're not going to want to see his show, are you?"

"I was thinking about it. Gods, look at the *size* of him. That's the only reason he gets away with having a Q'rin woman."

He was big all right, at least seven feet tall and maybe that wide. The scorpion woman went back to trying to shame all the Q'rin men in the crowd into ridding her of her husband (that's my guess, anyway); and the man who eats live lizards guffawed, turned his back on the crowd, and strolled off between the trailers. No one followed him.

We drifted away from the scorpion show and went past some aquatic tanks with some gratifyingly weird creatures inside, then headed for the big cat show. I wondered if they would have any Earth lions or tigers. I saw some Aesopians walking around, and for some reason the thought of a lion man being confronted by an Earth lion embarrassed me, as if the animal were a deliberate caricature of the man. That was ridiculous, but it was lurking at the back of my mind.

We did see a couple of lions. They looked tired and bored. But the six-legged Zorin tigers were spectacular. They leapt about and bashed into the transparency, looking more playful than angry. Tilli clapped her hands like a child. "Someday, I'll visit Zorin, I swear it," she said. "I've never been to the homeworld."

"I've never been to Earth, either," I confided. But somehow I was more interested in visiting Zorin.

We saw a sign indicating more six-legged cats just around the corner, so we went to investigate. We were confronted by a big tank with a freezer unit on the top. Moisture slid down the sides of the transparency, which was double-layered so that the defroster could make a window in the iced-up interior for us to see through. Inside was an Odinian ice cat.

It was just lying there, placidly chewing ice, looking rather unhappy. When Tilli and I walked up to the window, it looked at us curiously for a moment, then opened an extra pair of eyes over the usual ones and looked at us with those. I hadn't seen them do that on Odin—maybe these other eyes were for special occasions. The cat stopped chewing and stared at us in that fixated way cats have.

I tried not to feel bad about seeing the poor cat that way, but every minute we stood there, I was reminded more and more of the prisoners on Odin. What had this cat done to deserve the same kind of treatment?

"This is a crime," I said thickly. "This animal shouldn't be here. He should be sent home."

The owner, who was standing nearby, snorted and flipped me off.

Tilli grabbed my shoulders before I could jump at him. "You're a professional," she hissed in my ear. "And he's an animal. There's nothing you can do about it."

Somebody brushed against my back. I turned and saw a strange Lyrri standing behind us. He wasn't looking at me, so I started to turn around again; but then he said, "I agree with you. This wonderful animal shouldn't be confined. He should go home."

I stared at him, noting that he wasn't smiling like they usually do. He wasn't carrying a force gun either, just like Chaz never does, and maybe for the same reason. Maybe he did need it. I'm no expert on Lyrri, but I could tell he meant it about the cat, and I never doubted he would find a way to return it to its home.

I nodded to him, the only sign of respect I've ever shown a Lyrri, and took Tilli by the elbow. We left as discreetly as we could. Now that I was paying attention, I noticed that there were quite a few Lyrri hanging around the big cats display, and some of them had Q'rin companions. I was seeing more and more of that lately around town. More Q'rin with tinkers, too; probably because of the construction job Mr. Field was doing for Oshrii.

"So," said Tilli, "how about the man who—"

"No way!" I laughed. "I don't want to see anyone eat live lizards. I don't want to see anyone eat anything live at all."

The music we had been hearing all along became clearer as we moved away from the cats and toward the rear of the show. There were drums, horns, and cymbals—all crashing and clattering together—and singers. The singers were dancing with some bear-like creatures on a big platform. Aesopians crowded around this show, as mesmerized as the Q'rin had been by the scorpion woman. Tilli and I went over to watch, and stood there for quite a long time.

"I think it's some sort of religious play," Tilli whispered to me. She may have been right; certainly, a story of some sort seemed to be playing itself out. The dancers (the people, I mean), looked almost Human, maybe somewhere between Human and Q'rin, but with some interesting characteristics neither of us have. Like their ropy, bluish black hair, for instance; or their eyes, which had no whites at all, but were completely black. Or their perfect voices. The bear things howled along with the chorus, almost as if they understood the words.

A wolf man poked me in the ribs, and when I looked at him, he pointed to the show and said, "Zouanis. From Moasaii."

"Oh," I said, and thanked him. So these were the people from the planet I had almost gone to, three years ago. What a strange experience that would have been.

Tilli and I watched the Zouani show until we both got hungry; an amazing feat, considering the smell of that place. We went back across the field to one of the food shacks on the other side of the pits and ordered some Q'rin speared meat, which was a little like very spicy beef. I was having a wonderful time, and Tilli's eyes were shining like a child's.

"We should remember this, always," she said. "We should enjoy it as much as we can. Who knows how long the good time will last?"

She was right, of course. That was the last wonderful time I had on Z'taruh, because the very next day, Shade moved into the Q'rin complex, and my life began to take a downward spiral.

It wasn't Shade's fault, though. She came in like a refugee, looking for Donokh, and he took her in. I heard about it from Hazaar that very evening, at supper.

"Maybe we won't need to offer a contract," he said. "She doesn't seem to be in a position to bargain."

"Donokh might have something to say about that," I said, passing him the wine.

"He might, if he can keep her. What's that Human saying—? Oh yes, 'Possession is nine tenths of the law,' or something like that."

I ate the rest of the meal in silence. I didn't like his attitude at all. I was wondering if that "law" applied to me, too. I was only a few months from the end of my contract period by then, and I was having doubts about signing up again with Oshrii. The only thing that made me want to stay was Hazaar's hot lovemaking—that and the fact that Oshrii still had my ear.

"To be honest with you," Hazaar was saying, "I can't see what Donokh sees in Shade. He must be using her. Her body is like a child's, there's nothing there to work with."

"Don't be so sure," I said, thinking of the way Donokh and Shade had looked at each other when I saw them walking out of Packrat's Shack together. "He just has different tastes, that's all."

"Speaking of which," he said, pulling a small jar of honey out of a little paper sack, "I brought home dessert."

"Honey?"

"Yes."

"And no ice cream to pour it over?"

"I don't need ice cream," he said. "I have you."

See what I mean?

I saw Shade the next day. She came to watch me at knife practice. She was wearing one of Donokh's shirts, which on her was a dress, and her dog boots. She had lost the red wig, and her Deadtown cut had grown out into a sort of mad scramble. It looked kind of cute, in an untidy sort of way.

She still had the shades, of course.

She watched us avidly while we practiced, Tilli, Kallis, and I. Dorrin and I had managed all this time not to practice together—thank goodness—so he wasn't around. Kallis gave Shade some appraising stares—I don't think he would agree with Hazaar's assessment of her looks. She just watched us all with that funny little face of hers, sitting quietly by herself.

Hazaar came to watch about halfway through; but I didn't know if he was there to watch me, as he sometimes did, or if he was just keeping an eye on Shade. When I was done—just for the sake of curiosity—I went over to sit by Shade.

"So," I said, "another Deadtowner bites the dust, huh Shade?"

"Every day." She smiled. "When was the last time you went back?"

"I haven't set foot in Deadtown since Oshrii signed my contract. Why would I go back?"

"Have you made enough money to get off this planet yet?" she asked.

"Did that a long time ago."

Her mouth dropped open. "Then what are you still doing here?"

I thought about it. "Do you know anywhere else a knife fighter can make a living? I've got my own place here. I've got respect." (Most of the time, anyway.) "I've got a good lover." I nodded to Hazaar, who was watching us with a frown on his face.

She wasn't saying anything, and for some reason I felt compelled to fill the void. "I grew up on Hook. I was a military brat. If I hadn't run away from my old man, I probably would have—joined the service. I like the action."

I had almost told her about my Half-G dreams. I couldn't believe I was running off at the mouth like that. There was something about her that just seemed to pull information out of me. She was listening with her brows pulled together over her dark glasses.

"Wow," she said, half to herself. In some ways she was just like Alfred and Buster, or any other Deadtowner for that matter. Any other except me. I had *chosen* to come to Z'taruh. And I could leave it. They were trapped.

"I notice you've moved in with Donokh," I said. "Nice taste you've got there."

She got this funny little shy smile on her face. I'm not usually very sensitive to other people's feelings, but I knew then that I had been right about her and Donokh. They really were in love.

I left her there and went over to sit with Hazaar. I was ready to clobber him if he asked me what Shade and I had said to each other. I wasn't going to be anyone's spy. Fortunately, he seemed to sense that.

I think Hazaar tried to kidnap Shade a couple of days later. He came home late, looking really mad, and sat at the edge of the bed, brooding.

"What happened?" I asked him cautiously.

"We made her an offer, and she slammed the door in our faces," he snapped.

Uh-huh. I knew about those sorts of "offers." Those are the kind you can't refuse. Silently, I cheered her on.

A day later, they brought Knossos in to—you guessed it—stand trial for vagrancy. When I heard about it, I almost didn't attend the trial. I kept remembering him the way he had looked with a staff in his hands, or sitting across the table from me with my contract. But in the end, I went.

Shade got there before me. I went and sat down next to her. Her face was dead white. Knossos was supposed to be a good friend of hers.

"Can you translate for me?" she asked. "I don't understand much Q'rin."

"Sure," I said. I looked up to the judge's platform and saw Oshrii watching us, but I didn't care. "By the way. No hard feelings about last night?"

"Not toward you," she said.

"Good. No need to explain politics to a Deadtowner, because she already knows the score."

"Don't worry about it," she said, and she seemed to mean it.

The rest of the judges sat down, and finally Knossos arrived. I didn't recognize the men who brought him in. They may have been some of Donokh's men. I looked sideways at Shade and wondered how that fact sat with her.

Knossos looked a little worse for wear since the last time I had seen him. His clothes were more ragged, but he stood before the judges with enough dignity to put them all to shame.

"You are charged with vagrancy," Oshrii said. "What is your plea?"

The elephant man's massive shoulder rose as he drew

in breath. He said, "I, Knossos of clan Knossos, Lord of Ships of the Ragnir war and the War of Three Worlds, have lived as well as I can with no money and no ties with my homeworld, on Z'taruh for the last ten years."

"And what have you been doing for these last ten years, *ex*-Lord Knossos?" Oshrii asked him.

"I have endeavored to live with honor and justice," said Knossos. That sounds a little corny now, but it sounded right when he said it.

"How do honor and justice survive in a man who steals the clothing he wears and eats from refuse bins?" asked Oshrii.

"I live in humble circumstances, but I cannot unlearn virtue. I practiced it more faithfully than ever your Lyrri allies could."

There were some grumblings about that, some for and some against. Lord Bronnin and his group nodded their approval, and Oshrii looked like a thundercloud.

"Lord Knossos," Bronnin said, "are you conspiring to cause revolt on this planet?"

"No."

"How can you say that when you have been seen with members of your old crew?"

"Who else would I associate with on a planet of strangers?"

I thought that was an excellent point. Bronnin said, "I suppose the real question is what, in your mind, constitutes *association,* and whether or not it violates our laws."

"My lords," said Knossos, reasonably, "the question before you today is not whether or not I am a revolutionary. If you had evidence of that, I would not be standing before you now; I would be in a Questioning Cell or with the Lords of Torture. Today I am accused of being a vagrant. You must decide that I am, or I am not."

There was a good bit of applause for that, and the judges began to argue. It looked to me like one or two of Oshrii's steady pals were vacillating. Oshrii made a sharp comment to Knossos, but I didn't catch it.

"Very well," Oshrii finally said. "We find you guilty of vagrancy. You are fined fifty Z'taruh credits or three months in prison."

"My lords," said Knossos, "you know I have no money, and three months is far longer than the mandatory sentence for vagrancy."

"As I'm sure you know from long experience," Oshrii said coldly. "But that's our decision."

Shade was getting to her feet. "Larissa," she hissed, "loan me two credits, will you?"

I couldn't believe this girl's nerve. She was going to run right down there and bail him out. I had to admire that.

"Is three months to be the mandatory sentence from now on?" Knossos was demanding. "Will you feed and house every vagrant on Z'taruh for three months apiece?"

"No," said Oshrii. "Only the Aesopians."

That really pissed me off. I handed Shade the two credits. She charged down the aisle and went right up to Knossos.

"This man loaned me fifty credits when I was broke," she said. "Now I'm paying it back." She gave Knossos the money, and he whispered something to her. She turned a little paler, if that was possible.

"Sit down," Lord Bronnin told her.

Oshrii was smiling at Shade the way he did at me when I was defying him. I'll admit it warmed my heart toward her.

Knossos paid his fine, so they had to release him. Shade fled back to Donokh's place, and I went to knife practice. Later I watched Hazaar stomp around our apartment, looking frustrated.

I didn't say a word. I hardly knew Shade or Lord Knossos, but I was wishing I was with them, instead of with Oshrii.

* * *

About a month after that, Tilli was killed at the pits by a Deadtowner, someone I didn't know. He was killed himself, the very next day; so there weren't even any loose ends to tie up. Life in the complex flowed around and into the empty space she left, until she might as well have not ever been there at all.

Hazaar took me out to supper in the Spacer Sector and got me a little tipsy with brainbuster.

"You and Tilli were friends," he said.

"Yes," I agreed.

"Are you afraid the same thing that happened to Tilli will happen to you?"

When he saw that I hesitated, he said, "Speak freely. There are no bugs here."

"I'm not afraid. I'm just mad."

He stroked the back of my neck, considering his next words very carefully. "You don't have to renew your contract, you know."

"I do if I want my ear back."

"You're still beautiful." He ran a fingertip around the empty space. "If it really bothers you that much, I'll buy you a prosthetic."

"You would do that? Even if you knew I might leave?"

His face froze. His knuckles grew white as he gripped the brainbuster glass, until I was afraid he would break it.

"You want to leave me?" he whispered.

"You're not what I want to leave," I said. "You are the only reason I want to stay."

He hugged me and kissed me so hard, I was afraid he would break *me*.

"If you could just be patient," he said. "Once the fortress is built, Oshrii will be the most powerful man on this planet—eventually in this entire sector—and *I am his second.* I have a lot to offer you, Larissa."

"I know that."

"After your contract is up, you don't have to be a pit fighter. Do you want to be a lady-dog, a warrior?"

"That sounds rather interesting," I admitted.

"Think about it. You have six more weeks. You have many good options, Larissa."

I felt better for a little while. Hazaar took me to the hotel where we had first made love, and we spent the night there again. In the morning, we had breakfast in our room.

"Oh, by the way," he said conversationally, "we finally tracked down your friend, Shade."

"What do you mean *tracked her down*? I thought she was in the complex, at Donokh's—"

He gestured impatiently. "She left weeks ago. Slipped away. Didn't you know that?"

"No."

"Well, she's useless to anyone now, especially herself."

"What do you mean?" I asked, waiting for the worst possible news.

"She's become a meltdown addict."

That didn't make sense. "Meltdown? You mean that stuff the Skids drink?"

"Exactly."

So much for my good mood. It really wasn't any of my business, but I would have been happier not knowing. Much happier.

I ran into Donokh on my way to knife practice the next day. I think it really was an accidental meeting, because he looked as uncomfortable as me.

"Hello," I said, then on a sudden impulse, I stepped closer and put my thumb on the jammer button on the box at his belt. He stiffened, then leaned closer to listen.

"I was wondering if you could verify a rumor I've heard lately," I said. He frowned, and I could tell he thought I was going to ask him about Shade. But I didn't.

"You remember an act they had at the animal show, the man who ate lizards?"

He nodded.

"I heard he was murdered in a Midtown hotel. I

heard the knives they pulled out of him were Lyrri knives. Is that true?"

"Yes," he said. "Why do you care?"

"Did you see his body?" My thumb was beginning to get sore, but I held on.

"Yes."

"He was the biggest man I ever saw. Q'rin warriors were afraid of that man, you know what I mean?"

"And so?"

"I just wanted to know. I live a couple of apartments down from a Lyrri lectrowhipper. Timmy."

"I see," he said, beginning to catch on. "You don't like them."

"I don't. Listen, I don't mean to pry, but almost a year ago I was approached by a Lyrri named Chaz. He was looking for Shade—"

"—I know about that," he said curtly.

"Sorry," I said. "It's just that I thought if she knew someone who could get her off planet, she'd be better off. Someone who might be leaving in, say, six weeks? You know someone like that?"

"Are you asking for Shade?" he gave me a grim smile.

"Not necessarily," I admitted.

"I know someone who's leaving in five weeks," he said, softly. "And some others who are leaving in perhaps a month after that."

"Many others?"

"A great many."

We both stared at each other thoughtfully for a long moment, while my thumb got stiffer and stiffer. "You want me to do that for a while?" he indicated the box.

"Please," I said, taking my thumb back and shaking it.

"Don't you have—friends—who could help you with your *trip*?" he asked me. "Wrestling friends."

"Maybe, but I have to get out of the complex first. I have some things I want to take with me. And besides, my wrestling friends haven't asked me."

"Yet," he said. "But I have a feeling they will."

Someone was coming up the walk toward us, so we had to cut it short. I was sorry, because I had wanted to see if he knew what Shade was doing with herself these days. But maybe it was for the best. I didn't want to be the one to tell him such bad news. I gave him a nod and a grateful smile, and went on my way.

I ran into Donokh again, perhaps not so accidentally, at Packrat's Shack. I was looking for Rorra and the others, but couldn't find them. He waved me over to his table.

I ordered one drink and got through half of it while we made small talk about the weather and who was hot at the pits.

Then he said, in the same conversational tone, "Five weeks from tonight, at twenty hundred hours, my friend Lorrus is leaving for Kali. He'll be in a scout vessel—" and he gave me the ID number. "There's room for you if you want it."

"So if I don't show up at twenty hundred, he'll assume I'm not coming," I said.

"Right."

"Thanks," I said, and took my time finishing my drink.

"I know about Shade," he said when I was about to leave.

"Oh," I said.

"Some things you just have to get yourself out of," he said. "You have to find the strength yourself."

"Yeah," I said, uncomfortably.

"Good luck," he said, and left before I could get to my feet.

Chapter 19

Four weeks went by, and I saw almost nothing of Oshrii. I should have been on pins and needles, waiting for him to make another offer and to mention my ear. I assumed he would wait until the last minute, and then make my ear one of the terms of my new contract. That should have made me mad or impatient. But it didn't.

I was beginning to feel fatalistic about the whole thing. I knew sooner or later something would happen to propel my life off in another direction.

Finally something did. In fact, a whole bunch of somethings. It happened all at once. I was finishing up a fight at the pit, with Makrit, in fact, who was now the only fighter who could defeat me. That particular day I defeated him, but only just. We were walking back down the tunnel, when I was confronted by Lyadd and Lyanna, and several of their guards.

"My *dear,*" Lyanna said, "you are *wonderful*! We'll die if you don't come to lunch with us!"

I didn't say anything, and in fact, I tried to back away from them. Makrit stayed at my side, a look of cold hatred twisting his face. "What has she done to deserve the attentions of the Lords of Torture?" he snarled. "This is outrageous!"

Call me a dope, but I didn't know Lyadd and Lyanna were the Lords of Torture. I had only seen them at a couple of parties, and they both had acted like a couple of silly nitwits. Just like they were acting now.

"Don't be an idiot." Lyanna crinkled her nose at Makrit and locked her hand around my wrist. "We're talking about *lunch.*" She yanked on my hand, and I went sailing into her arms. "Whoops!" she cried.

Makrit made a move to stop her, but he was surrounded by Lyrri-dogs. Lyadd grabbed my other wrist, and the two of them pulled me down the tunnel between them, laughing like a couple of naughty children.

"The judges will hear of this," Makrit shouted. I looked back and saw him struggling with the dogs. Behind him, the announcer was coming in from the pits, but it was too late to call to him.

They pulled me down another tunnel, the one leading to the Lyrri surgeon's, but then took me off down a branch I'd never taken before. Their hair whipped in my face, and my wrists felt like they were being crushed in vises. "Don't hold me so hard!" I snapped, trying to work up some kind of bravado. But they just laughed.

We turned down several more tunnels, until I was hopelessly lost, and finally came out into the loveliest room I have ever seen in my life. They slammed the door behind us, and locked it.

"Well." Lyadd gave me a gentle shove toward a table laden with food. "At last we have you to ourselves. At last, at last."

"Thanks a lot," I said, rubbing my bruised wrists. "I don't enjoy being dragged."

"Sorry, dear," Lyanna pecked me on the cheek. "Sit down, won't you? We have a lovely spread for you. Do you like crab? It's my favorite, I'm positively addicted to it."

She pushed me into the chair, and the two of them sat down with me. I have to admit, the food was first-rate. And the furnishings were exquisite. I wish I could describe the curves and angles, the fine fabrics. I love fine things, but I'm not accustomed to them, even now. So I don't know the language.

"Do you like our salon?" Lyadd smiled and poured me a glass of wine. "These are all things from our homeworld. The Q'rin have some interesting notions about interior design, but we long for—'' he shrugged, indicating the room.

''It's lovely,'' I admitted, then wished I hadn't spoken when he stroked my hand.

''So are you,'' he said.

''Lyadd, stop,'' Lyanna said, without making a move to stop him herself. ''Larissa, my brother has the silliest notion that you might leave your Q'rin lover and stay with him. You wouldn't do that, would you?''

''It's not a silly notion,'' Lyadd said, before I could answer.

I kept my mouth shut.

''Try some brownwing fungi, my dear.'' Lyanna spooned the dish in question onto my plate. ''They taste very much like Earth mushrooms. Oh!'' Her hands flew to her face. ''But aren't brownwings poisonous to Humans, Lyadd?''

''I don't think so,'' he said. ''I never heard it.''

''You're making me very uncomfortable,'' I said, eyeing the rest of the food, not to mention the wine.

''Oh, I'm sure they're not poisonous,'' Lyanna said. ''I'm sure. Go ahead and try them.''

I nibbled at them, but couldn't quite bring myself to take a healthy bite. I was more at ease with the crab. Lyadd and Lyanna watched me avidly while I ate, trading mischievous looks with each other and occasionally stroking me with their fingertips. By the end of lunch, I was ready to go up the nearest wall.

I wiped my mouth on a napkin that looked twice as fine as linen, and pushed my chair back. Moving as one, they grabbed my chair arms. Suddenly they looked very much like the Lords of Torture, and not silly at all.

''Before you go,'' Lyanna said, ''one thing.''

''What?'' I asked, as if I didn't mind hearing the answer.

''Timmy is heartbroken that you and she have never had a chance to fight in the pit,'' said Lyanna.

''Well, I'm not. I don't intend to fight Timmy in the pit, or anywhere else.''

"But Oscar X does it," said Lyanna. I glanced at Lyadd, who seemed to be thinking about something else entirely. The top of his tongue peeked out from between his pale lips.

"Oscar X is a lectrowhipper," I said. "Lectrowhippers are crazy."

She frowned. "Why would you say a thing like that? Lectrowhippers are marvelous to watch, lectrowhipping is an art form."

You only say that because you torture people for a living, I wanted to say; but instead I said, "I didn't mean it as an insult. I just mean that lectrowhippers don't think like everyone else. Timmy's style and mine are not compatible. We are a mismatch."

"Why don't you ever fight in the Triad?" she asked, as if she hadn't heard me. "There's one tomorrow. You still have time to sign up."

"The Triad is fought to the death," I said. "I don't like that."

"But you've killed fighters in the pit, I've seen you." She closed her eyes, as if she were picturing it in her mind. "What's the difference?"

"The difference is that I don't like it," I said patiently. "I only do it to defend myself, not because it's in the rules."

"But Timmy will be so disappointed if you don't fight her tomorrow," said Lyanna.

"She'll have to be," I said. "I won't do it."

Lyadd and Lyanna exchanged long looks, then glanced toward an arched door at the back of the room. Soft blue light poured out of this room, like the light of the undersea. They looked at me again, and their hands flowed up the arms of my chair and over my hands.

"Come back here, Larissa," said Lyadd, thickly. "We want you to see our etchings."

Lyanna giggled, and then we all heard a distinctive, crisp sound. It came from behind us, from the locked door. Someone was unlocking it.

I craned my neck, and saw Oshrii open the door.

He had armed Q'rin warriors with him. "Well," he said, "have you enjoyed your lunch?"

"Uh," I said.

He strolled up to my chair and put his hands on my shoulders. "I need Larissa back, now," he said. "I have some things to discuss with her."

Lyadd and Lyanna withdrew their hands. I let Oshrii draw me out of the chair and toward the door.

"Let's do it another time, shall we Larissa?" Lyadd said hopefully.

I didn't bother to answer.

Oshrii kept his arm around my shoulder as we walked back down the tunnels to a place I recognized. "It's almost time to renegotiate your contract, isn't it?" he asked me.

"Yes," I said. I was sure he knew the time to the unit.

"Hazaar is already drawing up your new contract. I think you'll like it. You'll be getting more money."

As if I had already said yes.

"Oh, and some good news for you. I've scheduled an appointment for you with the surgeon. He'll put your ear back on."

"When?" I asked dreamily.

"Three days, at sixteen hundred hours. You won't want to miss it."

"I won't," I agreed. "That's Thirdday?"

"Yes."

That would still let me leave with Donokh's friend, Lorrus, in six days. If I chose to do that.

"Thank you," I said quite earnestly.

"You're welcome."

Once we were back out on the open field, Oshrii left me to my own devices. I decided to head over to Pakrat's Shack to get a much needed snort. And to wash the taste of Lyrri wine out of my mouth.

Across the field, at Pakrat's Plot, the animal show was coming down. It made me sad to see it. I remembered Tilli the way she had been when we went there together, the way she was smiling. My throat closed up and eyes swelled with unshed tears. I wished for once that people wouldn't stare at me, especially the Lyrri who were wandering around all buddy-buddy with Q'rin-dogs who should have known better, and the tinkers who seemed to be everywhere lately, laughing and drinking with the same Q'rin-dogs who allied themselves with the Lyrri. All of them were grinning at me, as if to say, *Well, we all know one thing men have in common. We all like girls!* I got tighter and tighter; my skin was itching from the inside. I felt like a character in a bad vid, and I wanted desperately to get off the screen.

My vision blurred, but I was too proud to reach up and wipe the tears or stop my determined march toward nowhere. I ran smack into something big and furry, something that wrapped its big arms around me and said "Ooff!" in Rorra's voice, then whispered, "I've been looking all over for you."

I blinked until I could see his face clearly. "Look who's talking," I said in a falsely normal voice. "I haven't seen any of you guys for a week."

He put his arm around me, and we took a casual stroll toward Packrat's Shack. "Lord Knossos's ship is leaving in three days," he said. "There's a place for you on it, if you choose."

That almost stopped me in my tracks. "Me?" I asked. "Three days?"

"Yes."

What else? The same day as my ear appointment. "I'm getting—" I pointed to the place my left ear used to be, but couldn't seem to finish the sentence. "In three days," I said.

"We can't wait any longer than that, Larissa. I understand that you may have other obligations, but you should get off this planet as soon as you can. If not with us, then perhaps with Donokh or Lord Bronnin."

"Oh, my," I said. "I need to think about this."

"If you decide to come, the field is landing field X, beyond the Spacer Sector, almost all the way to North

Outskirts. You take tran line Z to get there. We leave at eighteen hundred hours, Q'rin time."

Just two hours after my appointment. No way I could make both.

"Let's talk about it over a drink," I said.

"I can't. I just came to tell you. If you can't come"—he faced me, his big hands on my shoulders—"this may be good-bye. In case it is, Larissa—" He gave me a hug.

"You're a good fighter," he said, then turned and strode away.

I still felt like crying, but my eyes were short-circuited.

That night I had a dream. As usual, it told me how I really felt, and I couldn't understand it. I was walking down one of the tunnels at the pits, trying to figure out where I was. I walked for a long time.

Suddenly, to my right, there was a window in the wall. I looked through the window, and saw the Odinian ice cat. He was in a box in the wall. He had no ice to keep him comfortable, but he didn't seem to mind.

"Hello," he said. "I'm a cat!"

"Hello," I said back. "Do you know where I am?"

"Yes."

"Will you tell me?"

He blinked his eyes, then opened the ones above them and blinked them, too. "You're in the tunnel with me," he said.

"Do you know how I can get out?"

"I think if you just keep walking, you'll get out eventually," he said.

I was about to do that, but somehow I just couldn't leave him there. I put my hands against the glass. "How will you get out?" I asked him.

"Someone will come for me, soon," he assured me.

"Who?"

His tail flipped lazily up and down. "The Lyrri from

the animal show. Do you remember? He killed my owner, and now he's going to take me home."

"That's very—uh—nice of him."

"Lyrri aren't usually very nice, are they," he said, not really asking.

"Not usually," I said.

"A Lyrri killed Buster," said the cat, "and now Alfred is lost."

"That's true."

"Are you going to let a Lyrri kill you?" asked the cat. "I think that would be very sad."

"So do I. I think I'll leave before that can happen."

"Good idea," he said.

So I continued to walk down the endless hall. I didn't get out of the tunnel, but I did wake up, which is the next best thing.

I still wasn't any closer to a decision.

The next day was the Triad. I don't usually go to see those, but Hazaar talked me into it. He seemed reluctant, lately, to let me out of his sight. "We'll go for a drink together, afterward. Or to supper in the Spacer Sector. Would you like that?"

"Yes," I said, giving him a long kiss to reassure him. I wondered if it was a dishonest kiss or not, then just tried to forget about it.

We sat in Oshrii's box. I had only been there once or twice before—I usually sat in the fighter's box. Hazaar sat next to me, on Oshrii's right, and traced his fingertips lazily on my thigh. We watched the crowd slowly filling the colosseum. Hazaar's hand suddenly tightened on my knee.

"Look who's here," he said to Oshrii. "And with whom."

I looked, too. It was Shade. I don't know why I recognized her. She was thin, pale, scrubbed clean, and dressed in a short black thing. She was missing her dark glasses for once, and her eyes were spectacular—and scary. Maybe that's why I recognized her. She was with Chaz, who had hold of her wrist; and I didn't need to see the tension in her face to know how that felt.

"Tell the counters I want to know how she does, today," said Oshrii.

While Hazaar hailed the counter, I tried to follow Shade and Chaz with my eyes. They sat down in the Lyrri section. I didn't think Oshrii could get her out of there, even with armed guards.

The crowd settled in, and the announcer came out to announce the first fight of the Triad.

"The survivor of this round will go on to play in the next round! His or her opponent will not be handicapped, since this is a lectrowhip round.

"First fight, Janni and Ket! Fifteen units to place your bets!"

I had seen last year's Triad, so I didn't have any illusions about what to expect. I always thought you had to be either desperate for money or just plain crazy to fight in them; but with Lyrri thrown into the equation, that notion just goes out the window. For instance, there was Janni and Ket, two Lyrri lectrowhippers who were completely different in style. Janni was calm, cool, and never smiled. Ket was a sadistic animal who loved to see blood, and who usually fought Q'rin or Human opponents. I didn't even know what he was doing in this fight with Janni, unless he was pressured into it. But then, that's Human thinking.

Within the first five units, I knew Janni was going to win, so I stopped watching. I heard the *pow*! *pow*! of the whips connecting and the angry hum of the current, but I was much more interested in Shade and Chaz. They both sat completely still in their seats, Chaz occasionally stroking Shade's rumpled hair in an absent sort of way. He didn't look the way he had looked when he was toying with Buster. Maybe he was like Allaa, in love with a Human and consumed by his feelings. That's the way with the Lyrri. Either you must eat them or they must eat you; there's no middle ground.

I looked down in time to see Janni flip Ket onto the fire rods, a move Timmy had made popular this year. Janni did it even better than she did, and I wondered if she would be fighting him this round. But the second player was someone name Ono, another Lyrri male. Ono lasted ten units longer than Ket had.

By the time Janni was facing the third fighter, a Q'rin named Mardra. I was back to watching Shade again. I couldn't get over how strange it was to see her eyes in action. It was intimidating enough when they were covered up with the glasses; naked, they were almost too much to take. I rather hoped she wouldn't turn them in my direction.

"Her eyes are beautiful, don't you think?" Hazaar whispered in my ear. "They're her only good feature. No wonder that Lyrri likes her. Lyrri can't resist the eyes."

Janni certainly couldn't resist eyes. He blinded Mardra ten units into their game. She switched off her whip the same way Sasha the wolf man had done, and she made a dive for Janni. A brave move. But she wasn't as strong as Sasha, and Janni broke her neck, easily.

One of Oshrii's officers cursed. "A perfectly good female gone to waste," he muttered.

"It was her choice," Oshrii said, almost sadly.

So Janni won the first round. He retired with much applause, and then the mangler round started. I don't remember much about it, except blood and the sound of bones breaking. I did try to watch, but I kept looking at Shade to see what her eyes reflected. She never flinched from anything, never looked away. Lady Death must have eyes like hers, big pools full of compassion and avid interest.

I think a Q'rin won the mangler round, a woman named Bidde (which is pronounced Biddy), kind of a funny name for a mangler champion. She retired, and the freestyle round started. In this round, lectrowhippers could fight manglers and so on. Timmy came out in the first game, with her whip.

My stomach turned at the sight of her. She was still dressing in that negative-Deadtowner style, all pale silky wraps and hacked-up hair. Her lovely face and her hands were the only thing left exposed. The surgeon had kept her skin smooth, just as he'd done mine; but with her it was more of a feat, since she was burned so often.

I looked sideways at Oshrii when she came out with her opponent, a Lyrri named Fev—another lectrowhipper. Oshrii's face was cold. It didn't have that hot, half-lidded look of a Q'rin male who was interested in a woman. Even I had seen that look from him, so I knew he was capable of it.

He knew exactly what she was, I understood that, then. He knew it, and it was still worthwhile to him to use her, no matter what she did to others. Even if he cared, he didn't let his feelings influence him.

Timmy broke Fev's neck with her whip, which is a pretty astonishing thing to do to a Lyrri, even for another Lyrri. It was kind of sad to see Fev go limp and flop to the ground. Unanimated, he looked like a child. Maybe he was a child—it's hard to judge a Lyrri's relative age. Timmy squatted down to look into his eyes, then stood and wandered away. I almost expected her to smoke a cigarette.

Her second opponent was a Q'rin mangler-master, a fellow I'd never seen defeated whenever I had the stomach to watch him. His name was Vovvid, and he came out with a lunatic smile. I always kind of wondered about him, because it seemed to me that you could see more of the whites around his eyes than you should be able to see in a sane person's face. But the Q'rin loved him, and they went wild when he came out; especially the anti-Lyrri segment. Even Hazaar and Oshrii were affected, and I wondered if this wasn't Oshrii's way of getting rid of Timmy. Perhaps she was too dangerous even for him.

Since Vovvid only had manglers on his hands, he was allowed to wear force repellers on his arms and chest against a lectrowhipper. He had a good chance.

It seemed to me, as Vovvid faced Timmy across the sand, that her smile was a little strained. But that may have been wishful thinking. The betting period expired, and the announcer left the pit. Timmy switched on her whip, but Vovvid didn't give her a chance to build the charge up. He rushed her and pounded her with the manglers, knocking the whip right out of her hand. The whip twisted and turned on the sand, lashing both fighter's legs. I saw his manglered fists strike her face again and again, and I saw pink blood flying.

Most of the Q'rin crowd was on its feet then, cheering. I had to stand, too, if I wanted to see. I did.

Timmy was going right for Vovvid's eyes with her nails. His neck was strained backward to avoid them. She switched tactics suddenly, and tried to slither out of his grasp. He caught her, lost her, then caught her again. Again, she went for his eyes, and this time, caught him in the corner of the left one. He jerked his head away, and she danced back out of his reach.

I was horrified to see how little damage he had done to her with the manglers. It didn't seem fair. He had hit her in the face at least a dozen times; it should have been raw meat. She was looking back and forth between him and her whip, which was still lashing on the ground at his feet.

He lunged toward her, and the whip caught him around the ankle. He stumbled and tried to kick it loose, but it bounced back and wrapped around his knee. It emptied its charge into him. He screamed and his leg gave way underneath him. Timmy dove for the whip handle and got it. She flipped it away from him and danced back, waiting for the charge to build up again.

She skipped back and forth around him like a carefree little girl while he struggled to his feet and tried to get at her. His leg kept giving way.

"You cowardly bitch!" some Q'rin were shouting at her, but she ignored them. She waited until the whip was lethal and snapped it at Vovvid. He used the repellers to fend it off, and the cycle repeated itself.

Until she managed to get behind him and wrap the whip around his neck.

His head turned black, and his eyes smoked. I closed my eyes at that point, so I didn't see him fall. I heard the crowd screaming and cheering, and I think I heard the sound of someone puking.

When I opened my eyes again, Vovvid's body was being dragged from the pit. Timmy had a lot of cuts and bruises on her face; but her eyes were undamaged, and the bleeding had already stopped. She was ready for the next one.

I glanced at Shade again. She was still sitting quietly. Chaz was leaning toward her, stealing little glances at her eyes, looking aroused. She didn't seem to know it.

When I looked back to the pit, another fighter had come out, a Human knife fighter. She was a black girl, about my size. Sweat broke out all over my body, chilling me.

I never caught her name. She was wearing repellers just like Vovvid had. She had a hopeless look on her face, but a determined set to her jaw.

When the betting time was up, she charged Timmy the same way Vovvid had. I agreed with her strategy, it was her only chance. She managed to knock Timmy off her feet, but she couldn't make her knife blade go into Timmy's neck, and Timmy never lost her grip on her whip. She threw the girl off easily, and broke her neck with the whip. It all must have lasted about five units.

The Triad was over. The crowd got to its feet, and started to file out of the colosseum. A counter came over and whispered to Hazaar.

"She won every bet for him," he told Oshrii.

"Let's take the shortcut," snapped Oshrii. We were all on our feet and through the secret door in minutes, ten of us running through the tunnels toward an outer door. I just went along with them. If I had stopped, I probably would have been trampled. We burst out of the outer door and joined the throng.

"Where is she?" snarled Oshrii.

"Over there!" Hazaar pointed to a disturbance in the crowd, about halfway between the colosseum and the tran stop. We saw pale skin and flashing knives. Oshrii's men formed a wedge and marched through the crowd toward the disturbance. They plowed through a group of Skids, and one old guy shook his fist at them.

"Watch it you dirty Q'rin-nig—"

Hazaar casually punched the guy in the teeth as he marched past him. I felt a twinge of satisfaction, but it died quickly as I tried to keep up with the others, wondering if I was part of a rescue or another kidnapping attempt.

We got to the edge of the circle of spectators, then stopped dead. Shade was inside the circle with Chaz. She was breathing hard, facing him with a couple of those hand-altered Deadtowner knives in her hands. She held them, and herself, with a lot more finesse than most Deadtowners do; but Chaz had two knives of his own, elegant Lyrri monstrosities, and he was crouched like a lithe, powerful cat. He looked better than Timmy had in the Triad, a comparison that was not lost on Shade, judging from the desperate look on her face.

"Oshrii," I hissed, when no one made a move to help her.

"Shut up," he hissed back, punctuating the point with a sharp chopping gesture. Hazaar's own hand closed painfully around my upper arm, warningly; but by then it was too late anyway. Shade was moving.

She went for Chaz aggressively, and I grinned with approval as she landed dozens of cuts. I was amazed she was that good. But her cuts hardly marked him, and when he slashed back, he cut her pretty badly; though he didn't land as many cuts as he might have. They were moving so fast I could hardly see their strategy, but soon I realized she was moving just before he did, anticipating his moves.

It was astonishing. So this was why Oshrii wanted her so badly. She could tell what the enemy was about to do. She was dodging just as Chaz was lunging, turning what could have been a bad cut into a grazing slash. He would strike, but she would strike first, hitting him twice before he could change his tactic. If I could have done that, no one would have been able to beat me—no Human or Q'rin, that is. But against Chaz it was a losing battle, and Shade knew it. She knew it and she kept fighting, landing cuts that made only the slightest mark while she bled from too many wounds.

The crowd at the pits was getting its money's worth that day. I wondered if anyone had thought to place a bet.

Shade and Chaz broke off suddenly and stared at each other. He seemed mesmerized as he looked into her eyes. I was reminded of the Odinian ice cat, the way it had stared into mine. Chaz seemed to be caught in the same neurological trap. He might have stayed that way for hours. But he wouldn't. Any moment he was going to close in for the kill. My fighter's instincts told me so. She had to move, to find a way . . .

Shade lunged forward with her right knife and stabbed Chaz in the eye. Bells and whistles went off in my brain. *That's how you do it! That's how you kill a Lyrri!* It was wonderful, miraculous. He dropped his knives, and grabbed her by the shoulders.

"I want to see your eyes," he said. "Promise you won't cover them."

And then he died. She deserved a standing ovation, but she didn't get it. I felt Oshrii and Hazaar moving in on her, and saw a bunch of Lyrri-dogs doing the same. Shade turned and looked at us all. Her eyes passed over me, but I didn't think she recognized me. I felt very sorry for her.

The crowd surged against us, and I almost lost my footing. Knossos the elephant man was pushing his way toward Shade. Rorra and Ousa were with him. They cut through the dogs like a hot knife through butter, until they were at her side. Then Knossos scooped her into his arms and carried her away.

I think I may have tried to follow them then, but Oshrii and Hazaar pulled me back. At that moment, I felt very jealous of Shade.

Chapter 20

I went to sleep that night in the bed I shared with Hazaar; but when I woke up, I was in a sterile room, strapped to a table. I was only wearing panties and a T-shirt, and couldn't seem to wake up all the way.

"Whuzgoinon?" I said, then almost giggled at my own voice. "Whudz goinnon?" I tried again, just to see if I could speak normally if I tried hard enough. I couldn't.

The Lyrri surgeon came into my line of sight. "Uh-oh," I said.

"What do you mean?" He looked hurt. "It's time to reattach your ear. Don't you want your lovely ear back?"

"Yez."

"Of course you do." He was swabbing the place where my ear was supposed to go, and then he pulled out an enormous needle. It hurt like hell going in. I waited for the area to become numb, but I waited in vain.

"Are you sure you don't want some ritual scars, my dove?" He stroked my forehead.

"Nodfunny," I slurred.

He sighed and began to mess with some things he had on a tray. I occupied myself with trying to move and trying to think straight, two things I couldn't accomplish at the same time. Finally, I just gave up and tried to relax.

"Dodaythirday?" I asked.

"Thursday, yes," he said.

I didn't bother to try to say *Thirdday* again. He had

already told me what I wanted to know, anyway. I had probably missed the Aesopian ship. I felt a detached sort of sadness about that. But then I thought about Hazaar and the way he had made love to me the night before. Maybe it was all for the best. It hadn't occurred to me yet that he must have been the one who had drugged me.

"Don't try to move or talk to me now," said the surgeon. He had my ear in his hand now. I looked at it fondly, surprised at how happy I was to see it. He turned my head, gently, and began to work.

The pain was excruciating.

"Hey!" I shrieked.

"Don't speak! It will just take longer. You don't want it to take longer, do you?"

It was like having my nerves exposed and then plucked, one by one, by a red-hot wire. I made pathetic little whimpering noises, while he carried on a conversation with himself.

"Such a lovely little ear," he said. "I've had it on a shelf in my room, next to my shell collection. I was very sad when your Q'rin lover came to see me about it—by the way, did you know that the ancestors of the Q'rin originally came from Earth?"

Whimper, whimper.

"Yes, that was all some time ago. But anyone can see it. If you've ever seen a Zorin tiger, you know, with their six legs? Well, lots of Zorin animals have six limbs; but the Q'rin only have four. You'd be surprised, my dear, at how similar their cells are to yours. Yes, you would."

I was crying by then.

"The Aesopians used to tamper with all kinds of things in those days. They tampered with the Q'rin even before they tampered with themselves. They didn't always look the way they do now, you know. Like lions and bears, of all things! I don't understand them."

I had a sudden vision of a lion man sitting in a cage

at the big cat display, looking sleepy. I felt embarrassed again.

"It's all so fascinating!" he said. "Life has been so boring for the last thousand years or so. Nothing to do. And you wouldn't invite us into your Ragnir war; that wasn't very nice. That might still be going on if we'd had a chance to play with it. Well, the next war is going to be different, I can tell you that much. We haven't even begun to explore the possibilities."

I lost consciousness at that point. He continued to talk, but I only picked up bits and pieces of what he said, and those I only remembered in my dreams, later.

When I woke up again, he was almost finished. The drug he had injected into the area must have been wearing off by then, because the pain was almost bearable.

"Almost done," he said. "You won't even know there was a seam here in a day or two. Lovely, lovely. I shall miss it. My shell collection looks drab now."

"Unnh," I said.

He patted my arm, and then gave me another injection, this time in the butt. I slipped off into sleep. The last thing I thought about was that I hoped I would wake up in my own bed, next to Hazaar. I wanted to show him I was my old self again.

But when I woke up several hours later, I was in a cell.

I don't know how long I was actually in the cell before I woke up. I think it may have been as much as a day and a half, because I only had four meals and used the privy four or five times before some guards came for me.

They stared at my half-dressed body for a few moments, then wiped all expression from their faces and marched me out of there. I didn't attempt to get any information out of them. Once we were out of the cell, I knew where I was anyway. I was still in the catacombs under the colosseum. They took me even deeper, through some tunnels that didn't look like they were used too often. We went through a pair of large wooden doors, into a chamber that was all lit with torches. Rather a primitive touch, I thought.

It was the lower pit Kossos had warned me about.

Oshrii was standing on the other side of the pit. The room was about half-filled, with maybe forty or fifty officers and a few of their ladies. I noticed Katta was there, but Hazaar wasn't.

"I hope you've been doing something besides sitting since you've been awake," Oshrii said. "I have some work for you."

The pit was a lot smaller than the one upstairs, maybe twenty feet across. It was set about six feet into the floor and surrounded by a three-foot retaining wall that curved slightly inward. There were no chairs in the room. If you wanted to see what was going on in the pit, you'd have to stand next to the wall and look over. I walked to the wall and did just that.

Timmy was sitting cross-legged in the center of the pit. When she saw me, she gave me a gay smile and patted the whip that was coiled in her lap like a pet snake.

"This is murder," I told Oshrii.

He didn't even crack a smile. "No it isn't. Here are your knives." One of my guards tried to hand me my fighting knives and another stepped forward with some force repellers. I didn't put them on just yet.

"I didn't give my consent for this. My contract specifically states—"

"That contract was co-signed by a criminal!" he snapped. "It's not valid."

"If it's not valid, then I'm not bound to you by written agreement at all!" I yelled back.

"In that case, all we have is an oral agreement, and it is my word against yours." He looked around the room, at the officers and the ladies, some of who were now grinning. I didn't look to see if Katta was. "I think my word carries more weight than yours, here," said Oshrii.

Two of my guards picked me up and tossed me into

the pit. Timmy jumped lightly to her feet to avoid me. My knives and the repellers were tossed in after me. I stood up with as much dignity as I could muster and put them on.

Oshrii watched me over the retaining wall. "You have a fighting chance," he said. "You've watched the freestyle. I hope you learned from the mistakes of others."

I hoped I had, too, but I could see that Timmy certainly had. She was braced, waiting for me to try to tackle her the way she'd been tackled twice at the Triad. I wasn't sure I could knock her over. I would have to rely on my Half-G training, and that was a game I hadn't played in three years.

I made sure I had my Nefertiti mask in place, and looked Oshrii right in the eye. "I was ready to sign another contract with you," I half lied.

Now he did smile. "No you weren't. You were ready to leave with the elephant man. You have never committed yourself to me, your loyalties have always been divided."

Something about the way he said that made me wonder if I had made a big mistake with him from the beginning. I had never made any sexual advances to him. He was a powerful man, he might have thought it was his due.

"You're a beautiful, talented young woman, Larissa," he was saying, deepening my suspicions. "I could have made use of you. But that will never happen."

"You're assuming I can't win," I said desperately.

"Not so. You might win, Larissa. You might."

The others gathered around the rim of the pit, and Timmy switched on her whip. I lunged at her, but not to try to knock her over. Instead I went for her as I would for another knife fighter. I feinted for her whip hand, and she pulled it back. Then I changed direction and lunged for her eyes.

Her smile turned into a horrified grimace as I slipped my knife into her right eye. I tried to drive it all the way into her brain as I'd seen Shade do to Chaz, but she put a foot up on my chest and shoved me so hard I went flying. I felt myself falling, and then hit my head on the pit wall, hard. My skull filled up with red dots.

I wanted to get to my feet again, but my body just sort of twitched. I could hear Timmy's whip working up to its full charge. I pried my eyes open and saw her standing in the center of the pit, her head wreathed in the helix her whip created. Her right eye looked like the broken center of a cherry bonbon. Her other eye was open very wide.

She took one step toward me, and then another. I thought about all those vids I had seen where the hero is backed into a corner, and then he throws his knife and it hits the bad guy dead center. I'd never thrown a knife in my life, but I got ready to do it then. I concentrated on Timmy, and fancied that she looked like an evil angel bathed in holy light. As I watched, the light intensified, turned blue; and then Timmy was flying backward to hit her own side of the pit wall. Someone had shot her with a force gun.

I struggled to my feet. Timmy's good eye was closed and her whip was lying dormant on the sand. All the energy had been sucked from it. Only then did I dare to turn and look behind me, where everyone else was looking. I half expected to see Knossos the elephant man there. But it was Hazaar, his force gun still in hand. His personal guard stood behind him, but didn't draw their weapons.

"She's my mate," he told Oshrii, by way of explanation.

"She was my fighter before she was your mate," Oshrii said. He was icy calm. "You should have made your claim sooner."

"You knew I was waiting for the contract to expire," Hazaar said, bitterly.

"Yes, I did. Well." He signaled to my guards, and they pulled me from the pit. "You'd better register your claim as soon as you can. Otherwise it won't be official."

Hazaar put his arm around me and helped me from the room. His face was as calm as Oshrii's, but I could see the strain at the corners of his mouth. As we walked back up the tunnel together, his men watched our backs, and I think we were all surprised when no one attacked us.

Hazaar was strangely calm by the time we got back to our apartment. "Things aren't as bad as they look," he said. "He was angry with you. But you did well in the pit. Timmy has never been so badly wounded by anyone."

"So doesn't that mean he's even madder at me?"

"Maybe. Or you may have just rid him of a troublesome ally. He hoped Vovvid would do it for him at the Triad." He stopped when he saw the dazed look on my face and put his arms around me.

"You didn't object when I called you my mate," he said.

"No, I didn't." I didn't take that lightly, either. Hazaar could never have children with me—at least as far as I knew—and yet he was willing to call me his mate in front of his lord. It was a serious commitment.

He gave me a long kiss, then began to peel his clothes off. "Me first for the shower," he said. "That was a long run to the colosseum. I didn't know where you were—I thought they were holding you here, in the compound—" His voice trailed off as he went into the bathroom. I heard the water go on.

"Hazaar," I yelled, "What day is it?"

"Seventhday," he yelled back. "You were gone three days!"

I went to the bedroom and pulled on some clothes. Then I deactivated the stasis pad under my strongbox. The box was full now. I had thought about getting a bigger one. I put it in my suitcase, then checked the clock. It said 19:30. I had a half hour to get packed and get to the field. I set the clock alarm for 19:45.

I packed some essentials, and then threw in a picture of me and Hazaar. Tilli had taken it almost a year ago. I didn't have any pictures of her. I scribbled a quick note to Hazaar, apologizing, telling him I loved him but didn't trust Oshrii, saying I hoped he and I would meet again someday. But I wasn't really sure I wanted to meet him again. I thought he would hate me for leaving him.

I put the note on our bed, and checked the clock. It said 19:44. Something was funny about that. I could still hear Hazaar's shower running. His showers never lasted for more than ten minutes.

I had to go look. It was like when Mother was killed, when I had to go to the top of the stairs and look down.

No one was in the hall. I walked quietly to the bathroom, picturing him in the shower, soaping up that lean, gorgeous body of his, smiling at me invitingly.

His gun was on a chair, next to the shower door. I saw him through the rippled transparency. He was sitting down. I opened the door and looked at him. His throat was cut from ear to ear. It broke my heart to see the surprised look on his face.

My hands were shaking so badly, I could barely pick up his gun. Back in the bedroom, the alarm went off, filling the apartment with its obnoxious hum. I went back into the hall, holding the gun at a ready position, and ran into our bedroom.

I grabbed the suitcase with my free hand, and then out of pure habit, I put down the gun and switched off the alarm. The humming noise continued. Something whizzed past my face and snapped the gun right off the dresser. Then Timmy's whip flew up over her head and danced there.

She was standing on the other side of the bed. She had a bandage over her bad eye now, but pink stuff was leaking from underneath it.

"It was a shame to marr your lover's beautiful body," she said. "I had a bit of a crush on him, you know. I prefer men to women, don't you?" And then she sent the lash at me.

I was still wearing the repellers, but I used my suitcase as a shield. It worked quite nicely. The explosion knocked me back out the door, into the hall. I made a mad dash for the front door. I didn't look, but I knew she was right behind me.

As I burst out into the garden, I could hear the whip humming, building up its charge again. I made straight for Landing Field Road, noting as I passed that Hazaar's personal guards seemed to have vanished. In fact, there was no one on the road at all.

I saw myself running in one of the reflective windows, Timmy close behind me. When I looked again, she was closer. I decided not to look anymore, and threw everything I had into my legs. Her eye had to be slowing her down. It had to.

The landing field was lit up, but I didn't see the guards who were supposed to be at the gate. At the far end of the field, a scout was getting ready to lift off. The loading door was open, I saw a warrior leaning out. I waved to him and shouted. He saw me.

He stretched his hand out to me as the scout began to lift, and yanked me through the door. My suitcase went flying into some other cargo. I looked behind me at the dwindling ground, expecting to see Timmy there, maybe shaking her fist at me. But she was already gone.

The warrior slammed the door shut. "She turned back when she saw you were going to make it," he said. "She looked very disappointed." He turned to look at me, and I finally recognized him.

He was the announcer from the pits.

"I am Lorrus," he said. "Welcome aboard."

I collapsed into his arms and cried my eyes out.

Chapter 21

I was in a sad mood when my first officer, Theodore, and I left the vid theater on Kali after watching *The Butcher.* The movie had been upbeat at the end, but I knew the real story.

"That little girl in the movie was *you,* Captain?" Theodore teased.

"No," I said, taking the question seriously. The movie hadn't borne the slightest resemblance to my life, and I hadn't been sure how it was going to end.

We took the tran back to my ship, the *Dagger.* I like that name because it has a Q'rin sound to it, but Theodore always calls it the *Spiffer,* and *Spiffer* has caught on with the crew. All fifteen of them.

Yes, my dad's military blood runs true in my veins after all. I joined the navy right after I fled Z'taruh, and after three years of hard work on the frontier, I've earned my post. Of course, I checked to see if I had a criminal record before I joined. I was happy to see that I didn't. Maybe someday I'll find out who covered for me. Maybe it was even my dad. He might be proud if he could see me in my captain's uniform, sitting in my chair on the bridge.

I don't think he'd like my hair, though. It's grown out a bit in the last three years. I wear it in braids, dozens of them sprouting from my head like palm fronds. Theodore wears his hair the same way, so we braid each other's head. That's all we do for each other, though. I still sleep alone.

Sometimes I miss Hazaar very much.

I didn't feel like talking on the ride back to the *Dag-*

ger, and once there, I went to my private quarters immediately. Theodore and my other officers probably thought I was depressed because of the vid, but I was really thinking about the conversation I had with Lorrus the night before.

"War is no more than five years away," he predicted as he sat across from me in my anteroom, drinking the brainbuster I always made sure I had on hand for my Q'rin buddies.

"I thought it had already started," I said. "When Z'taruh and those other frontier colonies officially broke ties with the Emperor on Zorin—"

"That's just the talking stage." Lorrus grinned, without humor. "Later they'll have to back it up with muscle. And so will we."

When he said *we*, he didn't mean Humans, though I wish he had. Our government isn't ready to get sucked into something that expensive unless they absolutely have to. Not officially, anyway.

"I'm being sent to the Aesopian homeworld," Lorrus remarked as he watched these thoughts chase themselves across my face—my Nefertiti mask never fooled him. "They call it Home. You should see it some time."

"I hope I will."

"Captains defect from their navies all the time," he said, managing to make it sound like he was speaking generally instead of specifically. I allowed him a smile.

"You should know," I said, and he laughed.

We didn't talk about it any further that evening, but we both got drunk; and after he left I felt like going to bed early. But I had barely put my head on the pillow when I got a call from my communications officer.

"Top priority call, Captain," he said. "It's marked for your eyes only."

It was a recording from Admiral Nnaggenda, a woman I'd never heard of before. She got to the point immediately. "Captain Larissa Jones, due to your background in and special knowledge of Q'rin culture and language, and due to your acquaintance with Lord Knossos, the Aesopian, you have been chosen to be our Special Emissary to the Aesopian and Zorin Congress, which has been scheduled to meet on the planet Home in six solar months. You should arrive on schedule if you leave Kali within a week of the arrival of this message. All other orders are rescinded, and full priority should be given to your mission. Your communications officer has a fat file for you to review, Captain. I suggest you begin studying it immediately. Admiral Nnaggenda, out."

I sat there for several moments feeling very proud of myself. After all, I was the youngest captain in the fleet, and yet *I* was being chosen for this difficult and touchy mission. Then I realized what a dope I was. Of course they chose me. Despite my obvious talents, I was the most expendable candidate for the job. No experienced captain would be wasted in a conflict that Earth would just as soon never get mixed up in. It was my turn in the barrel.

"Lieutenant," I called my communications officer, "you have a file for me?"

"Just came in, Captain," he said. "It's *huge*."

I sighed, and got right down to work. I didn't quit until I had read all the way up to the chapter on the Great Change, that time almost a hundred thousand years ago during which the Aesopians changed themselves into a whole new race. Something was tugging at my memory when I put the file down, something the Lyrri surgeon had said to me when he was reattaching my ear. I could have sworn he had been talking about the Aesopians as he worked.

I was still thinking about him when I fell asleep, and I dreamed about the operation. I could even feel the pain. The Lyrri surgeon was yammering to me the whole time, while I drifted in and out of consciousness. Mostly he talked about the Q'rin.

"Yes," he said, "their ancestors—what did your science books call them—oh yes, Neanderthals. They emerged on Earth about a hundred thousand years ago,

I think. The Aesopians took some of the Neanderthals to Zorin and changed them so that they were better adapted to that planet. They made them smarter, stronger, more aggressive. Back on Earth, the Neanderthals had rather a bad time of it, you know.''

He chuckled and tortured my ear.

''They were always changing things back then. A little later, they changed themselves. Did I mention that before?''

''Who?'' I mumbled.

''Don't talk! See? Now I have to fix this. I'm talking about the Aesopians. They changed the Q'rin into what they are today.''

''When?''

''Now stop it! Didn't I warn you? They did it many thousands of years ago, back when . . .'' he paused, thoughtfully. ''Back when the Aesopians were still Lyrri,'' he whispered.

Now we're a week out from Kali, just getting started on our mission. But already I've received an urgent request from someone on Hook to hitch a ride to the meeting on Home. Hook is still pledging allegiance to the Emperor, but they haven't made up with the Aesopians yet. So they've decided to send a Special Service agent, unofficially; a guy who turns out to be a mutual friend of Lorrus's and mine.

He's Makrit, my old nemesis from the pits. I wonder if he joined the service before or *after* he turned professional knife fighter. Maybe he'll tell me.

Maybe my bed won't be empty much longer.

I'm worried about that piece of information the Lyrri surgeon gave me, about the Aesopians once belonging to the same race as the Lyrri. I couldn't find a reference to it anywhere in my official file, or in any of the unofficial sources I've plundered. The history of the Aesopians apparently begins at the time of the Great Change, period, end of story. But if what the surgeon said is true, the coming war is going to be a lot more complicated than I had thought.

In the past, I have run away from many things, from the Butcher, from Hook, and from Timmy. But this time I have to stand up and face whatever comes, even if that means telling the elephant man that he and his people are kin to the people they hate most in the universe.

I've put my knives away for good, but I'm ready.

I'm going Home to face the elephant man. But first I'm going home to Hook.